Between a Book and a Hard Place

A Devereaux's Dime Store Mystery

Denise Swanson

AN OBSIDIAN MYSTERY

OBSIDIAN

OBSIDIAN
Published by New American Library,
an imprint of Penguin Random House LLC
375 Hudson Street, New York, New York 10014

This book is an original publication of New American Library.

First Printing, March 2016

Obsidian and the Obsidian colophon are trademarks of Penguin Random
House LLC.

For more information about Penguin Random House, visit penguin.com.

ISBN 978-0-451-47776-7

Printed in the United States of America
10 9 8 7 6 5 4 3 2 1

Penguin
Random
House

*To all the librarians who keep the
information and entertainment flowing.*

CHAPTER 1

The Shadow Bend, Missouri, city council meeting didn't typically draw much of a crowd. Generally, fewer than a dozen of the community's four thousand twenty-eight citizens showed up, but tonight the residents had turned out in droves.

I wasn't sure what had sparked more interest—the application to turn a historic hotel on the village square into a rooming house or the UFO sightings east of town. But I was willing to bet the deed to my shop, Devereaux's Dime Store and Gift Baskets, that the majority of the folks hadn't come to discuss the same agenda item I was there to support.

Actually, *support* was too strong a word. I was present only because Boone St. Onge, one of my best friends, had nagged me into attending. Normally, I would have refused to squander what might be one of the last perfect summer evenings listening to Mayor Geoffrey Eggers drone on and on about rooming houses bringing down the tone and ambience of Shadow Bend, but Boone had been hard to refuse.

At some point, his ninety-seven text messages, phone calls, and Facebook posts had gotten to me and I'd given in to his relentless campaign. Our other BFF, Poppy Kincaid, was made of sterner stuff.

Certainly, Poppy had a better excuse than mine—business rather than pleasure. My dime store closed at six on Tuesday nights, but her nightclub, Gossip Central, was open until two in the morning. I wasn't buying it, though. She could have left her bartender in charge of the place. Instead, she claimed that the local motorcycle club's monthly get-together required her personal touch.

Translation: She was afraid if she wasn't there to sweet-talk them, the bikers would tear the joint apart. And the last thing she wanted was to have the cops called in to break up a fight. Poppy's watering hole had originally been a quarter mile outside the city limits, thus in the county sheriff's jurisdiction. But now, because of some recent restructuring of law enforcement districts, Gossip Central was in her police chief father's territory.

Since the change, Poppy had been extra careful to keep things calm in her club. No grown woman wants her daddy coming around to save her, especially a bad girl who wasn't on speaking terms with her father.

Which left me sitting between my friend Ronni, aka Veronica Ksiazak, and a stranger. Ronni owned the local bed-and-breakfast, and for the last ten minutes, she'd been hunched over, listening intently to the mayor's long, boring monologue. I wondered if she was concerned that if the city council refused the rooming-house permit, they might decide to rezone and disallow her B & B as well.

I'd tried to chat with the odd-looking guy next to me, but he didn't seem to have much of a sense of humor. After a couple of icy glares and his aloof silence, I reluctantly restrained myself from voicing any more of the many snarky comments running through my head about Hizzoner.

I would have preferred to sit as far in the back as possible—the better to sneak out after Boone's pet project was discussed. But because I had no idea this meeting would be so doggone popular, I had arrived only a few minutes before its scheduled start and had been lucky that Ronni had saved the chair beside her for me. Too bad it was so close to the front that I could count the nose hairs sticking out of the mayor's beaklike schnozzle.

I was nearly dozing off as Eggers droned on and on about the types of indigent people a rooming house would attract, when Ronni leaned over and whispered, "Dev, what do you think about an SRO moving into the old Desoto Hotel?"

The Desoto had opened in 1850, and for the next hundred years, it had been the town's social center. Supposedly, the hotel had thrown a party when Robert E. Lee had visited Shadow Bend. And during the War for Southern Independence, it had housed Confederate troops in its fifty-five rooms. But the place had run into hard times during the nineteen eighties and had been sitting empty for the past thirty years.

"I think Hizzoner has something up his sleeve. Something that will put money into his pockets." I raised an eyebrow. "Politics might be the second-oldest profession, but it bears an extremely close similarity to the first."

"You are such a cynic." Ronni snickered.

"That's not true." I lifted one shoulder. "I'm just an optimist with years of experience."

Ronni giggled, then said, "The Desoto is pretty close to your store, right?"

"Yep. It's two doors down." Actually, I had been thinking about that. "While I'm sympathetic toward the economically disadvantaged folks who often live in boarding houses, I'm concerned that their presence might drive away my regular clientele."

My shop ran on a very thin profit margin and I couldn't afford to lose any customers. When I had quit my consulting job at Stramp Investments and bought the dime store, I had reduced my round-trip commute from two hours to fifteen minutes and cut the time I spent at work almost in half. Too bad I had also shrunk my income from six figures to near poverty level. Which meant that no matter what, I had to keep my books in the black.

My altered lifestyle had been worth it because by making the change I'd been able to spend extra time with my grandmother Birdie Sinclair. Eighteen months ago, her doctor had informed me that Birdie needed me to be around more due to her memory issues; and knowing that it was my turn to help her, I had immediately begun to search for other ways to make a living. How could I do anything less when she had taken me in and loved me when I had nowhere else to go and no one else who cared?

When I was sixteen, my mother had dropped me on my grandmother's front porch with fifty dollars in my pocket and two suitcases containing all that remained of my previous life. My father had just been sent to prison, and Mom had been unable to handle the shame, loss of income, and reduced social status resulting from her husband's conviction. Having disposed of her burden, she'd headed to California to start over, leaving my grandmother and me to face the town's censure by ourselves. In the thirteen years she'd been gone, I'd heard from her fewer than a dozen times.

Ronni's elbow in my side brought me back from the past, and as I jerked my head toward her, I heard someone drawl, "As I live and breathe. Devereaux Sinclair. What are you doing here? You've never given any previous indication of being civic-minded."

"Wasting my time," I grumbled, glancing past Ronni to see Nadine Underwood sweep by me, trailed by Mr. Eye Candy, aka her health aide.

Up until a few months ago, Nadine had been a thirty-five-year member of the city council. However, because of a mysterious illness that none of her physicians could diagnose, she'd withdrawn, and her son, Dr. Noah Underwood, had been appointed in her place.

Nadine had never been one of my biggest fans, and now that I was dating Noah, she really had it in for me. In her view, I was not daughter-in-law material. I wasn't sure who was, but I suspected it was a mini-me version of Nadine. Someone who would step into her Prada shoes as belle of the country club set and president of the Confederate Daughters of Missouri. Someone she could bully.

Back when Noah and I had gone steady in high school, Nadine had manipulated him into dumping me, but Noah claimed to have learned his lesson. When we had started seeing each other again, he'd warned his mother to back off. He thought she had acquiesced, but I knew better.

Although there wasn't anything in particular I could point to, my guess was that Nadine had seen her son's words as a challenge and had taken her crusade to get rid of me and to destroy my family underground. Noah's mother had never been one to surrender that easily. After all, she still thought the South would rise again.

As I watched Nadine and Mr. Eye Candy take the reserved seats in the front row, Ronni narrowed her blue-gray eyes and muttered under her breath, "I wonder what Nadine's scheming about this time."

I smiled. Ronni may have moved to Shadow Bend only a year ago, but she'd learned quickly that Noah's mother always had an angle.

"I doubt Nadine is in favor of allowing a place that would attract the underprivileged and homeless to Shadow Bend's village square." I kept an eye on Noah's mother as she settled in, placing her Louis Vuitton satchel on her lap and nodding regally to those around her. "So I'm guessing she's here to make sure the city council votes against the rooming house."

Ronni grunted her agreement, and I realized that Nadine and I were on the same side on that issue. Feeling an unpleasant twinge, I wondered if I should reconsider my position on the matter.

No! As uncomfortable as it was to think that Noah's mother and I had anything in common, my family's livelihood was on the line. Without my income, Gran would experience financial hardship. And if my store went under, Dad would be unemployed.

A few months ago, after the truth had finally been discovered about my father's innocence and he'd gotten out of prison, he'd come to work for me at the dime store. And let's face it: Ex-cons didn't have a lot of employment opportunities, so finding another job would be tough.

As Mayor Eggers finally started running out of steam, I saw Boone and Noah put their heads to-

gether for a whispered conversation. It surprised me
that their tête-à-tête seemed so amiable. The rivalry
between the two men was legendary and had started
back when Noah was elected class president in sixth
grade.

The bitterness had continued throughout high
school and into their adult lives. During the years
Noah and I were dating, he and Boone had pretended to get along. But the minute Noah betrayed
me, Boone's true feelings reemerged. And from then
on, he'd never bothered to hide his contempt for the
good doctor.

Now that Noah and I had reconciled and were
going out again, I knew that both he and Boone were
trying for a détente in their hostilities, but I was suspicious about their new friendliness. Did it have anything to do with a certain ex–U.S. Marshal named
Jake Del Vecchio, the other man I was seeing? Or the
woman he had brought back to Shadow Bend after
his last case?

Both Boone and Poppy believed that I was crazy
to tolerate Jake's ex-wife, Meg, living with him and
his uncle Tony on the Del Vecchio ranch. Privately, I
thought I was a little deranged, too, but it was hard
to fault Jake for rescuing Meg from a psychiatric
facility. She was nearly catatonic, and had been that
way since being kidnapped by a serial killer. She
had been held captive by the psycho for months, and
he had threatened to carve her into a human statue.

According to Jake, Meg had no family and few
friends. Her doctors had said that there was nothing
physically wrong with her, but she needed rest and
time to recover emotionally from the trauma. If Jake
hadn't brought her to the ranch with him, she would

have had to go into a nursing home, where, with no one to make sure the staff was treating her okay, she would have been at the mercy of strangers.

The irony didn't escape me that while I had convinced Noah and Jake to tolerate me dating both of them, Jake was now living with his ex-wife. I hated irony.

Having learned early not to put the key to my happiness in someone else's pocket, I pushed aside my messed-up love life and refocused on Boone and Noah. Both men were now looking at me. What were they up to?

I sure wished Poppy were here. Few secrets ever remained hidden from her. Considering that her club was the most popular watering hole in the area, she was up on all the gossip. And if that didn't work, she had listening devices concealed by nearly every table.

Poppy liked to be aware of what was being discussed in her bar. She never shared the information with anyone except occasionally Boone and me, but she enjoyed the power of knowing facts others didn't. She had serious control issues—a gift from her father. Chief Kincaid made a drill sergeant seem like a laid-back surfer dude.

Digging my cell from my purse, I sent Poppy a quick text. She was probably too busy making sure the Brothers of Revolution didn't turn her tables into kindling or send one another to the emergency room to answer, but I was bored, so it was worth a shot.

While I had my phone out, I noticed a message that I'd missed from Jake. After I was finished with the meeting, he was supposed to come over to my house for pizza and a movie, but he was canceling. Meg was having some sort of crisis and he couldn't leave her alone.

Looking heavenward, I muttered, "Lord, give me patience."

I would have prayed for strength, but then I'd have to ask God for bail money, too, because I was beginning to wonder if Meg was less incapacitated than she was pretending to be. And if she was faking, I might not be able to control my impulse to slap her silly.

Maybe I was being unreasonable, but Meg seemed to have an emergency whenever Jake and I had a date planned. Was it possible she was trying to break us up and get her ex-husband back into her clutches? And if so, other than challenge her to a duel, what could I do about it?

CHAPTER 2

Mentally slapping myself for my paranoia, I quickly texted Jake that I understood, then vowed not to think about him or his ex-wife any more tonight. Instead, I would pay attention to the meeting and support my friend Boone's cause, whatever it turned out to be.

Boone had been secretive about the matter, and the agenda item had read "philanthropic donation to the town," so I had no idea what I was there to back. At least it looked as if Boone and Noah were on the same side, which made things a lot easier for me. I hated it when I had to choose between them.

The mayor finally shut up and allowed the guy trying to open the rooming house to have his say. When the man finished, the mayor asked for questions from the audience. Those who raised their hands mentioned lack of parking and the probability of increased criminal activity as reasons not to change the zoning.

There was a long pause, and when no one stood to speak, I thought the city council would vote. But before the mayor could call the question, Harlee

Ames rose to her feet. I found Harlee refreshingly levelheaded and was interested to hear her views on the rooming-house issue.

She had recently retired from the armed services, moved back to Shadow Bend, and opened Forever Used, an upscale consignment shop. We'd gotten off to a rocky start during the July Fourth cupcake contest weekend, but once she'd come clean about her past and cleared up my suspicions, we'd become friends.

Like Devereaux's Dime Store, Forever Used was located on the town square and might suffer a loss of customers if the tenor of the quaint downtown area changed. Her business was especially vulnerable since it catered to a more affluent clientele than mine.

Harlee slowly scanned the city council members, then cleared her throat and said, "My concern is that people who end up in rooming houses are usually low-income folks. Often they depend on public assistance. Because they lack resources, they frequently have difficulty taking care of themselves. They run out of food and other essentials, and this hinders their ability to function in general."

The man proposing the boarding house stuttered an objection.

Harlee stared at him until he stopped speaking, then asked, "Are you prepared to help these types of people? Because currently, Shadow Bend doesn't have any means to deal with them."

The man clearly had no response. His mouth moved, but no words came out.

Harlee nodded, as if that was exactly the reaction she'd expected, and sat back down.

Immediately, Winnie Todd jumped up, pointed her finger at Harlee, and said, "Which is a crying shame. We are in dire need of programs to help the residentially challenged. We can't just bury our heads and pretend the less fortunate don't exist."

Winnie's stance wasn't exactly surprising considering that she had come of age in the sixties. Certainly, her wardrobe still looked as if she were living in Haight-Ashbury. Tonight she had on a paisley maxi dress, a fringed suede vest, and leather toe-strap sandals.

Harlee gave Winnie a cool up-and-down glance, then lifted her chin and said, "I wasn't suggesting that we ignore anyone. Just that we need to be prepared if we invite them into our community."

Winnie frowned and threw open her arms. "Lack of preparation is just an excuse to exclude the needy from our town."

"That kind of disorganized thinking helps no one." Harlee began to tick items off her fingers. "We'll need a fully operational food bank, donated clothing, and enough medical personnel to handle the health problems many of the poor battle."

Winnie sputtered an incoherent protest, but while she attempted to voice an objection, Mayor Eggers pounded his gavel and declared, "As there are no further questions, the floor is closed." He turned to the city council members and said, "All in favor of rezoning to permit a rooming house within the Shadow Bend city limits?"

Silence.

"All opposed?"

Six voices rang out.

"Reclassification is denied."

With that, two-thirds of the audience got up and left the room. I noticed that the majority of the people who left were the folks who had relocated to our area and built their McMansions on the cheap land. The ones still seated were mostly the locals—farmers, ranchers, and factory workers who had lived in or around Shadow Bend all their lives. As usual, a huge chasm separated the two groups.

Just the other day, on my drive from home into town, I had noticed a new sign posted in front of a field. The notice read, THIS IS A FARM. IT CONTAINS ANIMALS THAT MAKE NOISE, PRODUCE FOUL ODORS, AND DON'T CARE WHO WATCHES WHILE THEY HAVE SEX. IF YOU DON'T LIKE THIS TYPE OF ATMOSPHERE, DON'T BUILD YOUR HOUSE NEXT TO THIS PROPERTY.

While I brooded about the rift splitting our town into haves and have-nots, a familiar voice broke into my thoughts. "Now that we've settled the issue of the poor moving into our town, can we talk about the extraterrestrial parasites that have begun to colonize Shadow Bend, infesting our children and using them as hosts for their own spawn?"

For a minute I thought we were all being punked, but the look on Nadine Underwood's face was deadly serious. Just when I thought she had hit an all-time low, the woman always managed to dig a little deeper.

I stared at Nadine as her health aide shot to his feet and tried to tug her back into her seat. She shook him off, then deliberately straightened the cuffs of her stunning Marc Jacobs white tux jacket. Her black linen slacks ended just above her still trim ankles and showcased her gorgeous Jimmy Choo Allure pumps.

Noah groaned and half stood. Evidently, he was trying to decide whether interceding would help matters or cause more of a scene.

As I watched, I saw Nadine's face rearrange itself into a scary semblance of a smile while her claw-like hand caressed Mr. Eye Candy's butt. Considering the aide was in his twenties and she was in her early seventies—she had been over forty when she'd finally produced an Underwood heir—I found her behavior a bit off-putting. Then again, no one would look twice if an older man flirted with a woman less than half his age, so I tried not to judge her too harshly—at least not on that issue.

No one had responded to Nadine's initial statement, and she pointed a bony finger at Mayor Egger and snapped, "Close your mouth, Geoffrey, and tell us what you're going to do about the aliens taking over the bodies of Shadow Bend's most precious resource."

Listening to Nadine's delusional rant about an invasion from outer space, I revised my opinion of her illness. Up until now, I had suspected that she was exaggerating her ailments to get her son's attention off of me and back on her, but now I wasn't so sure.

Her check engine light had been on for years. And I'd always thought that her motor needed finetuning. But tonight's performance proved that she required a major overhaul rather than a minor adjustment. Excessive good sense had never been a requirement for Shadow Bend's high society, but Nadine was pushing that tolerance limit.

Poor Noah. His handsome face was flushed, and he looked as if he wished the floor of the meeting room would crack open and he could escape into the hole.

While I couldn't help but feel bad for him, Nadine had been a thorn in my family's side for a long time. When my father had been under investigation for bank fraud, then convicted of manslaughter and possession of a controlled substance, she had black-mailed her son into dumping me.

Noah had recently disclosed that if he hadn't broken up with me, Nadine, as a member of the bank's board of directors, had threatened to involve Birdie in the embezzlement investigation. What a choice to give a sixteen-year-old boy—keep your girlfriend or save her grandmother.

Then a few months ago, when my father's innocence was proven and he'd gotten out of prison, I had finally discovered why Nadine hated my family so much. Birdie had revealed that although Nadine was many years older than Dad, they had dated, but when he chose my mother over her, she'd sworn vengeance on him and his descendants.

And anyone who doesn't believe feuds can last that long has never lived in a small town. Or dealt with a scorned grande dame.

Nadine's current fall from grace, and apparent loss of sanity, was delightfully karmic.

CHAPTER 3

Evidently, Noah decided that it was time for some damage control. He'd been sitting behind the conference table in the front of the room with the other city council members, but when Nadine's tirade continued, he reluctantly rose and walked to where she was standing.

Taking Nadine's arm, he attempted to usher her out of the area, but she wasn't cooperating. As he tugged her down the aisle, her voice rose and she continued to harangue the mayor about pod people.

The usually sleek, elegant, and aristocratic Dr. Noah Underwood was clearly ruffled by his mother's antics. When she stopped next to my row, leaned across Ronni, and poked me in the shoulder with her finger, I was afraid Noah was about to burst a blood vessel.

Nadine had never suffered from insanity—she'd always enjoyed every minute of it—and while her full maniacal attention was riveted on me, she didn't appear to notice that her only son was about to go into cardiac arrest.

Stabbing me repeatedly with her talonlike nail, she screeched, "Don't think I'm unaware that you and your family are collaborating with the enemy. My and my late husband's great-great-great-grandfathers may not have been able to substantiate that the Sinclairs were jayhawkers, but I'll prove that you all are harboring aliens."

"Seriously?" I hadn't heard that my people had been Union sympathizers. Was that all in Nadine's fevered imagination? Or was that why Gran had never participated in the Confederate Daughters of Missouri and had been so opposed when my mother signed me up?

"Socially, your family has burned every bridge in this county!" Nadine shrieked.

"And we've never appreciated a bonfire more." I refused to be intimidated.

Hearing several gasps from the people sitting behind me, I shrugged. My day was never complete until I had horrified a roomful of my fellow townsfolk.

When Nadine jabbed me again, I grabbed her hand and held it away from me. I was all for respecting my elders, but I wasn't about to allow her to continue to assault me. Noah's face had turned from ruby to scarlet, and he quickly yanked his mom back from me.

Putting himself between me and Nadine, Noah bent across poor Ronni, who looked as if she wished she'd let me have the aisle seat, put his lips to my ear, and whispered, "Meet me after we're through here."

"Why?" His warm breath tickled my neck, sending a *yee-haw* message to my girl parts. Both Jake and Noah could melt off my panties.

"Because I need to be with you after this fiasco."

Noah's slate gray eyes conveyed how much his mother's behavior was taking out of him.

"Okay." I glanced at the cell phone in my hand. "I'm suddenly free."

"His loss." Noah grinned widely. Then, with a new determination in his step, he put his arm around his mother and led her toward the door.

As Noah and Nadine's aide marched her to the exit, she turned her head and yelled, "Someone needs to check the Sinclairs' property for spaceships. I've heard there were glowing red lights hovering in the sky there every night last week and white flashing lights zooming around in a circle."

Nadine had been a teacup short of a place setting for years. But obviously the remaining saucer had cracked beyond repair.

I rubbed my temples. Gran always claimed that anything that doesn't kill you makes you stronger. If that's true, by this time I should be able to lift a pickup truck over my head with one arm.

Noah tightened his grip on Nadine's shoulder and hurried her out of the room.

Once she was gone, the audience buzzed for several minutes, and Mayor Eggers had to bang his gavel several times to get the meeting back under control.

When everyone had quieted down, Hizzoner said, "Next on our agenda is Professor Russell Hinkley, a renowned alientologist from the University of Eastern California. He has requested time to speak to us about the recent sightings above Shadow Bend."

The strange-looking man beside me rose to his feet, picked up the cane that had been resting by his side, and as he squeezed past me, he gave me a speculative glance. *Terrific!* Nadine's ravings had put my family on this lunatic's radar. Before we knew it, his telescope would be focused on the skies over our property.

I had thought the walking stick might be an affectation, but as Professor Hinkley made his way to the front, I noticed a slight limp. The hitch in his gait was subtle, but it was definitely there.

When the professor reached the podium, he said, "Large silent objects flying low and fast have been seen around these parts for several weeks. I want to assure you this is not a sign of the end of times."

There was a loud gulp from the audience, and the professor quickly continued. He spoke about cosmic pluralism, religions based upon early alien contact, and how to properly greet extraterrestrials when they arrived in town.

Midway through Hinkley's dissertation, Ronni used her hand as a screen and whispered, "This time Nadine has really gone off her rocker. What do you think poor Noah will do about her?"

"I suppose locking her in the nearest insane asylum is too much to hope for?" I knew there was no way Noah would commit his mother to a psychiatric hospital, but a girl could dream, right? I may try to see no evil and speak no evil, but I sure as hell thought about it plenty.

"I wonder what got her panties in a twist." Ronni wound a chocolate brown curl around her finger. "Unless it directly affected her, ordinarily Nadine wouldn't care about an alien invasion or the town teenagers."

"You're right." I nodded slowly. Nadine's concern was out of character for her. "I'll mention that inconsistency to Noah when we get together after this meeting."

"Didn't you tell me you had a date with Jake tonight?" Ronni raise a brow.

"He sent me a text saying that he had to cancel." I didn't look at Ronni, not wanting to see pity in her eyes. "Meg is acting up again."

"At this rate, Shadow Bend will have to open its own loony bin pretty soon." Ronni giggled, then jerked her chin toward the front of the room. "And we should reserve an entire wing for that guy."

I tuned in to the professor just in time to see him lean into the microphone. I studied him. If it weren't for the picket-fence teeth, Albert Einstein hairdo, and Mr. Magoo glasses, he might have been a nice-looking man.

After a dramatic pause, Hinkley said, "Extraterrestrial forms of life range from the simple microorganisms to far more complex beings that are superior to humans."

"Let's hope ours are the bacteria-like ones." I snickered. "Otherwise, we're in a lot of trouble. Can you imagine Hizzoner trying to negotiate with a really smart ET? Shadow Bend would be under alien rule before they could even get the probe up his butt."

Ronni laughed, but before she could respond, the professor said, "What I'd like to do is set up a series of large radio antennas and telescopes on the property where most of the unusual lights have been seen."

He glanced toward me, and I quickly turned my head. No way was I allowing this crackpot on Sinclair land. And I'd like to see him try to convince our neighbor Tony Del Vecchio to permit him on his ranch.

"Professor." Boone spoke from his place behind the conference table. "What do you hope to accomplish with the antennas and such?"

"Communication, my dear man." Hinkley rubbed the sparkly green glass ball on the top of his cane and gazed heavenward. "I want to welcome them to Earth."

With that statement, the spectators went wild. Voices rose and arguments started. Most folks seemed alarmed at the thought of receiving a visit from spacemen, but a few expressed some interest in meeting Alf, Mork, the Great Gazoo, and Marvin the Martian. One guy asked if any of them would look like Seven of Nine or Starfire.

I had to use my phone to Google that last one. Turns out that Starfire is a comic-strip character from the planet Tamaran. Considering the guy who asked about her was practically drooling, I was not surprised to see that she was drawn with huge boobs and a costume that resembled a couple of potato chips and a cracker.

I noticed that as the professor fielded questions from the audience, Boone kept glancing at his watch. He seemed relieved when Noah returned and took his seat at the conference table. The men put their heads together, then Boone pulled out his cell phone and I watched as his thumbs flew over the screen. What were those two guys up to?

Mayor Eggers spent the next fifteen minutes trying to regain control of the proceedings. Professor Hinkley was less than eager to relinquish the spotlight, and Hizzoner finally took the man by the elbow and escorted him down the aisle and back to his seat.

As Hinkley edged past me, he said, "So your family

owns the land near the contact site? I'd like to explore the area tomorrow morning."

"No." I figured short and succinct was the way to go with this guy.

"How about the afternoon?" He had a small leather planner in his hand.

"Never."

"But you must." The professor clutched my arm and demanded, "How can you even consider standing in the way of scientific research?"

"Let me make myself perfectly clear." I shook off his fingers and stared at him. "If I catch you with one foot on my family's property, I will call the police and have you arrested for trespassing."

"The mayor has given me permission to conduct any and all essential exploration for my study in and around Shadow Bend." Hinkley frowned and reached into his pocket. "Perhaps you'd like to see the document."

He tried to hand me a sheet of paper, but I refused to take it.

"Egger has no rights where my family's land is concerned." I skewered him with a sharp look. "And just FYI, the police chief is my best friend's father. Capiche?"

"But . . ." Hinkley stammered.

"Seriously? In spite of the look on my face, you're still talking?" With that, I pointedly ignored the professor when he continued to try to get my attention.

He was becoming more and more annoying when a voice from the row behind us said, "Mister, you need to leave these two girls alone."

Hinkley turned his head, and the glare on his face slowly faded, replaced with an expression I couldn't identify. His mouth snapped closed and he nodded at the man, his Adam's apple bobbing. I twisted my neck to see who had reduced him to blessed silence.

I didn't recognize our protector. He was an attractive middle-aged man dressed in a Western-style suit, cowboy boots, and holding a Stetson on his lap. I wasn't sure what it was about him that had caused the professor to shut up, but I gave him a grateful smile. He dipped his head in acknowledgment and crossed his arms.

While the professor had been bugging me, the city council had disposed of the remaining agenda items. Boone rose and stood next to the mayor. He and Eggers had a short conversation and Hizzoner waved my friend toward the podium.

Boone was a stylishly handsome man who wore expensive designer suits, Italian leather shoes, and Serge Lutens Bornéo 1834 cologne. His golden hair fell flawlessly across his forehead, and his straight white teeth were striking against his tanned face. I had rarely seen him nervous, but tonight he seemed jumpy.

After tapping the microphone, he cleared his throat and said, "As most of you are aware, Shadow Bend has been without a library for several years."

"Which is just a damn shame!" someone from the audience shouted.

"I agree." Boone shot a megawatt smile toward the person who'd commented. "Not only have we lost a vital resource for our town, but a magnificent piece of architecture is dying from neglect."

"We should sell that building," Colin Whitmore, the bank's computer wizard, bellowed. "Get rid of that old white elephant and put some money in the town coffers."

"Fortunately"—Boone paused and stared at Colin—"when Douglas Underwood's family gave the building to the community, the agreement stipulated that it had to be owned by the town and used solely as a library. Otherwise, the city government has to pay a million-dollar penalty to Underwood's heirs. And while Noah and his mother might waive that fee, there are other descendants, those who don't live in Shadow Bend, who undoubtedly would claim the money."

I had forgotten that the Shadow Bend Library was actually the Douglas Underwood Memorial Library. When the colonel was killed in the Battle of Shadow Bend, his widow had donated the building that had held his medical practice to the town in order to commemorate her husband.

"So what's your answer?" Colin asked Boone. "Let it rot away?"

"Up until now, we had no solution." Boone took a deep breath. "But recently I was approached with a very generous proposal." He beamed in my direction, and I felt a frisson of unease. "Mr. Jett Benedict has offered a three-year endowment for the library."

"Who is this guy?" Colin demanded. "And what's in it for him?"

"I'd like to answer that if I may." The guy who had quieted down the professor stood. "I believe I can explain it better than anyone else."

"Be my guest, Mr. Benedict." Boone motioned the man to the front of the room. "The floor is yours."

Jett strode to the podium and said, "When my wife told me about this wonderful town and its lack of funding for the library, I was concerned that unlike her daughter, the children of Shadow Bend would grow up without ever developing the joy of reading." He glanced around the room. "So when I was looking for a charity to support and she suggested endowing the library, I said, 'Yes sirree, Bob. Let's do that.'"

"Not out of the goodness of your heart, I'm sure," Colin sneered.

"Not entirely, no." Jett's smile thinned, but his voice was smooth. "All I ask is permission to examine the archives. My research leads me to believe that they contain information about this area's history that interests me." He shrugged. "I know it will take a while to spiff up the place and hire staff, but I'd like to have access before the library officially opens."

"A reasonable request that I feel the city council should approve." Boone shot a glance at the mayor.

Egger nodded and said, "Any other questions for our benefactor?"

The name *Benedict* had finally clicked in my brain, and I raised my hand.

The mayor pointed at me, and I stood. I really didn't want to know the answer, but I forced myself to ask, "Mr. Benedict, you mentioned that your wife told you about our town's need for a library. Is she from Shadow Bend?"

"Not originally, but she lived here for many years." His eyes twinkled.

"May I ask your wife's name?" My heart was pounding, and I could barely breathe.

"How about if I just introduce her to everyone?" Jett winked at me. "Although most of you already know her." He held out his hand, and a voluptuous blonde walked out from behind a portable whiteboard. He put his arm around her slim waist and said, "It's my pleasure to bring your own Yvette Sinclair Benedict back to Shadow Bend."

The audience was eerily silent as I stared at my mother's beautiful and traitorous face.

One of my best friends, along with a man who claimed to love me, had ambushed me. Mom was back in town, flaunting a new husband and his money. And I had a bad feeling that with Hurricane Yvette around, Shadow Bend would need to put up its storm shutters and take cover.

CHAPTER 4

Jett Benedict's little bombshell knocked me for such a loop that it took several seconds before I was able to put all the pieces together. When I did, I narrowed my eyes and glanced between Noah and Boone. Noah's expression was hard to read, but Boone, my up until now BFF, lifted one shoulder in an unapologetic shrug.

As I suspected, Boone had known for some time that the library benefactor was my stepfather, and that was why he'd been so insistent that I attend the meeting. My presence hadn't had anything to do with supporting the cause. The whole scheme had been a trap.

Boone was well aware that I would not have agreed to see my mother, and clearly, either Yvette or her loving husband had manipulated my friend into persuading me to come to the city hall. The only mystery was why Yvette would care enough to arrange all this. Considering that since dropping me on Gran's front porch, she'd made virtually no effort to be a part of my life, what had changed?

I didn't wait around to find out. Standing, I hurried

down the aisle. I could hear high heels clicking on the
hardwood floors behind me, and I doubled my speed.
With any luck, I could outrun a fiftysomething woman
hindered by her Louboutin stilettos.

City hall was divided into four spaces, half of
which was the mayor's elaborately and expensively
decorated office. The remainder was shared by a
postage-stamp-size reception area, the clerk's tiny
cubicle, and the large conference room where the
city council met.

Once I made it out of the conference room, I sprinted
across the lobby to the building's exit. As I pushed
through the frosted glass double doors, I heard my
mother calling my name.

Parking could be difficult around the town square,
and since the city hall was kitty-corner from my shop,
I had left my car in the tiny lot behind the dime store
and walked to the meeting. Now I was sorry I hadn't
attempted to secure a closer spot.

Thankful that I had on sneakers, I increased my
pace. Ignoring the sidewalks, I took the more direct
route from the city hall to my store. Surely Yvette
couldn't keep up in five-inch heels running across
grass.

"Devereaux Sinclair, you wait up for me," Yvette
ordered breathlessly.

She sounded closer. I peeked over my shoulder
and saw her closing in on me. Yvette had taken off
her shoes and was running barefoot. She really did
want to talk to me about something.

I hesitated. Maybe it would be better just to be
done with it. Mom was nothing if not persistent.
Especially if it was something she'd set her mind on
accomplishing. After all, she'd moved to a new town

fresh out of college, had married one of the most eligible bachelors—my dad—and had gone from a virtually penniless nobody to one of the movers and shakers of Shadow Bend.

No! I wasn't about to give in that easily. Besides, I wanted to speak to my father and grandmother before I dealt with Yvette. My mother had taken more wrong turns in her life than a shopping cart with a wobbly wheel, and I wasn't going to help her with whatever her current mistake might be.

I'd made it across the square and was heading down the alley between my building and the empty shop next door when I felt a hand on my upper arm. The grip was surprisingly strong, and when I tried to shrug it off, the fingernails dug into my flesh.

"Got you!" Yvette's triumphant voice echoed in my ear. "Now, let's talk."

I allowed her to lead me by the arm down the alley and into the parking lot, wondering why it was that when people decide to suck the life out of you, they don't take some fat along with it.

As we emerged from the dark passageway, we both blinked. After a body had been dumped behind my store, on the advice of the police chief I had installed halogen floodlights above the back entrance of the business. Even though it wasn't dark yet, I had them set to come on when the place closed, so their sudden brightness blinded me, and it took several seconds to focus.

I slowly turned and examined my mother. Yvette hadn't changed much since the last time I'd seen her. She was still model thin, her hair was still thick and a rich shade of honey blond, and if she had any wrinkles, I couldn't find them. Was her smooth skin a result of a face-lift or good genes? I certainly hoped it was the latter, since I'd never be able to afford cosmetic surgery.

While I had been inspecting my mother, she'd been returning the favor. Frowning, she rubbed my ponytail between her fingers and said, "Why are you wearing your hair like this? Women pay a fortune to get the cinnamon gold color you have naturally. And scraping it back instead of playing up one of your major assets is just stupid."

"Good to see you, too, Mom." I crossed my arms, ignoring her criticism.

Yvette had never been happy with my appearance. Even back in my teenage days, when I put a lot more effort into looking good, she'd been dissatisfied with my curvier figure and less than classically beautiful features. When she'd left me at Gran's, it had been a relief to stop trying to be the popular daughter my mother wanted.

"You know, Dev"—Mom leaned in as if she were about to reveal the secret of the century—"life is an unending battle full of disappointments and trials, but if you keep trying, you *can* finally find a hairdresser you like."

"My financial plan doesn't allow for the kind of stylist who knows how to handle the thickness and curls." I moved out of her reach.

Yvette waved away my words. "A budget is just a way to go broke on a schedule."

"Nevertheless." I knew it was senseless to argue. Any similarity between Mom's reality and mine had always been solely coincidental. "A good hairstylist is a luxury I've had to forgo since I no longer make the big bucks."

"I heard about your previous job." Yvette pursed

her lips. "It was certainly lucky that you quit before Stramp was arrested."

I wondered how she knew about that. Had she been keeping tabs on me the whole time, or when she'd found out she'd be coming to Shadow Bend, had she just done a Google search? The information would be easy enough to find. Ronald Stramp, the CEO of Stramp Investments, had been prosecuted for stealing investors' life savings.

A lot of people thought Stramp's employees were as guilty as their boss. Having left several months before he was exposed had not spared me from the accusations or the venom. And it hadn't helped that my testimony during his trial hadn't resulted in his conviction.

My silence seemed to annoy Yvette, and she snapped, "Being such a dutiful granddaughter certainly paid off for you. I wouldn't have been willing to sacrifice a six-figure salary to take care of Birdie."

"Of course you wouldn't." I sniffed. "You wouldn't even give up your social standing to stick by your husband or take care of your teenage daughter."

"That was different." Yvette dismissed her inexcusable behavior as if she'd tried to check out eleven items in the ten-or-fewer aisle rather than abandoned her only child and never looked back. "I knew Birdie would take good care of you and that in the long run, it would be better for both of us if I were able to make a fresh start while I was still young enough to marry well again. Kern wasn't the angel you thought he was."

"How did that remarrying-well-thing work out for you?" I asked, cringing at her insinuation about my father's character. "What number husband is Jett?"

Ignoring my question, she put a finger under my chin and tilted my head. Then murmuring half under her breath, she said, "Why don't you do anything to emphasize your gorgeous eyes? Do you realize people wear aquamarine contacts to get that color? What I could have done with your hair and eyes. I'd be married to Steven Spielberg by now."

"Doesn't he already have a wife?" I tapped my chin thoughtfully. "I'm pretty sure Kate Capshaw is still Mrs. Spielberg."

"That was just an example." Yvette seemed suddenly to realize where our conversation had led her and added quickly, "Of course, I love Jett to death and am thrilled that we're together."

"Of course." Tired of rehashing the past, I walked toward my car. "Now that we've reminisced and caught up on our lives, why did you chase me all the way across the square to talk to me?"

"Because I'm your mother and I haven't seen you in twelve years." Yvette clasped both her hands to her chest, her bottom lip trembling.

For a split second, I was thrown by her hurt expression. But then I remembered that she had been the star of our local theater guild. Her best role had been Lilly Dillon when the group had put on *The Grifters*. It wasn't until years later that I realized it probably hadn't taken much acting ability for Mom to play the inattentive, callous mother and desperate con woman.

"Thirteen years, Mom." I dug out my keys and pressed the button to unlock my BMW. "You haven't seen me in thirteen years."

"Details." Yvette pouted. "But now that I'm in town, we can spend some quality time together." She clapped her hands together. "I know. We can go shopping." She eyed my polo shirt, which bore the dime store logo, and my Walmart jeans. "I'll buy you some new clothes. Something pretty so you can close the deal and marry Noah Underwood." She smirked. "Won't that just chap Nadine's ass?"

Ah. That explained a lot. Now I knew why she wanted to see me. She must have a mole in town. Someone who kept her informed about what was happening in Shadow Bend. When I'd started dating Noah, she must have realized that if I married him, I'd finally be the daughter she'd always wanted—not to mention, getting one up on her archrival, Nadine.

The Underwoods and the Sinclairs were two of the five founding families of Shadow Bend, which made socializing with one another inevitable. Before my father's conviction, Nadine and Yvette had competed for the position of the town's belle of the ball. Both of the women craved attention like a smoker jonesing for his next cigarette. They each vied for the limelight and saw the other as an obstacle in their path to the top. When Dad went to jail, Nadine had claimed the victory. Now Mom was back for a rematch.

"Thanks, but no thanks." Opening the door to the Z4, I slid inside and quickly closed it in Yvette's face. When I turned on the engine, I lowered the window and added, "I don't need any new clothes. I don't need help landing Noah. And I don't need you in my life."

I backed up, and as I pulled away, I glanced in the rearview mirror. Yvette had a strange look on her face. I would have expected anger, or maybe even a little regret. Instead, her expression was speculative. Like she was already planning her next move.

Shuddering at the thought of Nadine and Yvette duking it out over Noah and me, I started home. If those two conniving women got involved, any chance that I might end up having a happily-ever-after with Noah was mighty slim. And with Jake's ex occupying his time, that relationship didn't seem too promising, either.

Maybe I shouldn't have fixed Ronni up with Cooper McCall. The new fire chief was hot, and he'd definitely shown some interest in getting to know me better. But since I was already having difficulty juggling two guys, I had done the right thing and arranged a blind date for him and Ronni. Now I had a bit of seller's remorse.

I pushed aside my man troubles as I turned into our long driveway. We lived on the ten remaining acres of the property my ancestors had settled in the eighteen sixties. A few premature deaths, some infertility, several families with only children, and everyone else moving away meant that Dad, Gran, and I were the last Sinclairs in Shadow Bend.

Fifteen years ago, when my grandfather died and my father showed no interest in farming, Gran had started to sell off the land surrounding the old homestead to Tony Del Vecchio. She used the money to pay the taxes and supplement her meager social security. Then, when Dad went to prison and I arrived on her doorstep, she sold off even more to provide for me.

Inch by inch, my heritage had vanished before I was old enough to realize what it meant. Now I cherished the acreage we had left.

Passing the duck pond, I slowed to gaze at my favorite spot. When Dad had gotten out of jail, this was where we'd had his welcome-home party. Smiling, I remembered the warm reception he'd received from our friends. I'd been especially touched that his old pal Chief Kincaid had welcomed him back as if he'd never been convicted of a crime.

I also loved our little orchard. The fall apples wouldn't be ready for another couple of weeks, but once they were, Gran would make her famous apple butter from the crisp and tart Jonathans.

As I drove the final quarter mile through the white fir and blue spruce lining either side of the lane, instead of the usual feeling of peace that coming home typically brought to me, tension crawled across my shoulders. How would I break the news to Gran and Dad that Yvette was in Shadow Bend? Birdie would want to shoot her, but I wasn't sure how my father would react.

Would her being in town remind him of the bad times? When he was on trial, she'd refused to come to the courtroom to support him. Would he be upset that she was here with another man? If he still loved her, Jett's presence would hurt like hell. Would Dad try to win her back?

Yvette was no stranger to divorce. So already having a husband wouldn't be much of an impediment. And if Dad and Mom did get back together, how would it be with her around all the time?

I found my father and grandmother in the living room. Before Dad's return, I would have sworn that Birdie was more of a boilermaker type of gal, but having him home seemed to have calmed her, and they'd grown into the habit of having a bedtime milk shake together.

Another change was Gran's use of the Mondae Siren milk shake glasses she'd collected as a teenager. The horizontal ribs below the four optical bull's-eyes were unique, and although I had begged to drink from them, they had always been for display only.

Kissing Gran and Dad on the cheek, I took one of the goblets from the china cabinet, walked into the kitchen, picked up the blender jar, and poured the chocolate ice cream mixture into my glass.

Returning to the living room, I sat beside Dad on the couch, put my feet on the coffee table, and asked, "Anything good on TV?"

Without looking at me, his interest riveted to the television screen, Dad answered, "The Discovery Channel is playing a *MythBusters* marathon. Jessi, Tory, and Grant are attempting to test how long someone can hang by their fingers. Like they do in the movies."

Birdie sighed. She was more a fan of *CSI* and *Justified*. Turning my attention to her, I asked, "How are you doing, Gran?" She'd had a summer cold, and I was worried that it might turn into pneumonia.

"Any day on this side of the flower bed, I consider a win." She cackled, then said, "I thought Jake was coming over."

I explained that Meg's crisis had terminated our evening plans. I didn't mention that I'd originally agreed to meet Noah later. Birdie was not a fan of the good doctor. I might have forgiven him for how he'd treated me when we were teenagers, but she had not. And right now I was seriously ticked off at him and Boone for tricking me into attending the city council meeting, not to mention the fact that he'd texted me, canceling our date because of his mother.

"Sweet Jesus!" Gran's face folded up into an accordion of wrinkles. The deep summer tan she'd gotten working in the back garden made her look like a golden raisin. "Tony thinks Meg is faking."

Although Tony was our nearest neighbor, he had never socialized with us. But six months ago, when I was accused of murdering Noah's fiancée, Gran had called him. She'd remembered that Tony's great-nephew was a U.S. Marshal and that he was helping out his uncle on the ranch while recovering from an on-duty injury.

When Jake had offered to look into the murder, he'd revealed that my grandmother and his great-uncle had dated when they were in high school. But Tony was a couple of years older, and while he was waiting for Gran to graduate, he'd enlisted in the marines. Then, near the end of the Korean War, he was reported MIA, and Birdie had married my grandfather. Which meant once Tony was rescued from the prisoner-of-war camp where he'd been held, things had been awkward between them.

Now that Birdie and Tony had both lost their spouses and reconnected, they were courting again. And both of them were intent on me marrying Jake. Meg's presence was throwing a monkey wrench into their plans, and neither senior citizen was happy about it.

When I didn't respond to her accusation about Meg, Gran said, "You need to do something about that woman and her shenanigans before she renews her title as Mrs. Jake Del Vecchio."

"Maybe Meg isn't as emotionally disturbed as she seems, but there's no way to prove something like that." I chewed my thumbnail. "And I can't really demand Jake abandon her without coming off like a total bitch."

"Hmm." Gran reached down, swooped up her cat, Banshee, and plopped him on her lap.

If I tried that trick with the ancient Siamese, I would have pulled back a bloody stump. Gran was the only one the feline allowed such liberties. He shot me a malevolent stare and settled across her knees.

Dad was still engrossed in his television program, and I decided to wait for a commercial to announce that Mom was in town.

Instead, I said to Gran, "I'm surprised you weren't at the city council meeting."

"Kern didn't want to go and so I decided to stay home, too."

Dad still wasn't comfortable around large groups of Shadow Benders. He believed that not everyone was convinced he was innocent and that he had been set up for both the bank fraud and the accident.

"Did you hear about the strange lights that have been sighted above our property?" I asked. "The mayor has brought in a UFO expert."

"That man makes an idiot look smart." She snorted, flipping her long gray braid over one shoulder. "It's not as if we've never had weird lights in the sky before. It usually turns out to be a kid shooting off illegal fireworks or a plane or something like that."

"True," I agreed. "Somehow Hizzoner is going to make money from all this."

"Duh." Gran rolled her pale blue eyes, then asked, "So what was Boone's big mysterious . . . ah . . . mysterious . . ." She trailed off, her face getting red.

"Philanthropic donation," I supplied. Her doctor had said it was best to provide the word she couldn't recall, rather than let her become stressed.

"Right." She shook her finger at me. "Get that worried look off your face. Lord a' mercy. Just because I misplaced something or can't come up with a word once in a while doesn't mean I'm senile."

"I never said you were." I held up my hands in mock surrender.

Gran's memory issues had improved dramatically with my father's return, but she still occasionally had trouble recalling the exact word she wanted. And she wasn't happy that I insisted she keep taking her medication and continue seeing the gerontologist. Thank goodness Dad was on my side and helped convince her.

I glanced at the television. My father's program had just gone to a commercial break. I had stalled long enough. This was my chance.

Clearing my throat, I said, "Dad, can you turn off the TV for a minute?"

"Sure." Looking at me strangely, he clicked the remote. "What's up?"

"The big news from the city council meeting is that for the next three years, some rich guy has offered to fund the library."

Now came the tricky part. Dad and I were trying to adjust to our new relationship, and I wasn't sure how to break the news about Mom and her husband to him. Half the time when I talked to him, I still felt like the sixteen-year-old I'd been when he went away. And the rest of the time, I felt like I was walking on eggshells because I hadn't believed or supported my father during his trial and incarceration.

"Holy crap on a cracker!" Gran asked. "Why would some stranger do that?"

"He's not actually a random visitor." I hesitated, then took the plunge. "His name is Jett Benedict, and he's Mom's current husband."

"Sweet baby Jesus!" Gran leaped to her feet as if she were eight years old rather than nearly eighty.

Banshee landed on the floor and ran screeching into the kitchen. Birdie smoothed the fabric of her purple sharkskin robe and tightened the sash. Her fashion sense was eclectic—one day she might dress like Doris Day in *Tea for Two*, the next like Ali MacGraw in *Love Story*.

Dad ran his fingers through his short auburn hair. Strands of gray glinted in the lamplight. He smiled feebly at his mother, then at me, and said, "I guess I should have warned you that Yvette was coming to town."

CHAPTER 5

Noah slammed through his front door and tossed his keys into the brass tray on the hall table. Lucky, the Chihuahua he'd inherited from his deceased fiancée, greeted him in the foyer. The look on Noah's face must have scared the little dog, because instead of his usual barking and tail wagging, the Chihuahua dropped the loafer he'd been chomping on and retreated down the corridor.

Feeling guilty for frightening Lucky, who normally would have never given up the shoe without a tug-of-war, Noah followed the pooch into the kitchen. After petting the Chihuahua and scratching behind his ears, Noah opened the back door so the little dog could relieve himself in the fenced-in yard.

While Lucky did his business, Noah preheated the oven. As he waited for the Chihuahua to finish and come back inside, Noah closed his eyes and groaned. His mother was going to drive him over the edge.

One day he wouldn't show up for work, and when his clinic manager sent someone to check on him, they'd discover him building a castle from mashed potatoes. Or doing something else that was bat-shit crazy.

Once Noah had removed Nadine from the city council meeting, he'd sent her home with her health aide, Beckham Janson. But just as Dev asked her question and Jett Benedict introduced his wife, Janson had texted Noah that his mother was trying to phone a Kansas City TV station to tell them about the UFOs.

Which meant that instead of following Dev and explaining that he didn't know St. Onge hadn't told her that the library donor was her stepfather, Noah had been forced to deal with his own family crisis.

After instructing Janson that under no circumstances was he to allow Nadine to contact the media, Noah had slipped out the conference room's side entrance and hastily driven to his mother's place. All he needed was the fourth estate getting wind of Nadine's fixation on the threat of a close encounter of the third kind.

It had taken Noah an hour to calm down his mother. She was convinced that an alien invasion was imminent and if they didn't contact the government to shoot down the spaceships, everyone in Shadow Bend would either be abducted or assimilated.

Finally, Noah had resorted to slipping an Ambien into his mother's cup of hot chocolate. Her doctor had prescribed the mild sedative to treat Nadine's insomnia, but she refused to take the medication. Knowing that zolpidem acts on the brain to produce a calming effect, Noah hoped that it would soothe his mother's fears.

Once she'd dozed off, Noah had made sure the security system was activated. Janson had assured

Noah that he kept the receiver by his bed and was a light sleeper, so he would hear Nadine if she woke. Up until now the health aide's main responsibilities had been to run errands and provide Nadine with company, but those duties seemed to be shifting. Noah just hoped the young man was able to handle the change.

After letting Lucky back inside, Noah headed for the refrigerator, grabbed a beer, and twisted off the cap. He chugged half the bottle of Coors Light, then set it on the counter and looked down. The Chihuahua sat patiently by his bowl, waiting for Noah to fill it with canned food and refresh his water dish.

Once Noah had taken care of the dog's needs, he got a pizza from the freezer and stuck it in the oven. He hadn't had time to eat supper before the city council meeting and he was starving.

He frowned. If Nadine hadn't had her meltdown, he might be having a late dinner with Dev instead of a frozen pepperoni pie with only the Chihuahua for company.

Just when Noah thought he'd gained an advantage on Del Vecchio in the contest for Dev's affections, his mother pulled this new crap and he'd had to flake out on Dev. Deputy Dawg might be hindered by his ex-wife's presence, but eventually she would recover and return to St. Louis. Nadine wasn't going anywhere.

When Noah had realized that he'd have to stay with Nadine until she fell asleep, he'd texted Dev that he'd had an emergency and couldn't meet her. He hadn't had a chance to check his phone since then. While he waited for his food to heat up, he pulled out his cell and looked at his messages.

"Son of a bitch!" Noah's roar startled Lucky, and the little dog growled before resuming his meal.

Taking a calming breath, Noah reread Dev's text. *Shit!* He'd been right. St. Onge *hadn't* told Dev that her mother would be at the meeting, and she was blaming both Boone and Noah for the omission.

Noah quickly tried phoning Dev, but she didn't pick up, so he left a voice mail explaining that he'd thought St. Onge had informed her about Yvette's presence. While he was at it, he sent her the same message via text.

Glancing at his watch, Noah saw that it was after eleven. Dev was probably in bed, but just in case she wasn't and she called back, he turned up the sound on his cell so he wouldn't miss it.

The timer *ding*ed, and Noah grabbed a dish from the cabinet and a potholder from the drawer. He removed his dinner from the oven and slid it onto the waiting plate. After cutting it into wedges, he picked up a slice, blew on it, and took a big bite of cheesy goodness.

When he was a child, his mother had never allowed processed foods in their house, and Noah's craving for the forbidden fare hadn't abated in the years he'd been on his own. As a doctor, he knew he should eat healthy, but this was his secret indulgence, and he wasn't giving it up anytime soon.

Savoring the rich tomato sauce and spicy pepperoni, Noah thought about how he would convince Dev that surprising her with her mother at the meeting had been St. Onge's fault, not his. He had slowly been regaining her trust, and this could be a real setback.

Had that been St. Onge's plan all along? No. Dev's BFF was too pissed about Del Vecchio's ex-wife living with him to try to sabotage Noah's relationship with her. So why hadn't he told Dev about her mother?

Noah finished his pizza, put the dishes in the sink, and then, too wound up to go to bed, he strolled into his den. Flopping down on the leather couch, he grabbed the remote. There was a commercial on, and as he waited for it to be over and *The Late Late Show* to return, he looked around the room.

This was the only spot in his house that felt like home. When he'd bought the place two years ago, he'd allowed the decorator free rein. But after she'd finished and he'd written her a check for an obscene amount of money, he'd gradually added his own stuff to the den.

He'd hired an interior designer because it had been simpler than fighting his mother. Noah had never liked conflict, and except in his role as a physician, when he was willing to fight for his patients, he prided himself on being an easygoing kind of guy. That was changing.

Nadine's reaction to his dating Dev had seen to that. There was no way he would allow his mother to get in his way. He loved Dev, and he would do everything in his power to convince her to marry him.

Up until six months ago, he'd been drifting, doing what was expected of him. He hadn't really been depressed, but neither had he been happy. He'd been numb. He'd settled into an engagement with a woman he didn't love, but when her murder brought Dev back into his life, it was as if his heart had been jump-started.

Dev was what he'd needed all along. And Noah wasn't about to allow his mother, St. Onge, or Del Vecchio to snatch her away from him.

Thinking about mothers made him wonder why Jett Benedict had made Dev's presence at the city council meeting a condition for his funding the library. He could understand a man wanting to make his wife happy by reuniting her with her daughter. But from what Noah knew about her, Yvette Sinclair Benedict wasn't the maternal type. So why did she want to see Dev so badly?

CHAPTER 6

A couple of weeks had gone by since the big reveal at the city council. Boone and Noah were both still on my shit list for setting me up, and because of that I hadn't spent more than a few minutes with either one of them. I was still debating Noah's claim that he thought Boone had told me Yvette would be at the meeting. And Boone's explanation that my presence had been Jett's only additional stipulation to funding the library's reopening, other than access to the archives, hadn't mitigated my anger toward him or the feeling of betrayal.

Adding to my discontent, Jake had been preoccupied with Meg's recent setbacks, so I hadn't seen much of him, either. Then, to top it all off, Mom had taken to popping into my store several times a day. I was having difficulty adjusting to her presence, and it was even more bizarre to see her and Dad together.

When I confronted my father about his relationship with Yvette, he said he believed that if you harbored resentment, happiness had no place to dock.

It had been all I could do not to roll my eyes at his hippie-dippie philosophy, but I'd kept my mouth shut and nodded without comment.

Now I twisted the ends of my ponytail as I watched my mother and father cooing to each other near the Fall into Autumn display. The scarecrows guarding the pumpkins seemed to be smirking as Dad stared soulfully into Mom's baby blues, all the while pretending to reposition the colorful paper leaves and bushel baskets.

It would serve him right if he stepped on one of the rakes in the arrangement and it smacked him square in the face. Maybe that would wake him up to Mom's manipulations and maneuverings.

I was aware that when Dad had gotten out of prison a few months ago, my mother had written to him. But I was taken aback when he'd revealed that since then, she'd been calling and texting him regularly.

I understood why he'd kept it a secret from Gran, but I was hurt that he hadn't confided in me. Then again, who's to say I would have been any more accepting of their renewed connection than Birdie?

Yvette and Kern almost seemed to have picked up right where they'd been when they'd parted thirteen years ago. Which was disconcerting, considering that she was now married to a different man. Not that I wanted to see it, but I half expected to find her doing the walk of shame out of my father's apartment one morning.

Before my grandfather died, back when the Sinclairs were prosperous landowners and farmers, the hired hand had lived in the studio above the garage. Although it had been empty for years, as soon as Gran had known Dad was getting out of prison, she'd cleaned it up and had it ready for him to move in when he arrived home.

This arrangement mostly worked, but with Dad, Gran, and me living in one another's pockets, none of us had any degree of privacy. The lack of it had severely curtailed my options regarding any love life I might choose to pursue. But now I wondered if my father might be suffering right along with me.

The sleigh bells above the front door jingled, and pasting a smile on my face, I welcomed the three elderly women who entered the store.

After returning my greeting, they took seats at the soda fountain.

"What can I get for you ladies?" I gestured to the blackboard. "Today's special is bourbon pecan ice cream served in mini pie shells."

They conferred among themselves, and then they each ordered a glass of water and one special to share. I served them their treat with three spoons, and while they ate, I allowed my gaze to wander around the store.

When the place was full, excited voices created a cheerful hubbub. I had decided against acoustical tile or cork matting for the ceiling and had kept the original tin tiles. I'd also saved the gorgeous oak hardwood floors by having them sanded, restained, and sealed.

Regardless of how disheartened or upset I might be, the old-fashioned charm of my shop made me smile. I had always loved this place. After every doctor's appointment, my mom had brought me to the soda fountain for a hot fudge sundae. Every Sunday Dad had taken me to the dime store to buy a dollar's worth of candy. And when I turned fifteen, Gran had taken me there to buy my first lipstick.

Which is why, when the ninety-one-year-old Thornbee twins had put the five-and-dime up for sale, I'd immediately submitted an offer. The sisters' grandfather had built the shop when Shadow Bend was little more than a stagecoach stop, and the thought of the place being turned into a Rite Aid or a CVS had spurred me into action.

Although I had doubled the interior space and had installed Wi-Fi, I'd tried to keep the character of the original variety store intact. In doing so, I had attracted several local groups who, in exchange for meeting space—square footage was cheap in Shadow Bend— bought the materials for their projects from me.

The Stepping Out Book Club, the Quilting Queens, the Knittie Gritties, and the Scrapbooking Scalawags all met at my store. In addition to their supplies, I also sold the members refreshments and any other odds and ends that caught their eye. All of which provided a nice steady source of revenue for my business.

I heard Mom's cell chime, and I looked over to where she and Dad were standing. She'd been ignoring her persistently trilling phone ever since she'd arrived at the store. However, this time she glanced at the text message, chewed her bottom lip, then sent a brief answer before turning a brilliant smile back to my father.

Frowning, I stared at my parents. How would my customers react to their obvious flirtation? Shadow Bend was an old-fashioned kind of town, and adultery didn't sit well with most folks.

I had to admit Kern and Yvette made a beautiful couple. Dad was tall and lean, with the erect posture of an army general. He had a few more lines than before he went to prison, but there was still the same twinkle in his bright green eyes that I remembered.

And time seemed to have stood still for Yvette. I wasn't at all thrilled that she looked more like my older sister than my mother, or that it was clear Dad was enamored of her. As I watched, he brought her hand to his mouth, and although I couldn't hear what she said, whatever it was brought a smile to his lips.

Finally, the ladies finished eating their ice cream pie, divided the bill three ways, and left the store. After washing up the dish, their water glasses, and spoons, I deposited the whopping six dollars—five ninety-five plus a nickel tip—in the till, then stepped over to the old kitchen table that I used for my workbench.

It was located in the space behind the register, and from that vantage point, I could keep an eye on my amorous parents *and* the front door. Not that I was expecting any shoppers. The hours after lunch were usually slow. I often didn't see a single customer from one to three, which was why Dad's official shift ended at noon.

But today, when Mom had strolled in at five to twelve, he'd suddenly forgotten that he was off the clock and had remained on the sales floor. I noticed that he'd finally stopped fussing with the autumn display and he and my mother had moved over to the candy case. He selected a Black Forest truffle, popped it into Yvette's mouth, and as I watched her lick his fingers, I made a mental note to dock his pay the two dollars and fifty cents.

Looking away from my parents' flirting, I thought about the next item on my to-do list—filling an order for one of my custom-made, personalized gift baskets. When I'd bought the dime store, I'd known I would need something extra to stay profitable, so I'd added the baskets.

That part of the business was extremely lucrative since I was selling my creativity more than the actual items. Now that I had hired my father, I finally had more time to devote to my sideline.

I had one steady customer, Oakley Panigrahi, who bought upward of twenty thank-you gifts a month. He was a Kansas City real estate tycoon who sold luxury properties. Oakley was persnickety, but he thought nothing of paying two or three hundred per basket.

Customarily, his orders were my top priority, but I had a request for one of my special creations, which I needed to complete by late afternoon. I usually worked on that kind of basket before the store opened, but a woman had offered me twice my price for same-day service.

My stomach growled, reminding me that I hadn't had lunch, so I ran into the back room and grabbed a container of Greek yogurt to eat as I worked on the rush order. Returning, I saw that my parents had left. I breathed a sigh of relief, and shoving aside the idea that they might have gone to sample some afternoon delight, I spooned the Yoplait into my mouth. As I ate, I examined the client's questionnaire.

The basket was for her girlfriend's birthday. My customer had forgotten until that morning that her life partner was born exactly thirty years ago today.

Looking over the half-completed form, I frowned. She was lucky I had a broad supply of merchandise that would please women of almost any preference or she'd be out of luck, because there was no time to order additional items.

Each of the baskets included my trademark—the perfect book for both the occasion and the person receiving the gift. While I was looking through my available inventory, my phone started playing Ross Copperman's "Holding on and Letting Go."

I dug the cell from my pocket, touched the speaker icon, and said, "Hello."

"Are you busy?" Noah's smooth tenor sent a delightful shiver down my spine.

"Always." I was still upset with him for his part in springing Yvette and her husband on me without any warning, but picturing his soft gray eyes smiling into mine was weakening my resolve to stay angry.

"I have some news about my mother." Noah's tone didn't reveal whether the info was bad or good.

"Oh." I was none too pleased with Nadine, either, so I stuck to one-word responses, hoping Noah would get the message.

"When you passed on Ronni's comment about Mom's general lack of interest in anything not directly affecting her, it made me wonder why she was so agitated about the aliens." He paused. "I knew questioning her directly wouldn't work, so I finally got Janson alone and asked him if he had any idea what had stirred her up."

"And?"

As I waited for Noah's answer, I started to work on the rush basket. Against the folds of a black satin robe, I placed *Heart of the Game* by Rachel Spangler and a pack of edible body tattoos. According to the package, the tattoos were totally lickable, and the recipient was supposed to apply them in a place they wanted their partner's tongue. Picturing Noah next to me, I could think of several locations where his mouth would be welcome. That is, if I weren't still mad at him.

Noah sighed. "Janson said he believes Mom had company right before they left for city hall. He'd run to the pharmacy, and when he got back there were two wineglasses by the sink. He thinks whoever visited must have said something about the invading aliens, because originally Nadine was attending the meeting because of the rooming-house issue, not the extraterrestrials."

"Interesting," I murmured. Nadine's reason was just as I had guessed.

I kept working on my special order. I needed to finish it before school got out and a swarm of starving teenagers poured into the store. No way could I be making an X-rated basket with a hoard of underage kids present, even if most of them would be hanging out in the recently created teen lounge on my second floor.

Which reminded me, I wanted to make sure my newest employee understood the rules of that space. On the recommendation of Mrs. Zeigler, the high school principal, I had hired Taryn Wenzel. After losing my two previous clerks—one to college and one for less auspicious reasons—I'd had to take on a couple of new staff members. My father was filling one vacancy, and per my policy of hiring from the school's vocational program, Taryn had started a couple of weeks ago.

I had recently hung up a sign in the teen lounge that read, "NO" IS A COMPLETE SENTENCE. Taryn needed to abide by that decree.

"Now all I need to do is figure out who stopped

by to see Mom and why." Noah's comment brought
me back to the present.

He sounded tired, and I couldn't blame him. Rid-
ing herd on Nadine was a full-time job.

"Good luck with that."

I tilted my head, considering adding a pair of
Naughty Ballerina crotchless bikinis to the basket,
but since my client hadn't filled in the blank for her
girlfriend's size, I reluctantly put them aside. It was
a shame, since the panties had cute little ruffles that
emphasized the wearer's derriere and a subtle peeka-
boo cutout so she could act out her own version of a
lap dance.

"Luck has never played much of a part in my
dealings with Mom," Noah muttered, then asked,
"Are you free tonight? A patient gave me two tickets
to the *Book of Mormon*. If we leave here by five, we
could make it to Kansas City in time for an early
dinner."

"You know the store is open until six on Tues-
days." I tried to keep the impatience out of my tone.
"I can't just close early. Some of us need our business
to turn a profit, in order to earn a living."

As the words left my mouth, I cringed. I was
being unfair to Noah. Although he was probably
one of the wealthiest men in town, his affluence
never stopped him from putting in long hours at his
practice.

After completing his education, Noah had returned to Shadow Bend and opened the Underwood
Clinic. The only medical center in a forty-mile ra-
dius, it was always packed with patients. Until recently, due to the long hours and low pay, he'd been
unable to entice another physician into joining his
practice, but a couple of months ago he'd finally

found an altruistic doctor who was willing to move to a small town, work ten-hour days, and settle for less money.

"I thought maybe your father could cover the store for an hour and close up for you." Noah blew out a frustrated breath. "But if you'd rather, we could leave here at six and eat afterward."

"Well . . ." I should say no, but I had wanted to see that show for a while and it had been sold out almost since day one. "I can't go to the theater in my jeans, polo shirt, and tennis shoes."

"How long would it take you to go home and change clothes?" Noah asked.

"If I have Dad come in to work the last couple of hours, he could bring me an outfit and I could change here," I admitted, then added, "If I can get ahold of my father, that is."

Returning my attention to the basket, I decided that since the panties were out, I'd include a Kissaholic Aphrodisiac Lip Stain and Melt Chocolate Body Fondue instead.

As Noah asked, "Does that mean you'll go out with me?" I heard the beeping that indicated someone else was trying to call me. I couldn't identify the number, so I tapped the IGNORE button. The only one for whom I would put another person on hold was Birdie.

"If I can get a change of clothes." My phone beeped for a second time. It was the same unfamiliar number, so I hit IGNORE again. "And this doesn't mean that I forgive you for springing Jett and my mother on me."

"As I've repeatedly tried to tell you, St. Onge didn't let me in on the fact you weren't aware they would be at the meeting." Noah's voice had an impatient edge. "But I am sorry that I didn't make sure he'd informed you."

"Fine." In my heart, I knew Noah was telling the truth. "I'll let it go this time."

"Thank you." Noah's smile was evident. "If you can't get ahold of your father, I could run out to your place and pick up an outfit for you, and we can leave later."

"Okay."

I stepped back to admire the birthday basket and nibbled my thumbnail. Something was missing. Rummaging through my "naughty box," I found the perfect finishing touch for my creation. Just as I was adding a Va-Va Voom Boa, my phone beeped once again. It was the same number as previously. That was odd. Most people would have left a message the first time they called, rather than continue redialing. A shiver ran down my spine. Something was wrong.

"Listen," I said to Noah. "I've got to go. I'll text you if I need you to get my stuff."

We said good-bye and I answered the incoming call. At first I didn't recognize the frantic voice coming from the cell's speaker, but when I did, I interrupted and said, "Dad, slow down. What's the matter? Are you hurt? Is it Gran? What happened?"

"I'm fine and your grandmother is fine." Dad sounded as if he'd been running. "But I need you to come over to the library right now."

"The library?" Had I heard him right? "It's not even open yet."

"The side door is unlocked." Dad murmured something to someone, but I couldn't make out what he'd said. "Don't tell anyone where you're going, and don't let anyone see you enter the building."

"Okay. I'm grabbing my purse and locking up the

back entrance as we speak." My father had never asked anything of me, so I sure wouldn't refuse him when he did. "But what's going on?"

"Jett Benedict is dead." Dad's voice cracked, and he cleared his throat before he continued. "And it looks as if he was murdered."

Before I could respond to that startling announcement, he hung up, and I stared at my cell. What was Kern doing at the library with my deceased stepfather? And why had Dad called me instead of the police?

CHAPTER 7

After turning on the neon CLOSED sign, I rushed out of the dime store's front entrance, locking it behind me. Then, my heart pounding and my pulse racing, I sprinted across the town square. The library was located between city hall and the movie theater, so this whole mad dash reminded me of running away from my mother after the city council meeting. Talk about bad déjà vu.

The library was housed in a redbrick mid-nineteenth-century Italianate building. Long, narrow two-story windows with crescent-moon stained-glass inserts stretched upward nearly to the roof. Keystones at the top of the arch gave the structure a look of permanent surprise. Facing the street, narrow slits marched across the top of the edifice, almost as if to provide snipers a location to repel an enemy attack.

I checked over my shoulder. Lucky for me, there were no adversaries in sight. Tuesday afternoon wasn't exactly prime shopping time, and the town square was completely deserted. Relieved that I wasn't being observed, I darted into the alley separating the library from the movie theater.

After hurrying to the side door, I twisted the knob. As Dad had promised, it was unlocked. Slipping inside, I hastily closed the door behind me. It took a moment for my eyes to adjust to the darkness, and as I waited, apprehension skittered along my nerves, tightening my shoulders.

Once I could see again, I discovered that I was in a short hallway. To my right was a storeroom and to my left was a staircase that I assumed led to a basement. I looked into the dark abyss and cringed. Ever since I'd been accidentally locked in my grandmother's cellar, I was not fond of dank, subterranean spaces.

There were no sounds of activity coming from the single large room in the front of the building, and I deduced that there wasn't any remodeling going on today.

"Dad," I called out softly. "It's Dev. I'm here. Where are you?"

Silence.

"Dad?" I lifted my voice.

Nothing.

A quiver of fear raised the hair at the back of my neck. What if the person who'd killed Jett had also murdered my parents and was now lying in wait for me?

Peeking into the storage room, I saw that cobwebs covered the boxes on the shelves and an old oak worktable was thick with dust. It looked as if no one had been in here for quite some time. Evidently, the library reopening project hadn't made it to this area yet. I wondered what was holding up the work.

Backing out, I eyed the stairs. Venturing into a dark basement after receiving a call about a murder was something a naive young heroine in a Victoria Holt Gothic romance might do, but certainly not me. At least not without some lights and a weapon.

I searched for a switch near the top of the staircase.

Strike one. There wasn't anything on the wall but an old sign advising the staff to use caution when descending the steps.

Wishing I had brought along my trusty Maglite, which was strong enough to turn the midnightlike darkness into high-noon brightness, I settled for the flashlight app on my cell.

Now that I could see my surroundings, I scanned the area for a weapon.

Strike two. I didn't see anything I could use to defend myself. Why was it that libraries rarely had swords lying around?

Just as I turned toward the storeroom, thinking there might be something useful in there, I remembered that after our first investigation together, Jake had given me a pepper-spray gun. He'd insisted that I keep the bright blue revolver with me at all times. I had thrown it into my purse, then promptly forgotten about it. Digging it out from beneath all the detritus that had settled on top of it, I tried to remember his instructions for its use, but all I could recall was *aim and squeeze the trigger.*

I slung my purse strap across my body, and then with the cell in my left hand and the pepper-spray gun in the other, I crept down the stairs. I kept the light trained on the step in front of me and hoped that if there was a bad guy—or girl—waiting for me at the bottom, my stealthy approach would give me an advantage.

With both hands occupied, I wasn't able to hang

on to the railing, and as I put my weight on the next
tread, I heard a sharp crack. Afraid I was about to
plummet to my death, I let out a scream.

Strike three. Whoever was down there now knew
that I was heading their way.

Scrambling upward, I decided that, despite my
father's warning, I needed backup. But before I could
figure out whom to call, I heard my dad shouting my
name.

I leaned forward and squinted. I could see a figure moving toward me.

A few seconds later, Dad grabbed me by the elbow
and said, "Hurry. Benedict's in the archives."

Having no idea where the library kept its archives,
I allowed Dad to escort me down into the basement,
but I kept both the pepper-spray gun and cell phone
light clutched in my hands, ready for any trouble.

As we passed through a large area piled with old
furniture, cartons, and trunks covered in spiderwebs,
I asked, "Whose phone did you use to call me?" I
would have recognized the number if it were his.

"Your mother's."

"Why?"

"She said hers was a prepaid disposable and couldn't
be traced."

My breath caught in my throat. Why did my mother
carry a burner cell? And more important, why didn't
she want my dad's call to me to be traceable? This situation had disaster written all over it.

Before I could put my questions into words, Dad
led me into a room lined with shelves and file cabi-
nets. Evidently, Jett had arranged for the electricity
to be turned on, because a bare bulb hanging from
the ceiling illuminated the scene.

The light was dim, but it was bright enough for me to see my stepfather's body collapsed over an open drawer, the back of his head a bashed-in, bloody mess. My hope that he really wasn't dead evaporated faster than a genie returning to his bottle after granting the third wish.

When the yogurt I'd recently eaten threatened a reappearance, I swallow hard and averted my glance from Jett's wound. Looking away from the carnage, I spotted Yvette slumped in an old wooden chair, her face buried in her hands. Mom's shoulders were shaking, but she wasn't making any sound.

Taking a deep breath, I turned to Dad and asked, "What happened?"

"Benedict kept texting your mother while she and I were talking at the dime store," Dad explained. "At first she didn't read his messages, but when she did, she said he wanted her to meet him at the library. We were in the middle of an important discussion, so she ignored his request, but he kept bugging her."

I raised a brow. My father knew darn well he and his ex-wife had been flirting, not ironing out a treaty for world peace.

Dad had the grace to look a little sheepish as he continued. "Finally, your mom said she'd better see what Benedict wanted and left to go to the library to find out what the fuss was about."

"I take it you didn't go with her." I was fairly certain Mom's new husband didn't know she had been spending so much time with her old one.

"Not all the way to the library." Dad refused to meet my eyes, finding the band of his wristwatch too fascinating to look away from. "I waited for her in my car. The plan was that she'd run over here, take care of whatever Benedict needed, and then we'd head to the barbecue place over by Sparkville for a late lunch."

"What happened next?" I asked, although I had a pretty good idea.

"Yvette walked across the square and used her key for the side entrance." Dad glanced over at my mother, who still hadn't lifted her head or moved from her perch on the wooden chair. "She knew Benedict was in the archives, so she went down here to find him."

"And?" I swear getting Dad to tell me the whole story was as hard as getting the last bit of caramel sauce from a glass jar.

"And your mother discovered Benedict like this." Dad pointed to the body of my stepfather. "It was obvious he was dead, so she called me."

"Why?" I narrowed my eyes and looked at my mother. She was now staring straight ahead. "Why didn't she get out of here and call the police?"

"Uh." Dad's eyes jerked to Mom, and then he shrugged. "I don't know."

It was more than a little creepy that we were calmly discussing the events leading up to discovering my stepfather's body while he was oozing blood a few feet away. But I needed more information before I could formulate any kind of sensible plan.

"So you came over here." I was perplexed by the whole scenario. Mom finds her husband murdered. Sticks around. Calls her ex-husband and waits for him to . . . what . . . resurrect Jett? "What next?"

"After I made sure there was nothing we could do to help Benedict, I called you." Dad cut his gaze to my mother. "I wanted to contact the police, but Yvette got hysterical at the idea."

Mom's actions didn't add up. Had she and Jett had a fight and she smacked him over the head with something? Then, when she'd seen what she'd done, had she decided to try to pin the murder on Dad?

Oh. My. God! Dad was on parole. He had been paroled rather than pardoned, because despite the fact he hadn't willingly taken the drug, he had run over and accidentally killed a woman while under its influence. He might have been able to get the conviction overturned, but taking parole had been cheaper and quicker than a new trial.

My heart raced. He could be sent back to prison. I mentally ran through the conditions of his parole. He hadn't traveled out of the state without permission or changed his residence. I could prove he was maintaining employment. Unless Mom was a convicted felon, he was avoiding contact with known criminals, because with the exception of Gran, the chief of police, and me, Yvette was the only person with whom he socialized.

He didn't do drugs or own a weapon. And he reported regularly to his corrections agent. As far as I knew, there was nothing about discovering a dead body in the rules, but I had a feeling that might fall under some sort of miscellaneous section.

My stomach clenched. I had to get him out of here right now, and then I had to make sure no one knew he'd ever been on the scene.

Grabbing both his hands, I demanded, "What have you touched?"

For a third time, Dad glanced at my mother. He was definitely hiding something, but we'd already been here way too long, so I couldn't take the time to pry whatever secret he was keeping out of him.

When he didn't answer my question, I raised my voice and repeated, "What did you touch?"

Dad's mouth dropped open. Even as a rebellious teen, I had never yelled at him before. Suddenly, his eyes widened, and he shouted, "Son of a bitch! You're afraid I'll be accused of murdering him."

"Not necessarily," I hedged. Privately, I thought Mom had more to worry about on that front, but now was not the time to bring up that idea. "However, I am concerned that this might affect your parole."

My father screwed up his face and then said slowly, "The outside doorknob, the banister, and Benedict's wrist when I took his pulse."

I dug around in my purse until I located a packet of tissues. Ripping one out of the cellophane wrapper, I handed it to my father and ordered, "Wipe everything you touched or might have touched."

"What about him?" Dad pointed at Jett. "Does skin retain fingerprints?"

"I don't think so." I tried to remember every forensic television crime show I'd ever watched and every dark mystery I'd ever read. "But if he's wearing a watch on the wrist where you took his pulse, clean that."

"His Rolex is on the other arm," Dad murmured.

When my father continued to stand there, I jabbed his shoulder with my index finger and said, "Move it. You need to get out of here right now."

"What about me?" Appearing to have recovered from her shock, Yvette jumped up from her seat. "I should leave with Kern."

"Whoa." I grabbed her upper arm as she headed out of the room.

"Let me go." Mom's voice rose, and she tried to break free from my fingers. "I have to get out of here.

They'll think I did it. In cases like this, the police always assume it's the spouse."

"Did you do it?" I asked, watching her expression carefully.

"No!" Mom's face crumpled. "How could you even think that about me?"

"Let me count the reasons." Sanity might be on back order in our family, but I had an unlimited supply of sarcasm. "On second thought, we don't have time for that list."

"Why are you being so mean to me?" Mom tried to get away.

I tightened my grip on her biceps, and keeping Yvette by my side, I pointed at Dad and instructed, "You, wipe off your fingerprints, make sure no one sees you leaving the building, and then drive straight home." When he hesitated, I foolishly promised, "I'll take care of Mom."

When he continued to hesitate, I threatened, "Unless you want to go back to prison, listen to me and do what I say right now."

Dad's fair skin turned an ashy gray and he nodded. He kissed Yvette's cheek, muttered that he was sorry, then hurried out of the archives.

While my father wiped off his prints and made his escape from the library, I had a few minutes before I could execute the second part of my plan, so I whirled on Yvette and said, "What's your game?"

"I . . . I . . ." she stammered, then out of the blue said, "The trouble with life is that there's no background music."

I was silent only because this was one of those situations where my supply of profanity was insufficient to meet my demands. Instead, I stared at my mother until she spoke.

Apparently, she correctly interpreted the "don't even try" look on my face and said, "Kern always fixed everything when we were married. I thought he could fix this."

"How?" I wrinkled my brow in disbelief. Maybe I had been right. Could my mother really think Dad could bring back the dead?

"I'm not sure." Yvette sobbed. "But Kern was always the smart one."

"Any idea who would want Jett dead?" I checked my watch. I'd give Dad five more minutes to get to his car. Then I'd call the police.

"Of course not." Mom shook her head vehemently. "Everyone loved Jett. He was giving the town back its library. Why would anyone harm him?"

"How about you?" I put myself between my mother and the door and released her arm. "You and Dad seem to be getting awfully cozy again."

"Don't be silly." Mom huffed. "Kern and I are just good friends now."

"Right." I looked at my Timex again. Dad should have made it to his Jeep by now. "Here's the story. You and I came to the library to pick up Jett for a late lunch. When we got here, we discovered him dead and called the police."

"But—"

I ran through the scenario we would tell the authorities and added, "Be vague about the time. Tell the police you don't know when we got here."

"Got it." Yvette nodded. "Late lunch. Found him dead. Called cops."

"Good."

I started to dial 911, and Mom grabbed my hand.

"We need to put our fingerprints back on the railing and the outside doorknob." Mom pulled me out of the room, then said over her shoulder, "Otherwise, the police will notice they've been wiped clean."

I stared at my suddenly calm and collected mother. How did she know stuff like that? I certainly hoped she came by her knowledge of forensics the same way I did, via TV and books. But she'd never been much of a reader, and her taste in television had run more toward *Sex and the City* and *Gilmore Girls* than *NCIS* and *CSI*.

CHAPTER 8

Istood in front of the library, trying to peer through the dirty windows. As soon as Chief Kincaid had arrived and assessed the situation, he'd sent me to wait outside and led my mother off somewhere for a chat. Along with watching the influx of cops, I'd been checking my watch every few minutes since my banishment.

Both ends of the street had been blocked, with an auxiliary officer manning each barricade. I knew they weren't the real deal because, instead of the standard uniform, they wore light blue shirts with navy epaulets and black pants. These volunteers provided traffic control, helped on searches, and supplied additional manpower on an as-needed basis. Unfortunately, the imitation cops were often a few doughnuts short of a dozen.

In addition to the auxiliaries, it seemed as if Chief Kincaid had called in every officer on the Shadow Bend force. The strong police presence was puzzling. True, there had been a murder, but the chief was treating the situation as if there were a bomb threat or a biohazard emergency.

Tired of pacing, I strolled up to the squad car parked on the sidewalk. It was barring the building's entrance and I peeked inside, but there wasn't anything interesting to see. The driver had gotten out and was arguing with the cop from another cruiser— the one positioned diagonally across the mouth of the alley.

I sauntered closer. Maybe I could overhear their conversation and get some idea of what was going on. However, as soon as they spotted me, they clamped their lips shut and frowned.

The officer closer to me was Jessie Huang, one of two female cops on the force. She and I had spent some time together during a previous investigation, and she had bonded with my grandmother's cat.

Hoping Jessie might give me a hint as to why the chief had rallied all the troops, I put a question in my voice and said, "Looks like Chief Kincaid thinks this is more than a simple robbery gone bad?"

"Hard to say." She looked somewhere over my head, clearly avoiding my gaze. As I opened my mouth to try another approach, the radio on her shoulder crackled to life. Stepping out of my earshot, she listened intently and nodded.

When she moved back to where I was standing, she said, "The chief's ready to talk to you. Meet him inside the library's rear entrance."

"Is my mother with him?" I asked, trying to gauge Jessie's expression.

"No."

"Oh."

A chill ran down my spine. I sure hoped my mother had stuck to our story and left my father out of it. She was a good liar, so she had no excuse to let anything about him slip into her account of the

events. If she got Dad in trouble, I would never forgive her.

Not that I planned to forgive her anytime in the
near future anyway, but if she screwed up my plan,
I'd be even less inclined to let her off the hook.

As I sprinted away, I heard Jessie mutter to the
other cop, "I wouldn't want to be Dev. The chief is
mad enough to chew nails."

Yikes! Why was Chief Kincaid angry? He liked
things neat and tidy, and murder certainly didn't fit
into that scenario, but, hey, it gave him job security.
At least it did if he solved the case. *Hmm. I probably
shouldn't mention that during our interview.*

Walking into the library from the dim alley, I
blinked, temporarily blinded by the eighteen hundred watts of illumination now flooding the building's back hallway. Half a dozen lights mounted on
tripods marched down the passageway in a straight
path to the stairs, where Chief Kincaid stood, ges-
turing for me to join him.

Several people wearing white Tyvek coveralls,
booties, and rubber gloves were swarming over the
tiny corridor and down the steps. I assumed there
were even more in the basement, dusting for prints
and gathering any other forensic evidence the killer
had left behind.

One of the coverall crowd was kneeling in the
storage room doorway, pawing through an unzipped
wheeled suitcase. He glanced up at me as I passed
by him, a speculative expression on his face, then
twitched his shoulders and continued digging around in the duffel.

Oh. My. God! I should have realized I'd be a suspect. Family was always under suspicion. But in my

haste to make sure my father wasn't implicated, I hadn't considered my own vulnerability.

Before I could panic, Chief Kincaid joined me and said, "Follow me."

"Where's my mother?" I asked, refusing to be ordered around like his pet dog.

"I sent her to the station to rest," Chief Kincaid answered. "Yvette claimed she felt ill and needed to lie down."

"I should go check if she's okay." What I really wanted to know is what she'd told the chief. "Maybe she should see a doctor."

"Yvette's tougher than she lets on." The chief started down the steps, but when I didn't immediately move, his head snapped back and he glared. "Don't just stand there. I need you to go over the crime scene with me." He raised a brow. "Unless you're feeling a case of the vapors, too."

No way was I admitting to Poppy's father that I didn't want to spend any more time with a corpse—I had my reputation as a tough chick to maintain—so I sucked it up and accompanied him back into the basement, hurrying to keep up with his rapid descent.

Eyeing the back of Chief Kincaid's heavily starched khaki uniform, I marveled that his clothes looked as if he'd just put them on a few seconds ago. Likewise, his gray buzz cut appeared to have been freshly barbered and his black shoes shone. Eldridge Kincaid demanded perfection from the folks around him, but even more so from himself.

As I had guessed, several more Tyvek-encased people filled that area. The chief stopped at the threshold of the archive room.

A man staring down into the professional-looking

camera that hung around his neck was blocking our way, and the chief barked, "Aren't you done yet?"

The guy jumped as if he'd been slapped, then skittered backward. "Sorry, Chief. Some of the images are blurry. I need a couple more minutes."

"I thought you knew what you were doing." The chief narrowed his steel blue eyes, and the man froze until Chief Kincaid snapped, "What in the Sam Hill are you expecting, an engraved invitation? Go."

As we waited for the photographer to finish, the chief took out a notebook and stared at the pages. Since he clearly didn't want to talk, I took the time to glance around the basement. When my father had hustled me through this area previously, it had been dark. But now, with the police lights, I could see that the whitewashed walls were stained and cracked. At some point, they had sustained water damage and hadn't been repaired.

Although the building housing the library wasn't very large, it seemed to me that this space and the archival room didn't equal the upstairs. I looked to see if there was another doorway, but didn't find any. The structure must only have a partial basement. The rest was probably a crawl space.

Chief Kincaid maintained his silence until the photographer emerged from the archives and gave him a thumbs-up. Then the chief tilted his head toward the doorway and said, "After you. Keep your hands in your pockets and don't touch anything, just point if you need to."

I nodded, took a deep breath, and forced myself to walk into the room.

The body of my stepfather was exactly as Mom and I had left it a couple of hours ago, and I looked questioningly at the chief, who said, "The county medical examiner was in Kansas City, attending a conference. We can't move the vic until he gets here."

I nodded, then waited with a patient air for further instructions. There was no rushing the chief. I'd find out what he wanted faster if I cooperated with him, a lesson his daughter, Poppy, had yet to learn—which was one of the many reasons they weren't speaking.

"What time did you and your mother get here?" Chief Kincaid asked.

"I'm not really sure," I hedged. "Sometime after one or one thirty maybe."

"Walk me through what you did once you arrived at the library."

"We came in the side door," I said slowly, wanting to get my report right. Our story had more potholes than MoDOT had left unfilled on I-70. "Mom had a key."

"So when you two got here, the door was locked?" He took a notepad and a mechanical pencil from his shirt pocket and made a note.

Shit! I wasn't certain how Yvette had answered that. "I'm not sure. Mom put her key in the lock, then turned the knob. I guess it could have already been open. What did my mother say about it?"

Ignoring my question, the chief asked, "Once you were inside, what did you do?"

"Mom explained that Jett was doing research in the archives, so we came down here."

"Did you touch anything besides the banister?" Chief Kincaid asked.

"Uh." I pretended to think, then said, "I may have leaned on the doorframe of the storage room. I peeked inside there when I walked past."

"I see." The chief jotted something on his pad. "How long was it between when you discovered your stepfather and when you called nine-one-one?"

"I don't know." I wrinkled my brow. "Everything seemed to go in slow motion once we saw him like that." I gestured toward Jett's lifeless form. "Mom was hysterical, so it took a while to calm her down."

"How about you?" Chief Kincaid tilted his head appraisingly. "Were you upset, too?"

"In the sense that someone was dead and it looked like murder, yes." I shrugged. "But I'd only met him once before—at the city council meeting—so we didn't have a personal connection."

"I see." The chief folded his arms. "You said he was dead. How did you know that?"

"It was pretty obvious from the wound, but I took his pulse."

"Did you notice this?" Chief Kincaid used his pencil to point to Jett's left hand. When I squinted, he said, "Take a closer look."

Reluctantly, I moved nearer and bent over to inspect my stepfather's fist. Immediately, I saw a shred of paper clutched between his fingers.

"I checked his other wrist." I glanced at the chief. "What's Jett holding?"

"Don't you know what it is?" Chief Kincaid's tone was frustrated. "We can't examine it until the ME gets here and takes it from the vic."

"Is that what you wanted me to see?" I asked, wondering why I couldn't have answered the chief's questions without returning to the crime scene.

"Do you know where your stepfather's cell phone is?" Chief Kincaid asked.

"No." I shook my head. *Shit!* I should have gotten

rid of both Yvette's and Jett's phones. If the police saw all his texts to her, they'd know our story about discovering the body was a lie. "Isn't it on him?" I crossed my fingers and asked the universe for it to be missing.

"No." Chief Kincaid indicated the empty phone holster on Jett's belt. "The murderer must have taken it." The chief frowned, then gestured to the floor and asked, "Was this here when you arrived?"

"What?"

Chief Kincaid tapped the toe of his shoe near a trace of what looked like sparkling gray sand.

"I didn't notice it." Although I kept my expression blank, I prayed that my father hadn't stepped in whatever material Chief Kincaid had discovered. Just in case, I'd have to make sure he got rid of the shoes he'd been wearing.

"Is there anything in this room that looks out of place to you?"

"How would I know?" I retorted. "I've never been in here before."

"Right." Chief Kincaid nodded. "So what was special about today?"

"What do you mean?" I felt my heart speed up. This smelled like a trap.

"Yvette said you were picking up your stepfather for lunch. He's been in town for quite a while now. Why were you getting together in the middle of a workweek?"

"Tuesday afternoon isn't exactly a busy time for me," I stalled.

"Perhaps." The chief's eyes drilled into me. "But previously, the only reason I've known you to lock up your store during business hours is in the case of an emergency." He stepped closer to me. "How is having lunch with your mother and her new husband an emergency?"

"It isn't." I wiped my suddenly sweating palms on my jeans, then wished I hadn't when I saw the chief notice my actions. "The thing is, Mom has wanted me to get to know Jett, but he's been extremely busy. So when he told her he was free for a late lunch today and she asked me to join them, I decided to close for a couple of hours. Business is usually slow between noon and three."

"What a good daughter." Chief Kincaid's voice held a hint of sarcasm.

"I try."

"I was under the impression from your father that you weren't really on very good terms with Yvette," the chief murmured.

"True." I met his gaze without wavering. "That's precisely why I made the extra effort to accommodate my mother's wishes." Thankfully, Yvette wasn't the only adept liar in our family. It was a skill I had picked up during my days as an investment consultant. "I was trying very hard to begin to rebuild our damaged relationship."

"I see." Doubt lingered on each clipped word he spoke to me.

"Was anyone else aware that you planned to have lunch with your mother and stepfather?" he asked. "Maybe you discussed it with a friend?"

"No." I bit my lip, remembering my phone call with Noah. *Hell!* I needed to warn him not to repeat our conversation should the police question him. Although I couldn't see why the cops would think to talk to him, better safe than sorry.

"Why is that?" Chief Kincaid wrote something down before looking up at me and asking, "It seems like a matter you'd discuss with Boone and my daughter before deciding what to do."

"It was a spur-of-the-moment thing." I paused to gather my thoughts, then added, "Mom just stopped by the store and asked if I could join them."

Chief Kincaid was silent, and I stared over his shoulder at a Tyvek-suited figure collecting dust and dirt samples in the other room.

I was still amazed that a town as small as Shadow Bend had such an extensive crime scene team and that we actually had a need for it. Not to mention the pimped-out white RV with SHADOW BEND POLICE CRIME SCENE UNIT painted in navy blue now parked in the alley near the library's side entrance.

It all came back to the infamous grant wars going on between Chief Kincaid and our esteemed mayor, Geoffrey Eggers. The chief and Hizzoner didn't get along, and because of that the city council had been voting down police department budget increases for years.

Frustrated, Chief Kincaid had applied for federal funds to remodel the station, then to train personnel, and finally to purchase up-to-date gear. Everyone had been surprised when the chief's applications began to bring in money and even more shocked when he'd been able to complete all three of those projects.

Eventually, Chief Kincaid had hit the mother lode and had been able to purchase his very own crime scene unit and mobile lab. The grant had even been large enough to pay for the training that allowed the chief's people to operate the elaborate forensic equipment.

The mayor had been beyond livid that the chief had managed to get what he wanted without financing from the town's coffers. Geoffrey Eggers hated being bested at his own game, and if I were Chief Kincaid, I'd be keeping a sharp lookout for Hizzoner's next strike.

Tapping his notepad with his pencil, the chief brought my focus back to him and asked, "How long were you and your mother together before coming over to the library?"

"An hour or so." I kept it as loose as possible. Nailing down a timeline could show too many cracks in our story. "As you said, I don't like to close up the store, so it took her a little while to convince me."

"Yvette would seem to be one of a very few people in these parts who might have some reason for wanting your stepfather dead."

"Like what?" My thoughts flew to her flirting with my dad, but I brushed that image aside and added, "If Mom wanted out of the marriage, she's obviously not averse to the idea of divorce."

"True." Chief Kincaid rolled his pencil between his fingers. "In that case, are you aware of anyone else who might have a motive?"

"No." I shook my head. "As I mentioned, I really didn't know Jett. To my knowledge, he'd never been in Shadow Bend before, so why would anyone here want to kill him?"

"Which brings us back to your mother," Chief Kincaid mused. "The logical assumption is that Benedict's death has something to do with her. Jealousy is a tried-and-true reason for homicide. And the only person I can think of who might be jealous of Yvette's relationship with her new husband would be her old one."

It took me a millisecond to grasp what the chief had said, but when I did, I gasped, a wave of dizziness sweeping through me. I had hoped that since Dad and Chief Kincaid were pals, he might not believe my father was capable of murder. Evidently, I'd been wrong about the depth of their friendship, because it was clear that Dad was one of the chief's top suspects in Jett Benedict's death.

CHAPTER 9

After Chief Kincaid blithely announced that my father was one of his top suspects, he escorted me to the police station and took my written statement. As I waited for Yvette to finish with her official account of the afternoon, I texted Noah that due to my stepfather's death, I wouldn't be able to go to the theater with him.

Assuring him that I would explain everything when I saw him, I requested that he keep quiet about our canceled plans, asked him not to call me, and suggested that we meet for lunch the next day. I told him to come to the dime store, where we could talk in private, promising him chicken salad sandwiches from Little's Tea Room and a full pot of his favorite French-roast coffee.

After getting Noah's okay, I texted Poppy and Boone to tell them about my stepfather and begged them to meet me at Gossip Central at eight for a much-needed drink and debriefing. They'd probably heard about Jett's murder, since they were both firmly tied in to Shadow Bend's rumor mill. In a town as small as ours, there was no way Chief Kincaid could cordon off a street and expect to keep the homicide from becoming the prime topic of local speculation.

Once both of my friends agreed to the get-together, my finger lingered over the picture of Jake on my contact list. I could certainly use his law enforcement expertise, but he rarely seemed to have time for me anymore, and I didn't want to bother him. Or at least I didn't want to feel like I was bothering him, which was even worse.

Sadness crept through me. I missed him. His humor. His warmth. His sexiness. We spoke on the phone every few days, and I could hear how frustrated he was with Meg's lack of progress, but he was too good a guy to dump her back into a psychiatric facility.

I knew that if I were a better person, I would be more sympathetic about Jake's situation. And intellectually I understood his position. But emotionally I felt neglected and abandoned. The same could be said for Noah's behavior. His mother occupied nearly all of the spare moments he could steal from his medical practice, which left precious little of his attention for me.

Disgust hit me in the chest. How could I whine about two such amazing guys? Yes, they had commitments that interfered with our relationship, but then again, so did I. And they'd both pushed aside their pride in order to allow me the space to figure out which of them I truly loved. There weren't many men around who would be able to overcome their macho need for exclusivity.

I was still trying to decide whether to text Jake when my mother joined me in the police station lobby.

Once we got into the car, I asked, "Did Chief Kincaid confiscate your cell phone?"

"He wanted to see it, but I told him I lost it." Yvette shrugged. "Eldridge didn't seem to believe me, so I told him to search my purse and pat me down." Her smile was smug. "Luckily, Kern forgot to give it back to me after he phoned you."

"Good." I gave my mother an approving nod. "I just hope the chief isn't able to get a list of Jett's calls from his carrier."

"He won't." Yvette studied her nails. "Both Jett and I use prepaid cells. He was a bit of a nut about privacy."

"Good." I mentally raised my brows. Had my step-father been hiding something, or had he just been paranoid? "I'll get your phone from Dad and dispose of it."

After my mother assured me that she'd stuck to our agreed-upon story, I warned her to make sure she didn't change any of the details and told her about Chief Kincaid's theory that her husband's death was connected to her. Yvette paled and swore to keep Dad's presence at the scene a secret.

Once I had dropped my mother off at the luxury condo she and Jett had rented near the country club and made sure she was settled in, I headed home.

When I turned in to our lane, I hit the brakes and stared at the new handwritten sign attached to a fence post facing the road. It read, NO TRESPASSING. ET HAS GONE HOME. WE DON'T HAVE THE MONEY TO BUY ANYTHING. WE'VE FOUND JESUS—HE WAS HIDING BEHIND THE COUCH. WE HAVEN'T VOTED IN TWENTY YEARS. REALLY, UNLESS YOU'RE GIVING AWAY CHOCO-LATE, DON'T BOTHER.

Evidently, the UFO guy had been back and Gran

had had enough. I just hoped the professor got the message, because if he returned, Birdie would probably put a load of buckshot in his britches. And the last thing we needed was another family member hauled into the police station.

As soon as I walked in the door, Gran put supper on the table, and while we ate, I brought her and Dad up to speed on what had happened since my father had left the library.

I was starving, and even their unending questions couldn't stop me from enjoying Birdie's chicken and biscuits. The interrogation continued through the homemade butterscotch-pudding cake, but they both finally ran out of steam as we washed the dishes.

My father wanted to go to Mom's condo to make sure she was all right, but I persuaded him that his friend the chief of police would have an officer watching Yvette and would see Dad's visit as evidence that he was still in love with Mom and had killed Jett to get her back.

We argued back and forth, and I finally snapped, "After how Mom treated you, I just don't understand why you're even talking to her, let alone care about her."

Dad put his arm around me and said, "I've made peace with my past, and you should, too. Otherwise, it will screw up your present."

I made a noncommittal sound, and when Dad promised to stay away from his ex-wife and throw the shoes he'd been wearing and my mother's cell phone down the old well, I headed to Gossip Central. I tore down the blacktop toward the bar with Adele's newest hit blaring from my radio.

As I drove, I passed farmhouses and freshly harvested wheat fields. A deer froze by the side of the road, staring at me as I zoomed by. I waved at the

inquisitive animal, loving the peacefulness of the
deserted countryside and relishing the lack of traffic
and congestion I'd faced every day when I'd com-
muted to Kansas City.

By the time I turned in to the club's parking lot, the
breeze had picked up, and the sign over the entrance
moved back and forth on its chains, emitting a gentle
squeak with each swing. Summer would be over in
another week, but it was still pleasantly warm, and I
enjoyed the soft night air.

Anxious for that first taste of the intoxicating goodness of lime and tequila, I sprang out of the Z4 and ran
up the side steps. Poppy was waiting for me at the
delivery door and swung it open, relocking it as soon
as I was inside. With her silvery blond ringlets, ame-
thyst eyes, and slight build, a lot of guys made the
mistake of believing she was an angel. However, they
quickly discovered she was more likely to wear horns
than a halo.

"Boone's already here. He's saving the Stable for
us," Poppy informed me as she pushed me in front
of her. "I'll grab a pitcher of margaritas and meet
you there."

Gossip Central had been a cattle barn before
Poppy bought it and turned it into the hottest night-
spot in the county. She'd kept the basic structure,
and the center of the building contained the stage,
dance floor, and bar, while the hayloft was now a
space that could be rented for private parties. Instead
of tearing down all the stalls, she'd converted them
into out-of-the-way little spots with comfortable
seating, themed decorations, and privacy.

When I entered our favorite alcove, one of the few
spots where Poppy didn't have listening devices installed, Boone was seated on the brown leather love

seat facing the doorway. His coppery face creased into a wide smile, and he leaped to his feet to hug me. Boone claimed that his skin was naturally bronzed, but both Poppy and I knew about the clandestine tanning bed in his back bedroom.

Which, I suppose, was only fair, since he knew all our deep, dark secrets. My biggest one was a tiny shooting-star tattoo I had gotten during a college spring-break trip to Mexico. Poppy's was how she had gotten the financing for the bar.

After releasing me, Boone said, "Your stepfather's murder is all anyone has been able to talk about, but no one seems to know any details. The police are being particularly closemouthed."

"I know."

Boone pulled me down on the sofa, and with an arm slung over my shoulders and an impatient look on his face, he said, "Spill."

Before I could start my story, Poppy strolled through the doorway. She placed a tray holding a pitcher and three glasses on the wood- and wrought-iron feed box that served as a coffee table, then dropped into one of the pair of saddle-stitched club chairs.

She glared at Boone, evidently because he'd tried to get the scoop without her. Then, as she poured the margaritas, she jerked her chin at me and instructed, "Start from the beginning."

"It's hard to know where that is." I grabbed my glass and took a healthy gulp. As the potent liquid entered my system, I relaxed for the first time since I'd gotten my father's call. "How much have you all heard?"

"Jett Benedict was found dead in the library's basement by his wife," Boone recited, as if reading from a newspaper. "Because of the overwhelming police presence, foul play is suspected. Devereaux Sinclair and Yvette Benedict spent a considerable amount of time as guests of the Shadow Bend Police Department."

Boone had barely finished talking when Poppy snapped, "I bet my dad loved that."

"Obsessed much?" I teased. Poppy was convinced that Chief Kincaid's every move as a cop was his way of getting back at her.

"Yes, she is." Boone's hazel eyes crinkled, and he leaned forward and tapped her knee. "Honey, you've got to get over that."

"I am not obsessed. I'm justifiably suspicious," Poppy protested. "Because I know what my father is capable of and you don't."

"We would if you would tell us," Boone retorted. "Which makes me wonder why you won't. We tell each other everything else."

I rolled my eyes. Although it was true we did confide in one another, I had no doubt we each had some things we didn't share. But I remained silent, because when Poppy and Boone started sniping at each other, it was hard to stop them. And tonight I didn't have the energy to waste that kind of effort on something futile.

"I'm not telling because you'll take his side," Poppy accused.

"No, I won't. I would never do that." Boone looked hurt. "Name one time when I haven't stood shoulder to shoulder with you and Dev."

When neither Poppy nor I could meet Boone's challenge, she said, "Well, you set Dev up when her mother and stepfather came to town."

"That was different. I just wanted us to have a

library again, and I figured there was no way she could avoid them in a place this small anyway." Boone glanced at me. "You forgive me, right?"

"I suppose I have to." It was too hard being mad at one of my best friends. "But don't ever keep something like that from me again." I finished my first margarita and poured another. "If you'd have explained, I would have attended the meeting voluntarily."

I hoped I was telling Boone the truth, but I wasn't sure. Would I have sacrificed myself for the town? Probably. Maybe. Possibly.

"Speaking of the library, what happens now that Jett is dead?" Poppy asked.

"Good question." Boone straightened the sharp creases in his designer jeans. "I'll have to see if the endowment was completely set up yet. There've been some hitches with the transfer of funds."

"That explains why the inside of the library is still filthy and looks as if it hasn't been touched," I murmured. Then his words sank in, and I asked, "What kind of snags are you talking about?"

"Oh. Wrong account numbers. Waiting for the right moment to sell stocks. Lawyers on vacation." Boone wrinkled his nose. "Stuff like that."

"In my former profession in the investment field, those types of issues would have thrown up a red flag." I frowned, thinking about what that could mean. "Maybe that's the motive for Jett's murder. Maybe he had money troubles and someone found out."

"Which leads us back to what the eff happened," Poppy huffed.

"You're right. I'm getting ahead of myself." I sat back and made myself comfortable. "It all started this afternoon when my mother stopped by the dime store and asked me to have lunch with her and Jett."

Taking a deep breath, I told them everything, except that it was my father rather than me who had been with Yvette when she'd found her husband's body. I had made Dad and Mom promise not to tell a living soul about his presence, and I wasn't sure if I could do any less.

"Do the cops have any idea who might have killed him?" Poppy asked.

"Unfortunately, that's why I needed to talk to you guys. Chief Kincaid has his eye on two suspects." My heartbeat skittered into high gear as I said the words aloud. "Mom and Dad."

"Was Kern brought in for questioning?" Boone asked, grabbing a leather pad and a slim gold pen from the pocket of his bright green Ralph Lauren polo shirt. "He shouldn't talk without a lawyer."

"Not yet." I sighed. "But I'm sure that's on the chief's to-do list. He probably wants to get all his ducks in a row first. You know, process the forensic evidence and check for witnesses."

I prayed no one had seen my father enter or leave the library.

"Do either of your folks have an alibi?" Boone had donned his attorney persona. His practice consisted mostly of family and real estate law, but in his heart he fancied himself as defense lawyer Will Gardner from *The Good Wife*. Before Will was gunned down, died, and disappeared from the show.

"We won't know that until they have the time of death." I nibbled on my fingernail, then glanced at the ragged edges. It was a good thing I no longer had the money to spend on manicures, or I would have just blown thirty bucks. "As I told the chief, Dad stayed late to finish up the Fall into Autumn display, so he was at the store until twelve thirtyish. And Mom was there from a little after noon until we went to the library together."

"Too bad you don't know when Jett died. That could solve all your problems." Poppy snapped her fingers. "Let me call a friend in the ME's office and see if they've figured it out yet."

"Whoa." Boone held up his hand like a traffic cop. "Do we really want it getting around that we're interested in that? It could make Chief Kincaid think we're trying to arrange a cover-up."

"My friend can keep his mouth shut," Poppy protested. "Besides, it's worth the risk. If Jett was killed while Yvette and Kern were in the dime store, Dev can quit worrying about them."

"I kind of doubt that he was murdered too much before we found him," I said slowly, giving myself time to make a decision.

"Why is that?" Poppy asked, leaning forward. "Was there still blood oozing out of his head when you got there? Was he still warm?"

Boone and I exchanged a glance. Poppy wasn't known for her tact.

"No. The state of Jett's body has nothing to do with why I think he was killed only a few minutes before we found him." It was getting tough to remember the sequence of events among all the lies I'd told. If I wanted my friends' help, they needed to know the truth. I trusted them with my life, and I would just have to trust them with my parents' lives, too.

I exhaled noisily and said, "I want your solemn vow that nothing we discuss leaves this room. It's vital that no hint of what I tell you gets to the police."

Boone pursed his lips, then said, "I still have your

retainer from last spring, so technically, I'm your attorney and anything you say to me is covered by lawyer-client privilege." He glanced at Poppy, dug his wallet out of his pants pocket, handed her a dollar bill, and said, "I am formally hiring you as my administrative assistant. You, too, are under the umbrella of confidentiality."

"Right." Poppy nodded soberly. "What are my duties? Should I take notes?"

"Nope." Boone chuckled. "Just listen and don't tell anyone what you hear."

Feeling slightly better about revealing my parents' secret, I leaned forward and said, "The reason I think Jett was murdered minutes before my mother discovered his body is because he was texting Yvette almost continually until the time she left the store."

"Won't the police see that?" Boone tilted his head. "That will help establish the TOD and could give your parents an alibi."

"Except Jett's phone is missing, and we got rid of Mom's," I admitted, bracing myself for my friends' reaction. "Since they both had prepaid cells, they can't be traced."

"Why in the hell would you do something that stupid?" Poppy screeched.

"It's a long and overly complicated story." I chugged my second margarita. "Let me start this grisly tale over." I explained that Jett had repeatedly texted my mother to come to the library while she ignored her current husband to flirt with her former one.

"Okay. I can see how that would look bad," Poppy admitted grudgingly.

"You haven't heard the worst." I hushed the panicky voice telling me to shut up. "I wasn't with Mom when she found Jett's body."

"Oh?" Poppy and Boone said simultaneously, both raising their brows.

"Mom was alone." I crossed my arms. "She went to the library to find out what Jett wanted, then planned to have lunch with my father."

"Shit!" Poppy swore.

She looked as if she would have liked to use a stronger word, but the three of us had made a pact to stop dropping the F bomb. Boone rarely swore, but Poppy and I had gotten pretty bad about it.

"When Mom found Jett dead, she called my father, who, like an idiot, hurried right inside to do I don't know what." I couldn't keep the annoyance I felt for both of my parents out of my voice.

"Dumb move with him being on parole and all," Poppy commented.

"You think?" I snapped. "Anyway, Dad called me, and since I wasn't sure if he could be sent back to prison for being at a crime scene, I had him leave. Then, before I called nine-one-one, I concocted the lunch-with-Mom-and-stepfather scenario to account for my presence."

"So you lied to the police, tampered with evidence, and are shielding a suspect." Boone frowned, then used his thumb to smooth the line between his brows. "Not your smartest moves, Dev."

"We're talking about my father." I scowled at Boone. "What should I have done? Thrown my dad to the wolves in order to protect myself?"

"Kern would have probably been okay." Boone didn't sound convinced.

"Really?" I barely stopped myself from screaming. "Because, as Chief Kincaid so helpfully pointed out, Jett is new in town, so the only obvious motive for killing him seems to be one that centers on my mother. Like, say, a jealous ex-husband who wants her back."

"There is that." Poppy collapsed back against her chair, subdued.

"Damn it all to hell!" I screamed, so frustrated I thought my head might explode.

"What's done is done." Boone rested his chin on his fist. "Assuming Dev isn't going to tell the police what really happened, we're the only ones with all the facts. Which means, if the crime is going to be solved, we have to figure out who killed Jett."

"Any ideas?" I asked, turning my gaze on Boone. He was one of the smartest people I knew, so maybe he had a plan to exonerate Dad.

Poppy and Boone shook their heads, and the three of us sat in silence until Poppy jumped up and said, "Time for another round." She headed to the bar. "Booze always helps me think much more clearly."

After Poppy returned with a fresh pitcher, she said, "If we take love and jealousy off the table, what other motives are there for murder?"

"Hatred, robbery, revenge, obsession, mental illness, drug deal gone wrong, the victim knowing too much." Boone pursed his lips, clearly racking his brain for more reasons someone would kill.

"You know," Poppy said, tapping a perfectly manicured fingernail against her glossy lips, "we're overlooking the obvious."

"The money." I leaned forward, a flicker of hope in my chest. I had almost forgotten Boone's statement about the delay in the library's endowment. "Why was the funding he promised late? We need to investigate Jett's finances."

"How will we do that?" Poppy asked.

"I could probably get that information for you," a sexy baritone drawled from the doorway.

I jerked my head up and saw Jake leaning against the wall. My insides melted and relief oozed through my veins. Like Dudley Do-Right, my very own ex–U.S. Marshal had appeared to save the day.

CHAPTER 10

When I eventually tore my eyes away from the sexy ex-lawman, I looked at Poppy and Boone. They glanced at each other uncomfortably, then back toward the doorway. Following their gaze, I saw a tall, gaunt woman step from behind Jake. She had to be his ex-wife, Meg.

I could tell that at one time she had been a gorgeous redhead. Long, limp ginger hair framed her once beautiful face, and her empty green eyes were fringed with thick, dark lashes. Her vacant stare and shrunken cheeks only hinted at the person she had been before her ordeal at the hands of a serial killer.

Struggling to sort through my feelings, I finally forced myself to stand and walked over to the woman. I held out my hand to her and said, "I'm Dev Sinclair, and you must be Meg . . ." It dawned on me that I didn't know her last name. Did she still go by Del Vecchio? I really hoped she didn't.

When Meg didn't respond, Jake placed her flaccid fingers in mine, and as I shook them, I raised a questioning brow in his direction.

He lifted a shoulder, then guided his ex to a chair

and said, "These are my friends Poppy and Boone." Jake turned to them and asked, "Could you two keep Meg company while I talk to Dev?"

"Sure." Poppy nodded, then asked the eerily silent woman, "Can I get you something to drink?"

"Dr Pepper," Meg whispered, surprising me when she actually spoke.

"Coming right up." Poppy turned to Jake. "How about you, cowboy?"

"When we get back, a Shiner Bock would sure hit the spot." Jake cupped my elbow and said to the others, "See you in a few." He glanced at his ex-wife, then said to Poppy and Boone, "Call me if there's a problem."

"Will do." Boone nodded. "I've got your cell number right here." He tapped the device clipped to his belt, then turned toward Meg and said, "Let me tell you about our charming town square. It has quite a history. During the Civil War, there was a standoff between the Union and the Confederacy."

Before I heard whether Meg responded to Boone or not, Jake said, "Let's go sit in my truck. I'm pretty damn sure we should talk in private."

"Good idea."

I followed him as he wound his way through the packed bar. Jake was at least six four, with the type of powerful, well-muscled body produced by hard work on his uncle's ranch rather than hours in a fitness center. Although considering the sculpted biceps and triceps visible below the short sleeves of his white T-shirt, I was certain he spent time at the gym as well.

I shivered as a flash of unexpected heat sizzled through my body, leaving me breathless. The first time I'd seen Jake, his arresting good looks had totally captured my attention. And even during his long absences, said hunkiness had kept him in my thoughts.

While I was drooling over Jake's hotness, I completely missed the fact that he had stopped moving. Slamming into his back, I stumbled and would have fallen if not for his quick reflexes.

Once Jake steadied me, I peered around him to see what had halted our progress. At first all I saw was a large group of people gathered near the stage that was usually used only during the weekends, when Poppy hired local bands or DJs to liven up the club.

Then I noticed the man clutching the microphone. It was the alientology professor who had spoken at the city council meeting. He wore a white tunic with a gold-embroidered insignia over his left breast. Squinting, I could just make out that the patch seemed to depict a solar system, although not one I recognized.

While Jake fought to clear a path for us through the mob, I heard Professor Hinkley say, "Despite the nonbelievers who have refused to cooperate and have hindered my research, I've managed several sightings and have communicated with our extraterrestrial friends."

Immediately there was a high-pitched buzz from the spectators, several of whom also claimed to have spotted hovering lights. Hinkley paused, clearly waiting for the noise to die down.

I tapped Jake's shoulder, pointed at the professor, and asked, "Did that guy try to get your uncle to allow him to set up his ET equipment on the ranch?"

Jake flicked a glance at the stage, then turned to me and said, "Yeah. But Tony told that nut job if he caught him on our property, we'd set the bull loose. When the guy started arguing, I reminded him that we had a lot of acreage to hide a body."

"Gran pretty much told him the same thing." I snickered. "Except she threatened him with Banshee instead of a bull. Hinkley thought that was hilarious until the Siamese shredded his pants."

"Knowing that cat's temperament, the guy was lucky it wasn't his leg." Jake chuckled.

We were distracted as the mike screeched and Hinkley said, "Khrelan Naze has indicated that he will meet with us in the town square on what we earthlings call Saturday noon. At that time, he will present a gift for mankind."

The professor's announcement whipped his audience into a frenzy, and they all pressed closer to the stage. Seeing our opportunity, Jake took my hand and towed me in the opposite direction.

Just outside the bar, Jake paused and did a swift recon of the parking lot. Evidently there were no aliens or assassins hiding among the rusted pickups, shiny motorcycles, and dusty family sedans because he led me to his black Ford F250, opened the passenger door, and helped me scramble inside the cab.

He'd finally stopped teasing me about my inability to hoist myself up into the hulking vehicle. The enormous truck reminded me of its owner—solid and rugged, with just a hint of sexy playfulness. I briefly wondered how difficult it would be to hoist myself up Jake's hard length, but banished that naughty thought from my mind. Or at least hid it somewhere in my subconscious.

As I settled on the butter-soft brown saddle

leather, I watched Jake climb into the driver's seat. He seemed to get better-looking every time I saw him. His thick black hair was longer than he'd worn it when he was working as a marshal, making me want to run my fingers through the silky strands. And his full lips tempted me to slide over for the kisses I'd been missing.

Jake seemed to read my mind, and his sapphire blue eyes darkened. But when I scooted closer to my door, his mouth twitched downward. He was aware that our relationship had taken a hit when he'd brought Meg to the ranch and devoted so much attention to her.

It had been more than three weeks since Jake and I had managed any time alone, and I wished I had bothered to apply makeup, fix my hair, and put on something other than a polo shirt and jeans. But then again, I'd had no idea he would pop up at the bar.

When Jake remained silent, I glanced at his chiseled profile, noticing for the first time since his arrival that the bronzed skin pulling taut over the elegant ridge of his cheekbones appeared tighter than usual. Clearly, the caretaker duties he'd assumed for his ex-wife were putting a strain on him.

Jake continued to stare mutely out of the windshield as if the dark parking lot held the answer to his troubles. When I saw the muscles in his strong throat move as he swallowed, I figured he was trying to figure out how upset I was and what to say to make things better.

Without any warning, he flipped up the console, reached over, and tugged me closer. I tried to scoot away, but he cradled my cheeks between both his callused palms and rested his forehead against mine, softening my resistance. I couldn't deny the heat I saw in his expression, but there was more than just raw sexual desire. There was wonder and a look of peace, as well. Almost as if he could finally relax.

I breathed in the enthralling scent of what I thought of as eau de Jake—a mixture of lime, saddle soap, and sexy man. He smelled so damn good.

"I'm sorry I haven't been around much," Jake murmured. "I promise that will change right now." His eyes were so dark with a mixture of remorse and desire that I was nearly hypnotized.

Being with him like this reminded me of how much I was attracted to him, and erotic images began flickering through my mind. I had promised myself that until I decided between Jake and Noah, I wouldn't sleep with either of them. But at times like this, I was sorry I'd made that vow.

Clearing the lust from my brain, I asked, "How are you going to accomplish that? I don't think they're cloning humans yet."

I knew I sounded snarky, but I'd been hurt by his casual neglect. And with Jake's lips a fraction of an inch from mine and his gaze searching my face, I needed to remind myself of that pain.

Jake's jaw clenched, but he continued to caress my cheeks with his thumbs as he said, "A home health aide is starting tomorrow night. Meg is better during the day, and Uncle Tony's housekeeper has been keeping an eye on her while I'm working out on the ranch. But for some reason she's more agitated in the evening, and I couldn't ask Ulysses to watch her then."

I bit my tongue to stop myself from suggesting that Meg might be exaggerating her symptoms when Jake was around. That was a conclusion he'd have to draw on his own. Instead, I concentrated on ignoring the feeling of his body pressed along the side of mine. The sensation made me hotter than a curling iron.

Gathering my scattered wits, I said, "What made you decide to hire someone? It's been quite a while since she came to the ranch."

"I've been working on it all along," Jake hedged.

"So, why are you here now . . . ?" The warmth of his palms as he slid them down my shoulders made me gasp. And when he moved his hand to the neckline of my shirt, his fingers trailing over my collarbones, a delicious shudder shot up my spine. I gritted my teeth and focused. Once I could breathe normally, I continued. "Instead of waiting until the aide took over?"

"Your stepfather's murder." Jake must have realized that he couldn't seduce me into forgetfulness. He sighed, withdrew his hand from under my polo, and said, "Birdie called Tony."

"Of course she did." I slid back to the passenger seat. "So the only reason you think it's important to free up some of your time is because your uncle asked you to help me." I didn't add *again*, but I could have, since that was how Jake and I had met.

"Son of a bitch!" Jake roared. "I knew that was what you would think."

"Because it's a logical conclusion." I crossed my arms. "Why do you think I didn't call you myself? I don't want the only reason I see you to be because I need rescuing. I'm not a damsel in distress." Knowing that I had made my point with surgical precision, I refrained from pushing the scalpel in any deeper.

"Look," Jake growled, evidently holding on to his temper by a thread. "Granted, the timing is suspicious, but I swear I've been trying to find an aide ever since I brought Meg to Shadow Bend. You know damn well that I want to be with you. You told me you understood about her and weren't upset that she was here. Say the word, and I'll ship her back to the psychiatric clinic."

"No." Feeling lower than pond scum, I shook my head. Jake didn't lie. If he said he'd been trying to hire someone, he had. "Sorry for sounding like a jealous bitch. I guess I missed you more than I realized." I scooted closer and trailed my fingers across the Levi's covering his muscular thighs. The denim was faded and as soft as velvet. "I appreciate that you want to help me."

"Actually, it sounds more like your dad is the one in hot water this time." Jake captured my hand and brought it to his lips.

"I guess." I kept my gaze on our entwined hands. How much did Jake know? Had Dad told Birdie that he was with Mom at the library, not me? He'd agreed not to, but Gran was good at ferreting out info from him. Had she told Tony? "It sounded like Chief Kincaid thought both my parents might have a motive to kill Jett."

"Yep." Jake slipped an arm around me and cuddled me to his side. "Spouses and exes are always high on any law enforcement department's suspect list, so your idea to look into your stepfather's finances is a good one. What made you think of it?"

After I explained what Boone had told me about the delayed library funding, I said, "As a former investment consultant, the situation made me suspicious."

"Right," Jake agreed. "You would think that Benedict would have had the financing all lined up before he presented it to the city council."

"I'm also curious as to exactly what Jett was re-searching." I tried to ignore Jake's lips nibbling along the side of my neck, but my pulse began to pound in my ears and I was having trouble concentrating.

"Why is that?" Jake continued to kiss his way down my throat.

"It just seems odd to me that he couldn't wait until the library was reopened to use the archives." I gasped. The chemistry zipping between us was taking all the oxygen out of the truck's cab.

"Maybe because Benedict never really intended to donate the money."

When Jake tugged me into his lap and drew my top over my head, I didn't even pretend to resist. Murmuring, "Good point," I returned the favor and took off Jake's T-shirt.

He was the kind of man who would look good wearing anything or—even better—nothing at all. It was a testament to my sadly lacking sex life that I was thinking entirely inappropriate thoughts a few hours after my dad had become a suspect in my stepfather's homicide.

I was losing my train of thought, but there was something else niggling me about Jett's murder. Just before Jake's mouth came down over mine, I squeaked, "The scrap of paper in his hand."

"What? Who?" Jake jerked his head up, his blue eyes unfocused.

"Jett was clutching a scrap of paper in his fist."

"I'll look into that," Jake rasped. "Tomorrow." He tightened his embrace and said, "It's been so long since I had you in my arms."

"It has." His expression made my mouth go dry

and chased off any lingering thoughts about my stepfather's murder investigation.

"All those nights lying alone in my bed, I thought about running my fingers over your soft skin. It was all I could do not to drive over to your place and throw pebbles at your window until you came outside so that I could hold you and taste you."

I tried to inhale, but his mouth was so near, I could barely draw enough breath to ask, "Why didn't you? All you had to do was text me."

He gathered me closer, pressing me against his hard length and making me hotter than the cheese on a pizza. Then, when he moved his hand to my breast, a delicious shock wave radiated southward.

What was it about Jake that had my body commandeering the control from my brain? How did he sweep away all my doubts, anger, and common sense? We needed to concentrate on finding out who killed my stepfather, but I couldn't find the strength to stop Jake as he placed his lips on mine.

The desire in his kiss destroyed the little restraint I had held on to, and I was overcome with a primitive need for him. I slid my hands over his rock-solid pecs, and he groaned his approval before licking into my mouth as he held me against him. His heat warmed me and made me feel safe. I scraped my nails down his back, loving the texture of his firm muscles under my fingertips.

His hands were fumbling with the button on my jeans, when a chorus of laughter jerked me out of my sensual fog. I thumped Jake on the shoulder, and it took him a long moment before the voices penetrated his sexual haze. He glanced over my shoulder and swore.

It suddenly dawned on me that not only had we forgotten about the murder, but we'd overlooked the fact that we were in a public parking lot. Whimpering, I looked around for my bra and top.

With a groan, Jake grabbed them and helped me re-dress, then put on his own T-shirt. An instant later, his cell rang. When he answered it, all I could hear was a woman screeching the word *Jake* over and over.

Apparently, Meg was having a meltdown and our alone time had come to an end.

CHAPTER 11

Jake glanced at his ex-wife as he drove out of Gossip Central's parking lot and turned his pickup toward home. She was rocking back and forth in the truck's passenger seat, making pitiful mewling sounds, her ragged nails digging into the armrest. When he and Devereaux had rushed into the bar, Meg had been standing with her back to the wall, her hands covering her face, shrieking his name.

While he'd tried to calm her down, Boone and Poppy had explained that one moment Meg had been sitting quietly sipping her Dr Pepper and the next she'd leaped from the chair and begun screaming. They had no idea what had triggered the outburst.

Once Jake had cajoled Meg into taking her medication and she'd stopped howling, he'd quickly hustled her out of the club, yelling over his shoulder that he'd call Devereaux the next day. Dev had smiled her acceptance and waved good-bye, but the look of abandonment that had flashed across her face had torn at his heart. If the home health aide didn't work out, Jake knew he would blow his chance for a life with Dev, because she would end up married to Underwood.

Jake ground his teeth in frustration. He needed time to persuade Devereaux that he was the man for her. That Dr. Doolittle was her past and he was her present. But what woman in her right mind wanted a future that included a crazy ex-wife? Dev was certainly no Jane Eyre, but he was starting to feel a lot like Mr. Rochester.

Jake knew he'd been neglecting Devereaux, but there was never enough time. Between tending to Meg in the evenings and his increasing responsibilities on the ranch, he barely had a chance to breathe. He'd almost been happy when Birdie had called and asked for his help in solving Jett Benedict's murder. The situation had given him an excuse to be with Dev, one that didn't seem selfish and that his sense of duty couldn't demand he ignore.

When he'd bundled Meg into his truck and lit out for Gossip Central, Jake had known Devereaux wouldn't be entirely happy to see him, especially with his ex-wife in tow. Not to mention that once he told her about Birdie's telephone call to Tony, Dev would assume he was there out of obligation, not desire.

Devereaux was such a strange mix of tough businesswoman and vulnerable female that he hadn't been entirely sure how she'd react to his presence. She never did exactly what he expected her to do, and although he normally hated being caught by surprise, she always managed to charm him.

It had been a relief that Dev believed him when he told her about the aide he'd been trying to hire. And that she hadn't demanded he stick Meg back into the nuthouse. He would have done it, but he wouldn't be able to think about Devereaux in the same way he had before. Abandoning his ex-wife would have eaten at his gut, and the resulting guilt would have eventually ruined things between him and Dev, just as much as keeping Meg at the ranch might.

Jake clenched his jaw as he pulled the F250 up to his uncle's front door. If only his ex could have managed to hold on to her sanity for a little while longer. He'd needed just a few more of Devereaux's kisses to tide him over. It had been so long since they'd been together that his hunger for her had grown into an insatiable craving.

Jake could still taste her sweetness. Sighing, he got out of the pickup and went around to the passenger side. Meg had fallen asleep, and he certainly didn't want to wake her and risk another screaming fit, or worse.

Slipping his arms around his ex, he eased her from her seat and nudged the door closed with his shoulder. Her lashes fluttered, but instead of stirring, she burrowed against his chest and clutched his neck. It felt as if she weighed less than a newborn calf. She refused to eat unless he hand-fed her. She was only a ghost of the strong, independent U.S. Marshal she had once been.

Jake stared at the dark house. It was a few minutes past eleven, and Tony and Ulysses would both be asleep. Most ranch folks went to bed right after the ten o'clock news and got up before dawn. This schedule had been a bit of an adjustment after Jake's life in law enforcement, especially his undercover work, but now he loved watching the sunrise.

As he climbed the front steps, he winced. This late in the day, his leg always ached. The docs had told him that although his wounds had healed, he'd have some permanent pain. The injury, a gift from the gun of a fleeing scumbag who sold underage girls to the drug cartels in Mexico, was one of the reasons he'd retired.

Although he'd been deemed fit for duty, once he was back on the job he'd realized that he'd never be a hundred percent. And he wasn't willing to risk his team's safety should his leg give out in a crucial moment. Not when his weakness could endanger all their lives.

Ignoring the twinge, Jake went inside and headed to the den, which had been turned into Meg's sickroom. When he placed her on the bed, he had to pry her fingers from his shirt. He slipped off her jeans and shoes but decided she could sleep in her T-shirt and underwear.

Jake waited until he was sure she wouldn't wake up, then headed for the refrigerator. He needed a beer or three. He grabbed a bottle and the opener, walked into the living room, and flopped down on the old leather couch. After popping off the cap, he took a swig of the icy brew and lunged for the remote. Stopping midreach, he flopped back on the sofa. He wasn't in the mood for TV.

As he drank, his thoughts skittered to Devereaux and Dr. Dweeb, making Jake's stomach churn. He'd never been good at sharing. Had Underwood been worming his way into Dev's heart while Jake was AWOL? At the image of her in that asshole's arms, a wave of fury nearly choked him, and he fought the urge to punch something.

Toeing off his Durangos, Jake set his stocking feet on the coffee table. After he'd swallowed his anger, along with most of his beer, he made a mental note to pump Tony for information on Devereaux's activity with Frat Boy during the time Jake had been

MIA. Surely Birdie would have kept his uncle in the loop since she was firmly on Team Jake.

He frowned. At least she had been before his vanishing act. What if Devereaux's family had changed sides? Her father seemed friendly enough, but he hadn't indicated which man he thought would be better for his daughter. If Birdie switched teams, Kern might follow.

Jake got up and paced the length of the living room. Devereaux had haunted him over the past three weeks. He'd tried to steal a few minutes to stop by the store to see her, but something had always come up. She was constantly on his mind. He should have let her know that.

She had asked why, if he missed her so much, he hadn't texted her to meet him one of those nights when he'd lain awake thinking about her. But that would have felt too much like a hookup.

Which would have been just fine with him with any other woman. *Hell!* Until he'd met Dev, a night of wild sex was the only reason he'd felt the need to be with a gal. But that wasn't what he wanted from Dev. Or at least, it wasn't *all* that he wanted from her.

It had been sheer torture sitting hour after hour with his ex-wife when all he wanted to do was spend that time with Devereaux. While he felt sorry for Meg and he hated to see her the way she was, he'd had to ask himself why he'd ever married her. How had he thought he loved her? The only thing he felt for her now was pity.

After chugging the last of his Corona, he walked into the kitchen and put the empty beer bottle in the trash can under the sink. Then he pulled out a chair, sat at the table, and leaned back. There was no use going to bed. He wouldn't be able to sleep. He knew he'd just lie there and fantasize that he and Devereaux were together in their own house and she was in his arms.

Instead of wasting his time staring at his bedroom ceiling, he turned his thoughts to the murder. If Dev's parents hadn't killed her stepfather, who had? They needed to know time of death, what was on the paper Benedict had been holding, and the vic's financial situation. He could call in a few favors in order to get some of that information, but without any authority, his options were limited. He needed the power of a badge.

It was nearly two a.m. by the time Jake headed to bed. In the hours he'd sat watching the clock above the sink tick off the seconds, he'd come to a decision. It was time to get a PI license.

He'd been considering the possibility since he'd first realized he would have to retire from the marshal service. He needed to get online and find out the requirements in Missouri to be recognized as a private investigator, but he doubted there would be any credentials he didn't already possess.

With autumn around the corner, things would slow down a little on the ranch, which meant this was the perfect time to start the accreditation procedure. As long as the home health aide resolved the situation with Meg, this might be his chance to keep his finger in the investigative pie and to spend more time with Devereaux in the process. A win-win scenario if he ever saw one.

That night Jake's sleep was plagued with dreams of Devereaux walking down the aisle with Noah Underwood. Every time Jake turned over, the pain in his leg woke him up, and he alternated between gazing out the window and at the clock. Finally, he gave up, and by five a.m., he was already dressed and outside doing chores.

It looked as if today's late-summer weather would be a repeat of the past week—warm and blustery. But this morning there was a hint of something strange in the air, and the cows were acting oddly. Jake chuckled to himself, thinking that Professor Hinkley would probably blame the herd's bizarre behavior on the extraterrestrials.

Jake had actually seen an array of lights in the sky a few nights ago, but they looked more like distant fireworks than a flying saucer. What would the alientologist do when ET was a no-show in the town square next week? Having dealt with his share of scam artists, Jake figured the professor would have some excuse for Khrelan Naze's failure to put in an appearance. And sadly, many of the suckers would believe the charlatan's lies.

Shrugging at the gullibility of the masses, Jake went back to work. The cows had to be tended to, no matter what the conditions, and the last crop of hay was nearly ready to be harvested from the field. Once it was baled and in the barn, there would be a short break before the winter work began in earnest.

While he labored, Jake considered what he knew about Jett Benedict's murder. If neither Devereaux's mother nor her father was guilty—and that was a big *if*—then who else had a reason to want the vic dead?

Unless someone had followed Benedict to Shadow Bend, he hadn't been in the area long enough for the killer to have a personal motivation. An unfamiliar individual lurking around the square certainly would have drawn someone's attention. Had anyone noticed a stranger in town?

If the reason for the homicide wasn't love or revenge, Jake's bet was on the money. Why hadn't the funds for the library arrived as promised?

As Jake treated a toe abscess on one cow, the injured tail of a second, and the cracked hoof of a third, he considered his next move.

Heading back to the house for breakfast, he decided that a trip to the police station was in his future. Without a badge, he'd have to charm the information he wanted out of someone. He hoped that the woman who had flirted with him on his previous visit to the PD was on duty. Dispatcher Barbie had seemed more than eager to help him in any way that his heart or any other part of him desired. Maybe he'd bring Devereaux along again. On their last visit, he'd enjoyed her reaction to the woman's flirting, and it would be good to let her see what it felt like to be jealous.

When Jake entered the kitchen, Ulysses nodded at him, then placed half a dozen sausage links on a plate and poured pancake batter into a sizzling-hot cast-iron griddle. Jake had known the housekeeper for more than twenty years and he hadn't changed at all during that time.

Ulysses was a short, chubby man of unidentifiable age and ethnicity who had always reminded Jake of a genie. A mythical being that materialized from a magic lantern and returned to the lamp every evening without ever revealing anything about his history or future plans. An otherworldly creature that refused to answer any questions.

Jake greeted the housekeeper, then said good morning to his uncle, who was sitting at the head of the table reading the local newspaper. Jake rarely bothered to do more than skim the *Shadow Bend Banner*. National and international stories were given less than a couple paragraphs of coverage, while the area sports teams took up most of the remaining pages. And unless you had a kid in the game, the stats weren't all that interesting.

Tony lowered the paper and asked, "How did it go last night? Did that ex of yours behave herself long enough for you to talk to Dev? Or did she pull her usual hysterical act?"

Jake sighed, knowing his uncle thought Meg was faking, or at least exaggerating her condition. He was beginning to suspect Tony might be right, that his ex-wife wasn't as bad off as she pretended, and Jake was developing a plan to test that theory.

"Devereaux and I had some time together before Meg lost it." Jake didn't bother to lie. Everyone in Gossip Central had heard his ex's breakdown. Her screams had been loud enough to wake the dead. Or at least the drunks at the bar. And all eyes had followed them as he'd led her through the club and outside to his truck.

"What a surprise." Tony skewered his nephew with a piercing stare, lifted a bushy white eyebrow, and asked, "How did Dev take that?"

"She said it was fine."

"And you believed her?" Tony shook his head. "The speed that a gal says 'fine' is inversely proportional to the intensity of the shitstorm that's coming."

"Devereaux's not like that."

"Every lady has her limits." Tony shrugged. "You need to wise up soon."

"Probably in more ways than one." Jake walked to the coffeemaker on the counter. "Want a refill?"

He knew his uncle had a point and that he would drive home that point until he was satisfied Jake was on the right track again. Not out of meddlesomeness, but out of concern.

Tony had been more of a father to Jake than his own dad had ever been, and he had earned the right to have his opinion respected. Jake's parents had shipped him off to military school when he'd turned eight, and since that time, they had rarely spent more than a day or so with him. He saw them only on those rare occasions when their demanding social life left them with a few free hours and nothing better to do than to visit their only son.

Tony was the one who had taught Jake how to clean a fish, hunt a deer, and to be a real man. He was the one who was there to listen when Jake shared his hopes, dreams, and troubles. The ranch was Jake's true home. His parents' opulent houses, condos, and villas felt more like hotels than places to kick off his boots and relax.

"Don't mind if I do." Tony held out his mug. "Caffeine *is* the elixir of life, and when you're so far over the hill that you've started up the next one, coffee is the only thing that gets you going in the morning."

"What are you talking about?" Jake grabbed a cup for himself, filled it, then emptied the rest of the pot into his uncle's white crockery mug. "You're the youngest octogenarian I know."

"Thanks." Tony leaned back and took a long sip. "But I'm so old I remember when porn cost money and water was free."

Jake chuckled.

Tony grinned, then returned to the subject of his nephew's love life. "So was Dev pissed at not seeing you lately?"

"She wasn't happy," Jake admitted. "But she understands."

"I bet." Tony wiped his mouth with the back of his hand. "If she's anything like her grandma, she'll 'understand' for only so long. Then she'll take a real hard look at Underwood and decide he's the better option. Is that what you want?"

"Hell no!" Jake settled into the wooden slat-back chair, and Ulysses silently slid a full plate in front of him. "It's just that I've been so dang busy I'm not sure if I found a rope or lost a cow. But the aide's first shift starts at three today, and I plan to be at the dime store by three fifteen."

"Good." Tony quirked his mouth. "All it took was another murder to get you back on track."

Jake grunted.

"And that reminds me." Tony tapped the tabletop with his fingers. "I was at the bakery the other day, and I heard Nadine Underwood and one of her CDM friends talking about Jett Benedict."

"Oh?" Jake wasn't sure where Tony was going with this, but knew his uncle wasn't prone to idle chitchat. "What did the cream of the Confederate Daughters of Missouri have to say about Devereaux's stepfather?"

"I didn't get much of the conversation." Tony pursed his lips. "But it had something to do with Benedict poking his nose in places it didn't belong and making him sorry if he didn't stop doing it."

CHAPTER 12

When my radio blared on Wednesday morning, I woke up with a start, batting at the snooze button repeatedly until the damn thing stopped blasting "Love the Way You Lie"—one of my least favorite tunes. I mean seriously, who wants to hear lyrics about a couple's refusal to break up despite their abusive relationship? Considering my parents' present situation, the words hit way too close to home.

The annoying song distracted me, so it took me a few seconds to remember what I had been dreaming about. When I did, the warm, tingly sensation that had greeted me when my eyes opened was explained. Jake and I were back in the cab of his truck, but in my dream version we hadn't been interrupted by either onlookers or his phone.

Hell! My fixation on a man so wrapped up in his ex-wife's life wasn't healthy. I wiped the smile off my lips and trudged into the bathroom. Meg and the barflies had actually done me a favor. Having sex with Jake before I chose between him and Noah was a bad idea on so many levels.

The chemistry between us was too strong for a

fling. I needed to make such an important decision with my head and my heart, not just because my girl parts wanted to enjoy themselves.

It was time to buckle down and concentrate on my father and/or mother's impending arrest. Just because I hadn't been with anyone but my battery-operated boyfriend for the past several years didn't mean it was okay to forget about the very real possibility that my dad could end up back in prison. And this time, dear old Mom might be occupying the cell right next to him.

Gran was washing the window over the sink when I entered the kitchen. She was sitting on the counter with her feet in the basin, swearing at the mechanism that refused to latch the pane back into place.

I quickly hopped up next to her and held the glass so she could return the window to its full upright and locked position. Her obsession with Windex never failed to mystify me, but there was no talking her out of using her trusty blue bottle and her old flour-sack dishcloths to make every glass surface in the house gleam. Even if the sparkle lasted only until the next rainstorm or fingerprint.

As I returned to terra firma, I glanced around for Banshee. He was in his preferred spot, perched on top of the fridge. It was one of his favorite places from which to launch himself onto the top of my head as I walked by him.

Giving him a superior smirk, I avoided his likely trajectory and peeked into the warming oven. Gran had waffles with a side of crispy bacon waiting for me. I grabbed the plate, poured a cup of heaven from the Mr. Coffee, and settled into my seat at the table.

Noting my father's absence, I asked, "Did Dad

already eat?" Even on the days he worked an afternoon shift at the store, he generally had breakfast with me, or at least sat with me while I ate mine.

"Nope." Birdie shook her head. "I haven't seen him yet this morning. Maybe he slept in."

"I hope so." I wrinkled my brow, wishing I could make sure without violating our unspoken agreement to respect each other's privacy.

I really wanted to run up to his apartment right now and see if he was there. But since I didn't want him checking on whether I spent the night in my own bed—should I ever choose to fulfill my Jake fantasy—I'd have to curb the impulse to check up on him.

Worried that Dad had gone back on his word and spent the night with my mother, I rubbed my temples, trying to ease the headache I could feel approaching. My father wasn't a stupid man. He had to recognize that pursuing any relationship with Yvette would make him look even guiltier in Chief Kincaid's eyes.

Maybe I should telephone Mom and see if he was there. Luckily, the condo she and Jett had rented came with a landline, since Dad had disposed of her cell. No. I shook my head. The problem with that plan was that I couldn't count on Yvette telling me the truth. And considering our less-than-loving relationship, calling her might nudge her into doing something just to provoke me.

The best plan was to wait and telephone her later. She was always a late riser and wouldn't appreciate being woken up to see how she was doing. When I phoned her, I'd subtly remind her that when the police talked to her again, as I was sure they would, she needed to keep quiet about Dad's part in yesterday's scenario.

I'd make sure she understood that I'd help her only as long as she protected my father. After deserting me when I was a teenager, she didn't deserve and couldn't expect anything more from me.

Gran interrupted my thoughts by handing me the bottle of Aunt Jemima. As I poured the syrup over my waffles, she demanded, "Did Jake show up at Gossip Central last night?" When I nodded, my mouth too full of deliciousness to answer, she asked, "Was that hussy with him?"

I nodded again, but before I could fork another bite into my mouth, Gran scooted my dish out of reach and said, "Tell me what happened."

Eyeing the rest of my breakfast, I quickly summarized my evening, leaving out the part where Jake and I almost provided a peep show for the patrons of Gossip Central, and ended with, "So our talk was interrupted when Meg freaked out. Jake said he'd contact me today about our next step in investigating Jett's murder."

"Like I said before, Tony thinks Meg's faking." Gran returned my plate to its rightful place in front of me. "He says he's going to catch her acting . . . uh . . ."

"Sane."

Gran nodded, then continued. "Tony's going to prove to Jake that his ex is just trying to worm her way into his life and make him send Miss Meg packing. Tony told me he'd drive her to St. Louis himself if he thought he could get her into his pickup."

"Good for him," I mumbled around a gulp of ambrosia. Gran made the best coffee.

"Tony says Meg has the manners of a two-year-old," Gran continued.

"Evidently she never experienced the joys of attending Miss Ophelia's etiquette classes on excruciatingly correct behavior." I crunched a perfectly crisp piece of bacon between my teeth.

"Which goes to show you how fortunate you were to have had that experience," Gran deadpanned.

"Does it?" I had hated those lessons.

"When is Jake going to call you?" Gran snatched my now empty dish off the table, along with my fork, and put them in the sink.

"I'm not sure."

"He didn't say?" Gran's blasé expression didn't fool me one bit. While she was truly worried about her son's situation as Chief Kincaid's prime suspect, she wasn't about to miss the opportunity to get Jake to spend more time with me.

"The store's open until nine tonight, so there's no rush." I glanced at the clock on the microwave. It was nearly eight a.m., which gave me less than an hour to shower, dress, and drive to work. "If Jake doesn't get in touch with me by then, I'll text him."

"You should wait for him to call." Gran crossed her arms. "In my day, a lady didn't pursue a gentleman."

"But this is the twenty-first century," I teased.

"I like living in the past." Gran smiled. "It's cheaper back there."

Chuckling, I escaped from the kitchen and went into my bedroom to get dressed. Since there was a good chance I'd be seeing both Jake and Noah today, I put on my best, most slimming jeans and an aquamarine Devereaux's Dime Store polo, which brought out the color of my eyes. Feeling a little foolish, I brushed on some bronzer and a few swipes of mascara, but I drew the line at curling or flat ironing my hair, so I gathered it into its usual ponytail.

As I headed into town, I noticed that the wind was really strong and there were no birds in any of the trees. The air seemed to crackle with electricity, and I wondered if we were in for a thunderstorm.

A few minutes later, I crossed into the city limits and cruised the four blocks to my store. On my way, I passed the Greek Revival building that housed the bank, the unadorned cinder-block newspaper office, Little's Tea Room in its Queen Anne–style house, and the movie theater with its limestone facade and Art Deco entrance.

Although Shadow Bend looked like a postcard of an idyllic Midwest small town, I had learned with the past couple of murder cases that it had a dark underbelly. It didn't show itself on the surface, but I had become adept at sniffing out the community's secrets.

The influx of new residents who had moved to the area to raise their families in a more wholesome atmosphere than most city neighborhoods could offer had brought some of the crime they'd been trying to escape.

Not that the newcomers were the only ones whose pasts created problems. Native Shadow Benders intent on maintaining the way of life in which they had grown up wanted their world to remain a safe and orderly place—even if it meant getting rid of someone who threatened that security. Country folks, even more than urban dwellers, understood the concept of survival of the fittest.

I'd worked in the city for many years, but I'd always lived in Shadow Bend. I endeavored to see both sides' point of view and to make my store a spot where everyone could feel comfortable. Unlike Brewfully Yours, which catered to the commuters, or the feed store, whose sign out front—GUNS, COLD BEER, BAIT—said it all, my goal was to offer a neutral zone where the two groups could find some common ground. I hoped this new murder wouldn't be a setback.

I was proud that Blood, Sweat, and Shears, the sewing club that met on Wednesday evenings at the dime store, had nearly an equal number of townies and move-in members. And I was particularly pleased that the kids who hung around the new teen lounge in my store's second floor had accepted my declaration that if I saw any evidence of cliques, discrimination, or bullying, everyone would be kicked out. It was too hard to determine who was guilty and who was innocent, since often the ones who were caught weren't the ones who'd started the problem.

Maintaining this progress meant that in addition to clearing my parents' names, I needed to find out who'd killed Jett before fingers started pointing and the town split in two once again.

Despite my aversion to being rescued, Jake's offer to help was a godsend. He knew how to manipulate the legal system and get the information we needed to move forward on the investigation. Without him, Poppy, Boone, and I could only gather rumors and pump people for gossip. That might be fine if Jett were a local, but with him being from out of town, pickings would be mighty slim.

Soon after I opened the store for the day, my fears were confirmed. I overheard a group of women chattering about the murder. It was a stroke of luck that the ladies didn't seem to realize Jett was my stepfather. I sure didn't want to have to field a lot of "you have my sympathy" comments, but it was a shame the rumors were already flying.

"I had an interesting phone call this morning," a middle-aged woman dressed in Levi's and cowboy boots said, rocking on her heels.

The crowd around her chirped excitedly, offering guesses as to what had been said.

When they finally quieted, she continued. "You know that Irene Johnson cleans for several of the Country Club Cougars, right?"

Boone had coined that nickname for the ladies who hung out at the country club on the prowl for husbands, and it had caught on.

"Of course we do, Emma," a young mother wearing shorts and flip-flops said. "They brag about it anytime they can. It's always 'my housekeeper' this and 'my nanny' that. Sure wish I could afford some help."

"Anyway," Emma continued, "Irene and I are in Knittie Gritties together. She called to tell me she'd found some yarn I've been looking for and that she'd bring it to the next meeting. Then, when we were chatting, Irene mentioned that she heard one of the cougars on the phone complaining about the library reopening."

"Why in God's name would she object to that?" Ms. Flip-flop demanded.

Not wanting to miss a word, I edged closer to the group. To disguise my interest in their conversation, I pretended to straighten a display of autumn-themed coffee mugs.

"Well, Angie, the cougar claimed that after the initial funding ended, local taxes would need to go up to support the library, and since they had the biggest houses, theirs would increase the most." Emma crossed her arms. "The woman also claimed that libraries were dinosaurs and people could just download whatever stuff they wanted to read and look up info on the Internet."

"Sure." Angie glared. "If you're rich and can afford to buy all the new books."

"Not to mention that around here our Internet service is limited, and if we go over a certain amount, we have to pay extra," one of the others chimed in.

"Exactly." Emma's voice reeked with spite. "Not that any of those country club people have a clue that the rest of us struggle to pay our bills."

It took all of my self-control not to groan. *Damn!* It hadn't taken long for sides to be drawn. I didn't stamp my foot at the stupidity, but I may have tapped my toe a couple of times.

"I bet one of those rich snobs killed that poor Mr. Benedict," Angie said. "To stop him from helping us regular folks."

"Can I find something for you ladies?" I stepped up to the group. It was time to break this up before they formed a lynch mob.

"I need to order a gift basket for my niece's baby shower." Emma moved over to the register. "I want something special. It's her first."

After I took the basket order and rang up everyone else's purchases, the women headed for the exit. As they walked out the door, Angie was describing the strange lights she'd seen in the sky last night.

I was still mulling over how quickly the townies and newcomers had become divided when Taryn Wenzel arrived. He worked four mornings a week for me as a part of his high school vocational program. I wouldn't say that my newest clerk was short, but he would have to look up to a Hobbit.

I was uncertain as to why he was in the voc-ed program, since he'd made it clear he'd be attending the University of Central Missouri's software engineering program when he graduated. Maybe he planned on owning his own company and wanted practical experience in running a small business.

He watched me refilling the book rack for a minute, then asked, "Are you okay, Dev?" Taryn tilted his head, and his wire-rimmed glasses slipped down his nose.

"I'm fine."

"Then why are you putting the new Stephen King book where the romances go?" Taryn was a keen observer and a voracious reader.

"Well, horror and romance have a lot in common. Neither is too realistic and both can keep you up at night." My feeble attempt to distract Taryn with witty repartee didn't work. The boy had no sense of humor. Or at least, none that I'd been able to find.

"True." Taryn narrowed his eyes. "I hadn't thought about it like that, but you're right. Maybe I'll use that premise for my next English paper."

"Probably not a good idea." *Hell!* I couldn't let the poor guy do that. I doubted his teacher would buy the idea, and he'd end up with a failing grade because of me.

My day didn't improve when the phone rang at eleven thirty. It was Noah, and he said, "I am so sorry about your stepfather, Dev. And I wish I could be there for you, but we have an emergency."

"Oh." I cringed. What had happened now? Was his mother acting up again?

"One of the patients in my waiting room just

went into labor." He paused to give someone on his
end several lengthy directions, then said, "I need to
accompany her to the hospital."

"I understand." How could I be upset with a doctor saving a life?

"Sorry. Elexus has her hands full at the clinic. The
patient is two months early and a high-risk preg-
nancy." He paused again. I heard a commotion, and
then he said quickly, "I've got to go. The ambulance
is here. I'll call you when I get back to town."

He hung up before I could answer, which was just
as well. There was nothing to say. He had his obligations and I had mine. Several of which were await-
ing my attention. So instead of an intimate lunch
with Noah, I dealt with unreliable vendors, disgrun-
tled customers, and a three-year-old shoplifter who
grabbed a candy bar and shoved it into his mouth
before his mother could stop him.

The frustrations continued to mount, and I was
close to locking myself in the bathroom and screaming when my father arrived at three fifty-five. He
took one look at my scowling face and wrapped me
in a hug.

I enjoyed the novel sensation of having my dad
around to comfort me again, then eased out of his
embrace and, as casually as I could, said, "I missed
seeing you at breakfast. Did you sleep in?"

On Wednesdays, when the store was open in the
evening to accommodate one of my craft groups,
instead of his usual morning shift, my father came
in from four to eight.

"No." He raised a brow, indicating that I wasn't
fooling him. "I had an appointment with my parole
officer over in Kansas City at nine, so I had to leave
early in case traffic was heavy."

"Did you make it in time?"

"Yep." Kern smiled. "And afterward, I treated myself to a nice lunch and a matinee of the latest Bruce Willis Die Hard movie." As I opened my mouth, he added, "It wasn't as much fun alone, but it was still nice."

I hid my relief that Dad hadn't been with Yvette, but the twinkle in Dad's eyes said that he knew what I'd been thinking. He pecked me on the cheek and headed toward the storeroom to put his things away before starting to work.

As I watched him walk away, I went over to the soda fountain and poured myself a cup of coffee. I had just settled on a stool when the sleigh bells over the entrance jingled. I twisted my seat toward the sound and my heart sped up. Six feet four of hot man strode through the door. And this time Jake was alone.

CHAPTER 13

Jake threw his leg over the stool next to mine, and I said, "I'm surprised to see you here. I thought you were going to call." Trying to ignore the electricity zipping between us, I asked, "What's up?"

"After I introduced the health aide to Meg and got him squared away, I hightailed it away from the ranch so fast that my pickup left skid marks in the gravel." Jake's smile was both devastating and contagious. "I was hoping we could talk to some folks about your stepfather's murder."

"How did Meg take the change in nursing staff?" I sipped my coffee and watched Jake's reaction from behind my cup.

"She was screaming fit to be tied, but the aide said that was normal and he'd handle it. I sure hope the poor fellow has earplugs." A dimple at the corner of Jake's lips appeared. "Tony and Ulysses decided this was a good evening to go eat barbecue in Sparkville and catch the latest action movie."

"Smart men." I traced the rim of my cup with my index finger.

"Yep. That they are." Jake leaned back, propping his elbows on the counter. "So what do you say we do some investigating, then grab a bite to eat at the new Mexican place out near the highway?"

"I wish I could, but this is my late night at the store," I reminded him.

"Can't your father cover for you?" Jake coaxed. "I'm hoping to get some info from the dispatcher about what the police have on the case."

"I'm sure Miss Perky Boobs will tell you a lot more without me there." I bared my teeth in a fake smile. The woman had practically gotten on her knees in front of Jake the last time we were at the PD together.

"I thought you could talk to your friend Chief Kincaid while I charmed Bambi."

Bambi wasn't her real name, but Jake had explained that it was a tag the marshals use for a woman whose IQ is less than her bra size.

"The chief is only my pal when I have something to trade," I retorted, then remembered the gossip I'd caught that morning and murmured, "I wonder if Chief Kincaid heard the rumor going around that Jett was killed to stop the library from opening."

"Why would anyone want to do that?" Jake's dark brows drew together.

I gave Jake the short version of Emma and Angie's conversation.

"Who was it that this housekeeper overheard complaining about the library?'

"The women talking never mentioned a name." I grinned and elbowed Jake. "Guess you'll have to go out to the club and poke around."

His normally tanned cheeks paled. The last time

Jake had tried to get information from the country club ladies, the cougars had nearly made him the main course on their hot-guy menu.

"Back to tonight's agenda." Jake's chiseled face relaxed into a sexy smile. "Now that you do have something to trade with the chief, how about going with me to the PD and using it to find out what he knows?"

"I'm not sure Dad is ready to handle Blood, Sweat, and Shears by himself." I bit my lip. "That group might eat him alive."

"If Kern survived prison"—Jake twirled the brim of his cowboy hat on his finger—"he can manage a ladies' sewing circle."

With Winnie Todd as the club's president, I wasn't so sure. Still, it was probably worth the risk to get to the bottom of Jett's murder. Just because the chief hadn't questioned my father yet didn't mean he wasn't building his case before he pounced.

When I'd spoken to Yvette earlier in the afternoon, she'd informed me that there was a police car sitting in front of her condo, watching her. I'd advised her to stay home and hibernate. She'd giggled at my suggestion and informed me that she had nothing to hide. It had taken all my self-control not to laugh in her face.

"There's one other person I should talk to ASAP." Jake broke into my thoughts. "And I know you'll want to be along for that conversation."

"Who?" I didn't like the tiny grin playing around Jake's lips.

"Nadine Underwood." Jake grabbed the cup from my hand and chugged the rest of my coffee. "Tony overheard her and one of her CDM friends saying that your stepfather needed to stop poking his nose in places it didn't belong or he'd be sorry. I'd sure like to know what places those are and why Nadine was so bent out of shape about it."

"I would, too." My father's voice startled me. I hadn't noticed him come out of the back room. "That woman is always up to something."

Jake and I both swiveled our stools to look at him. He stood by the register, frowning, with his hands shoved in his pockets.

"You go with Jake," Dad ordered in a tone I wasn't used to hearing. "I'll handle the sewing ladies and close the store for you."

"But—" I protested.

"Devereaux Sinclair," Dad interrupted, crossing his arms and staring at me, "surely you have enough faith in me to let me sell refreshments without your supervision?"

Giving in, I didn't quite meet his eyes when I said, "Of course I do." My father had played the trust card, and after how I'd behaved when he was wrongly convicted and sent to prison, there was no way I could do anything but agree to his wishes.

"Good. I promise to straighten up afterward." Dad nodded to himself, then said, "Since you won't let me see her or call her, check on your mother while you're at it."

"Okay." I smiled at Dad, then turned to Jake and frowned. "But I'm not going to blindside Noah by popping in on Nadine without warning him."

"Look at it this way." Jake lowered his voice. "If it's his mother getting into trouble versus your father returning to prison, who wins?"

"Dad." I sighed. "But I'm still sending Noah a text. I'm sure he won't interfere, and he deserves to know what's happening."

"Maybe." Jake shrugged. "But Underwood has a history of caving in to his mother."

"Not lately," I argued. Jake didn't have to remind me about Noah's past betrayals. It wasn't something I was likely to forget. Raising a brow, I lasered a sharp look in Jake's direction. "But we all have obligations that interfere with our personal lives."

"Some of us have seen what's really important and made the necessary adjustments." Jake's gaze burned me like a branding iron.

Unwilling to allow him to distract me, I stood and said, "We're wasting time. Chief Kincaid usually heads home for dinner by five and it's four forty, so if we want to talk to him, we need to get going. Let me grab my purse and I'll meet you out front."

The Shadow Bend PD was located between the hardware store and the dry cleaner. Jake and I made the short walk across the square in silence. I had no idea what was going through *his* mind, but I was thinking about my aversion to entering the police station.

The building's square cinder-block structure, recently installed front window bars, and overall crushing atmosphere reminded me of where my dad had been incarcerated.

Which was a problem for me, because during my one and only visit to the penitentiary, I'd developed a sort of claustrophobia that kicked in whenever I stepped into anything that resembled a prison. It had been hard enough yesterday, but I'd been nervous about what Mom was saying to the cops and the distraction had been enough to get me inside without fainting. Today I had nothing to worry about except the oversexed dispatcher tackling Jake and having her way with him. I was fairly certain he could avoid that touchdown, and if he didn't, I'd put on my helmet and intercept her myself.

Before I was ready, we were in front of the station and Jake had opened the door for me. Although the anxiety I felt had lessened somewhat with my father's release, my chest tightened and I still experienced a moment of panic as I walked through the entrance.

I was in the process of working myself into a full-on state of alarm, when I was sidetracked by the crowd of strangers milling around the lobby, wearing odd costumes and carrying posters. I paused and nudged Jake, then pointed to a sign that read, EARTH WELCOMES OUR NEW INTERGALACTIC FRIENDS. BEAM ME UP, KHRELAN NAZE.

Jake snorted and continued his march toward the short flight of concrete stairs that led into the rest of the station. I followed, scowling when I spotted Nympho Barbie behind the counter. Jake's luck was holding out. The dispatcher manning the desk behind bulletproof glass was the same one who had practically drooled on his cowboy boots the last time we were here together.

Seeing Jake, she licked her lips, unfastened the top button on her uniform shirt, and slid the window open. She leaned forward, exposing enough cleavage to hide an aircraft carrier, and drawled, "Well, if it isn't Marshal Hottie." She fluttered her false eyelashes and pouted. "I'm mad at you. You were supposed to call me for drink."

"Was I, darlin'?" Jake rested a hip against the desk and smiled seductively. "I'm sorry if I broke my word to you. That's not right."

"I'll forgive you this time." She sucked on her finger.

"'Cause you didn't exactly promise, and I'm sure she"—the dispatcher jerked her chin at me—"keeps you on a mighty tight leash."

It was all I could do not to tell her exactly what I thought about women like her. If I didn't watch it, I'd end up in an anger-management class. Of course, I wouldn't need to manage my anger if other people would just learn to manage their stupidity.

Jake shot me a smirk, then said to Ms. Boobs, "Dev here needs to talk to the chief. And while she's busy, maybe you and I can have a little chat, too. You know, catch up on what's been happening."

"I might be able to arrange that." Her sultry tone made it clear that in her mind, chat was another word for getting naked and doing him. "Chief Kincaid's hiding out in his office. He told me to let him know when the alien hunters leave the building."

"We saw them in the lobby." Jake flashed her a sexy smile, his straight white teeth gleaming. "What do they want with the chief?"

"Permission to camp in the town square until ET shows up." The dispatcher fluffed her bottle-blond curls and allowed her gaze to sweep every delectable inch of Jake's six-foot-four frame. "Their weirdo leader was here earlier, but he cut out after the chief threatened to lock him up for trespassing on private property. Seems there've been several complaints."

"Yeah. He's been nosing around my uncle's ranch," Jake murmured, then said, "So how about Dev goes on back and talks to Chief Kincaid and you and I get better acquainted?"

"Sounds good." She winked at Jake, then shook a long pink fingernail at him and said, "You stay right here, handsome." Flipping open the counter, she pointed at me and marched off, shouting over her shoulder, "If you want to see the chief, get the lead out!"

Biting my tongue, I followed her down the hall, nearly hypnotized by the sway of her backside moving to some primal rhythm only she could hear. Once again, it had been a bit unsettling to witness Jake turn on the charm in order to get what he wanted. It made me wonder how sincere he was in our relationship.

Miss Bodacious Tatas knocked on the chief's door, then opened it and announced, "That dime store woman is here to see you." When Chief Kincaid grunted his okay, she turned on her heel and hurried away.

As I stepped into the chief's lair, I heard her deliberately raised voice float down the hall. "Sugar, now that the ball and chain is taken care of, you and I can really get to know one another."

It took considerable self-control not to run back there and throttle her. She was one of those folks who really needed a hug around the neck . . . with a piano wire.

Instead, I gritted my teeth and greeted Eldridge Kincaid. His uniform was as starched and pressed as if he'd just started his shift, but his face sagged with exhaustion and his eyes were bloodshot. Clearly, handling a murder and a mob of extraterrestrial chasers at the same time was getting to him.

Once I was settled in a chair facing his desk, the chief said, "What can I do for you, Dev? Did you remember something you noticed when you discovered your stepfather's body?"

"I wish I could help you with that, but no." I sat forward, put my palms on the desktop, and tried to use some of my own charm. "I know this case is difficult for you and I appreciate that you haven't brought in my father. I'm afraid the people around here who still think he should be in prison would stir up trouble for him if it looked as if he's one of your suspects."

"I've been keeping that in mind." The chief laced his hands and stretched. "But I will have to speak to him soon. I've just been waiting for the crime lab to finish up the forensics before I do."

"Would it be possible to drive out to the house in your personal vehicle and speak to him there?" I asked, knowing I was pushing his friendship with my father to the limit. "Or maybe stop by the store tomorrow morning and meet with him in the storage room?"

"That would work." Chief Kincaid rubbed the back of his neck.

"Thank you." Despite his quarrel with my best friend and his rigidity, I liked Eldridge Kincaid. I admired his dedication to his job and his loyalty.

"I did reinterview your mother today." The chief tented his fingers and gazed at me impassively. "Her memory is as bad as yours."

"Maybe it's not our memory as much as it is that we just didn't see anything," I countered, glad Mom had evidently stuck to the designated story.

"Yvette denied knowing anything about her husband's business or finances, which surprised me." Chief Kincaid tapped his chin. "I would have thought his money would be high on her radar, but she claimed that as long as her credit cards worked she didn't care about the details."

"That sounds about right." If the chief thought I would try to defend my mother's morals, he was sorely mistaken. "I'm guessing Mom didn't have any knowledge of what Jett was researching, either."

"Nope." Chief Kincaid hollowed his cheeks, then blew out a breath. "Yvette said that Benedict was a history buff and loved to hear her talk about Shadow Bend's past. Then one day he announced that they were coming here so he could access the library archives."

"I bet she was thrilled." I didn't bother to hide the sarcasm in my voice.

The chief smiled, then asked, "If you haven't recalled anything more, why did you want to see me?"

"It's probably nothing." I faltered before I took a breath and blurted out, "But I overheard a conversation this morning that I thought might interest you." I told him about the country clubbers' opposition to the library, adding, "I know it's not much of a motive, but it does show that there were people who had a grudge against Jett and who wished he was out of the picture."

"Interesting." Chief Kincaid dipped his head. "I hadn't heard that. Anything else?"

"Uh." I paused, realizing Jake and I hadn't discussed whether to share Nadine's comment with the chief. Hurrying, before Chief Kincaid realized I was holding something back, I added, "The funding for the library still hasn't come through."

"No one has mentioned that, either." The chief made a note. "I'll have to check on it with the city council."

While he was in a grateful mood, I asked, "Did the medical examiner determine the time of death yet?"

"The victim suffered an extensive cranial hemorrhage sometime between twelve thirty and one." The chief fingered his shiny brass nameplate, then raised his head and said, "Which was pretty close to when you and your mother must have arrived. Are you sure you didn't see anyone on the street or near the building?"

"Not that I noticed." I shrugged. "I wasn't paying attention." Of course, in truth, I had arrived later. Had Mom or Dad seen anyone?

"Too bad." Using his handkerchief, the chief rubbed off the mark his thumb had made on his nameplate, then looked up at me and asked, "Anything else you overheard or want to share with me?"

"Uh." Should I mention Nadine? No. Jake and I should talk to her first.

"Dev?" Chief Kincaid adjusted the leather blotter so that it lined up more perfectly with the edge of his desk. "Did you remember something?"

"No." I shook my head. "But I'll keep thinking." Maybe tomorrow, when he came to the store to interview my father, I'd tell him about Nadine's comment.

Seeming reluctant to let me go, the chief said, "That trace of glittery dust I pointed out to you at the crime scene was a magnesium alloy. Any idea why your stepfather would have that in his possession?"

"Something about his health?" I guessed. "Don't people take magnesium for lots of medical reasons?"

"Not this form."

"Then I have no idea." I wondered what else contained magnesium. Maybe it had something to do with preserving rare books.

After several more minutes of idle chitchat, I stood up and edged toward the door. Saying good-bye and promising to keep him in the loop, I made my escape.

I found Jake and the sexpot at the dispatch desk, laughing together. When she spotted me, she narrowed her heavily made-up eyes, heaved a dramatic sigh, and said, "Looks like your warden is back."

Jake ignored her comment and said, "Thanks for your help, darlin'."

"Anytime." She licked her overly glossed lips and said, "Now, don't be a stranger."

She glared as I took Jake's hand and tugged him down the stairs and into the street.

Swallowing my jealousy, I pasted a smile on my face and said to Jake, "How did it go?"

"The police don't have any witnesses, but the dispatcher did tell me that the fragment of paper in the vic's fingers wasn't from this century."

"Oh?" I raised my brows.

"It was a hundred and fifty years old."

"It must have been from the archives Jett had been researching." I stopped and stared at Jake. "What in the world did he find?"

"More importantly." Jake raised his brows. "Was he killed for it?"

CHAPTER 14

Jake had parked his truck in front of my store, and as we approached it, I said, "I think we should go see Mom before tackling Nadine."

"Why is that?" Jake opened the pickup's passenger door and helped me inside.

"For one, I promised my father I'd check on her." I fastened my seat belt and dug through my purse, looking for my cell.

"You could just call her." Jake swung into the driver's seat and backed the F250 out onto the street. "What's the real reason?"

"Chief Kincaid reinterviewed her, and I want to find out exactly what she told him." I tapped the messaging icon on my phone, then looked up from the screen to give Jake Mom's address. "Do you know where that is?"

"Sure. One of Tony's pals lives in that same complex."

"Great." I turned my attention back to my cell, selected Noah's number, and typed, JAKE AND I ARE GOING TO TALK TO YOUR MOM RE AN OVERHEARD

COMMENT SHE MADE ABOUT JETT. HOPE YOUR
PATIENT IS OK. LUNCH TOMORROW?

I looked up just as Jake glanced at me. He evidently
assumed I was texting Noah, because he frowned.

Tucking the phone into my purse, I asked, "Find
out anything else from your new girlfriend?"

"Jealous?" He grinned, then said, "Bambi mostly
told me everything the police don't know. For in-
stance, there were no usable fingerprints and no
weapon was found."

"Time of death is between twelve thirty and one
thirty, and the glittery stuff they found at the scene
is a magnesium alloy." I tilted my head. "Any ideas
about that?"

"One type of alloy is used in engine parts, rock-
ets, and missiles." Jake twitched his shoulders. "But
there are lots of different kinds of magnesium."

"Crap! I should have asked for more specifics." I
shrugged. "But I doubt the chief would have told
me. He wasn't too impressed with the info I had
about the country clubbers opposing the library."

"Hard to pin something like that down." Jake
turned the truck into the condo's parking lot. "It's
too nebulous to be very useful."

"Yeah. He did perk up about the delay in the
library funding." I waited for Jake to give me a hand
down from the pickup. Then, as we headed inside, I
added, "I didn't mention Nadine."

"Probably best." Jake cupped my elbow as we
walked down the hallway to Mom's unit. "We'll get
more information from her if she hasn't already been
questioned by the police. Plus it gives you another
piece of info to trade."

"Good point." I pressed the doorbell, and Mom

answered wearing a short black-and-white Diane von Fürstenberg wrap dress and strappy white sandals. Her hair was carefully arranged around her shoulders, and her makeup was flawless. If this was how she dressed for a causal evening lounging around the house alone, I'd hate to see what she put on to go out on the town.

Yvette stepped back, put her hand to her chest, and said, "Dev, I thought you were . . . uh . . . the take-out guy." Her eyes flickered from my face to Jake's, and she said, "This must be Tony Del Vecchio's nephew."

I made the introductions, and she invited us inside. An ultramodern white modular sofa, matching chair, and metal-and-glass occasional tables occupied the living room. The condo was furnished like an upscale hotel. Beautiful, but about as welcoming as a hospital room.

Once we were seated, I explained, "Dad asked me to make sure you were okay. Did you get a new cell yet?"

"Jett always had a couple extras." Yvette picked up a notepad and pen from the coffee table and scribbled something across the page. Handing me the paper, she said, "Here. Give the number to your dad."

"That's not a good idea. As I told you yesterday, it's best if you and he aren't seen together until Jett's murderer is found. We don't want to give Chief Kincaid a reason to be any more suspicious of you two."

"I wasn't suggesting Kern come over here just to give me a call. I'm not stupid." Yvette made herself comfortable on the chaise, adjusting the flap of her skirt as she scooted back. "Eldridge has never been one of my biggest fans. He'd love to throw me in jail."

"Glad to know you realize the consequences of

your actions." I bit my tongue to keep from pointing out that in the past she hadn't always been so cautious. "We don't want you *or* Dad behind bars."

"I suppose your boyfriend knows all about our little deception?" She glanced at Jake and narrowed her eyes. "Is that wise?"

"Jake is a retired U.S. Marshal and is helping me look for Jett's killer." *Shit!* I hadn't decided whether to reveal Dad's presence at the crime scene to Jake, but I could tell by his expression that now I would have to come clean. "He'll be cool." At least I hoped he would, since now there was no way to keep it from him.

"Good." Yvette didn't look entirely convinced. "Anything else?" She glanced at the clock above the mantel, then at the front door.

"I heard the chief talked to you again." I wondered why she was so nervous. Maybe takeout wasn't all she was expecting. I was fairly certain Mom hadn't been in love with Jett, but it surprised me that she didn't even try to pretend she was mourning her husband's death. "How did it go?"

"He sent an officer to pick me up in the middle of my yoga class." Yvette frowned. "I think Eldridge did that deliberately to rattle me."

"Did it?" I knew she would hate being seen in public all sweaty.

"No." Yvette pressed her lips together. "I just kept repeating what we rehearsed. And I denied knowing anything else."

"Is that the truth?" I asked, fairly sure my mother would want to know where the money was coming from and how much there was to be spent.

"Pretty much." Yvette's smile was self-satisfied. "Jett's family is in the oil business. He had plenty of cash, and he kept me in the manner I had grown accustomed to, which is all that mattered to me. Whenever he had a business meeting, he sent me shopping."

"Of course that kept you happy," I muttered. It sounded as if my stepfather had kept his wife and his wheelings and dealings far, far apart. Was it because she had no interest in how he earned a living, or was it because he had something to hide?

"Hey. I know you think I marry my husbands for their money, but that's not true." Yvette lifted a slim shoulder and giggled. "Money is why I divorce them."

When I didn't respond, my mother continued. "If there's one thing I've learned, it's that regardless of how sizzling a relationship is at first, the passion fades and there had better be something else to take its place. And for me that something else is cash." She shot a look at Jake, then added, "Something you should consider when choosing between Mr. Hot and Steamy here and Noah's kind of security."

I ignored her advice and asked, "Have you been in touch with Jett's family?" I was ashamed to admit that I hadn't even thought about them. "Did he have children?"

"No." Yvette shook her head. "He's the last of the Benedict line."

"So you inherit it all?" I asked. Had she killed her husband?

"I don't know." Yvette wrinkled her nose. "Jett would never let me see his will."

Evidently, my stepfather hadn't completely trusted his wife. Wise man.

Changing the subject, I said, "You told the chief that Jett encouraged you to talk about Shadow Bend's past and was interested in the town's history. And that's why he funded the library." When she nodded, I asked, "So what exactly was he researching?"

"I haven't a clue." Yvette shrugged. "I usually stopped listening when he started talking about boring stuff like that. Why does it matter?"

Up until this point, Jake had been allowing me to steer the conversation, but now he leaned forward and said, "It's hard to know what's important in a murder investigation. Do you have any idea the time period that your late husband was the most interested in?"

"The Civil War." Yvette rolled her eyes. "Why he cared about some stupid stuff that happened a hundred and fifty years ago is beyond me. But lots of people around here are the same way."

I refrained from reminding Mom of her own interest in the Confederate Daughters of Missouri because I knew that her wanting me to join the organization had been a purely social move.

Jake asked a few more questions, but it was clear that Yvette didn't know anything more and was anxious for us to leave.

When she hustled us into the foyer, I said, "You do recall that Chief Kincaid has an officer watching this building?"

"Your point?" Yvette smoothed her hands over her slim hips.

"Any gentleman callers will look bad." I raised an eyebrow, daring her to protest her innocence.

"Eldridge may have a cop on the entrance, but I doubt he can spare two officers, which means the back door isn't under surveillance."

"I imagine it's kept locked," Jake said.

"It was, but it isn't now." Yvette's smile was coy.

"What if the chief does have someone in the rear, too?" I couldn't believe my mother was being so rash.

"Look." Yvette nearly pushed us across the threshold. "There are twenty condos in this building. Who's to say which resident anyone is visiting?"

With that I gave up, said good-bye to my mother, and headed toward the parking lot. As much as I wanted to stick around and see whom she was expecting, I realized that the policeman watching her condo would surely notice if we sat in the truck for very long.

Besides, I was pretty damn sure Chief Kincaid wasn't dumb enough to have surveillance only on the front. Maybe he'd be willing to tell me who had used the back door. I just had to figure out how to ask him without admitting that that person was visiting my mother.

As we drove out of the parking lot, my stomach growled, and Jake sent me an amused smile. I shrugged. Hey, my lunch had been a day-old pastry that I had scarfed down in between customers.

"Maybe we should eat dinner before we stop by Nadine's," Jake suggested.

"I *am* hungry." That Danish had been a whole lot of empty calories, but I'd forgotten my yogurt. "Still, I think we should tackle Nadine first. It's already six thirty, and if she's like a lot of the women around here, she'll be glued to the TV tonight."

"Why?" Jake kept his eyes on the road. We were on the stretch between town and the country club subdivision, a spot where deer were notorious for darting across the asphalt. "What's so fascinating on TV?"

"The *Dancing with the Stars* reunion episode is tonight, followed by a sneak peek of the next *Bachelor*."

I watched his baffled expression as I answered. Obviously, his uncle Tony was not among those shows' devotees.

"You're kidding me." Jake's brows disappeared into his hairline. "They do know all those reality programs are faked, right?"

"I wouldn't mention that to Gran if I were you." I smirked. "Those would be fighting words to her. She gets so involved that she actually flings things at the TV screen when her favorites go home."

"Then I guess we better go to Nadine's now." Jake shook his head. "If Birdie gets that violent, I'd hate to see what Underwood's mother is like watching those shows."

After giving Jake directions and promising to explain my mother's remark about her and Dad's "little deception" over dinner, I grabbed the few minutes it took us to get there to check for missed messages. There wasn't anything from Noah. Was he still at the hospital? It had been several hours since our canceled lunch. What else would keep him too busy to look at his cell phone?

There was a text from my dad asking how Yvette was, so I sent him a short reply reassuring him that she was fine. It saddened me that he still cared so much when I suspected she was already sinking her hooks into another rich guy and only amusing herself with my father.

Nadine's place was more of a manor house than a home, and when we arrived, the outside was lit up like a movie set. Lights outlined the driveway, emphasizing the meticulously trimmed shrubs, sweeping steps, and massive double doors intending to impress and intimidate. The Underwoods were old money who sneered at the nouveau riche who had moved to town and built their shiny new McMansions around the country club.

Enormous white columns and a wide porch made for quite the curb appeal, and as we exited the truck, I could see that Jake's shoulders were stiff. I wondered if the setting reminded him of his parents' property.

He didn't like to talk about his folks, but I had managed to wheedle a little information from him. His father was a plastic surgeon who had grown rich promising vain men and women eternal youth, and his mother was a trust-fund baby who had inherited a fortune.

Both images were hard to reconcile with what I knew of Jake, and I wondered what Yvette's attitude would be if she realized that he stood to inherit just as much as Noah. Maybe more if you threw in his uncle's ranch.

We rang the bell, and as the seconds ticked by, I realized that Nadine might decide not to come to the door. Noah had mentioned that his mother's long-time housekeeper had recently retired and that she hadn't been able to find anyone else she found suitable. If it was her health aide's night off, she might ignore the doorbell.

After another couple punches of the bell, the queen of Shadow Bend swung open the huge oak portals. Shockingly, she didn't seem pleased to see me and didn't extend her sympathy for the loss of my stepfather.

"Devereaux, Mr. Del Vecchio, what a surprise." She wore tailored khaki slacks and a blue oxford shirt with a tan cardigan flung over her shoulders. "I certainly wasn't expecting you."

Pasting a neutral smile on my lips, I said, "Sorry to just drop in on you, Nadine. But we have something to discuss with you that is better said privately." Knowing that she loved to gossip but not be the subject of the rumor mill, I emphasized the last word.

"Well . . ." She clutched her sweater. "I'm not really prepared for company."

"This will only take a few minutes." I stepped over the threshold, forcing her to either bodily block me or move out of the way.

Nadine prudently chose the latter. I had a good thirty pounds on her. Maybe more, since she appeared skinnier than ever. She truly adhered to the obnoxious saying, "You can never be too rich or too thin."

"I can't imagine what's so important that you couldn't call before coming over." Nadine may have been a beauty at one time, but years of sun and spitefulness had taken their toll, and the furrows around her mouth became even more noticeable when she scowled.

"We were running other errands in the area." I motioned Jake to follow me inside. "It seemed easier to clear things up right away."

Nadine allowed me to edge us farther into the impressive foyer. Then she glanced at her diamond-encrusted watch and said, "I have an important engagement at seven. I can only give you fifteen minutes."

"That's fine." I shot Jake a knowing look. *Dancing with the Stars* came on at seven. "Perhaps you'd be more comfortable seated."

"You mean you would be." Nadine sighed and said, "This way."

She led us into a formal parlor. The graceful lines and perfect proportions of the impeccably preserved antique furniture were spectacular. Nadine seated herself on a cross-stitched Victorian floral upholstered Sheraton chair, then motioned for Jake and me to take the divan facing her across the marble-topped mahogany coffee table.

"What's so vital that you had to interrupt my evening?" The pleats of skin on her face rearranged themselves as she talked.

Jake leaned forward and said, "You were overheard remarking that Jett Benedict was poking his nose in places that it didn't belong."

"If you say so." Her voice oozed condescension. "I don't recall."

"Then the rumors that your memory is becoming problematic are true?" I raised my right eyebrow, a trick I had mastered in graduate school and had put to good use in my prior career, but which I hadn't felt compelled to employ as much lately as the proprietor of a dime store.

"That is completely false," Nadine snapped. "My mind is as sharp as ever."

"Then you do remember saying that about my stepfather." I gave her my most maddening grin. "So what exactly did you mean by it?"

Nadine ignored me and pouted at Jake. "Young women nowadays are so disrespectful."

"I've heard many ladies of a certain age feel that way. My mother would undoubtedly agree." His contrite smile was insincere. "But we do need to know what you were referring to when you mentioned Mr. Benedict. As I'm sure you're aware, the man's been murdered."

"Of course I heard about his unfortunate demise. Poor Yvette doesn't seem to be very lucky with her

choice of husbands." Nadine's expression bright-
ened, clearly cheered at the thought.

"My father was proven innocent of the embezzlement charge, and he certainly can't be blamed for the
car accident, since he was roofied," I reminded her.
"I'm certain you would agree that having her husband murdered isn't something my mother could
have predicted."

"And yet he's dead." Nadine's tone oozed condescension. "Surely you can't ignore that, since I understand *you* were with Yvette when she found the
body."

"Which is why Jake and I are trying to figure out
who could have wanted Jett gone." I clenched my
jaw but managed to keep my tone civil.

"Perhaps his wife found out that he was a fraud
and wanted to be free to pursue greener pastures."
Nadine's eyes sparkled with malice. "Yvette was
always looking for a way up the social ladder."

"What do you mean by 'fraud'?" I put a steel edge
in my voice, daring her not to answer. "How would
you know something like that?"

"Observation." Nadine crossed her legs and stretched
her arm along the back of the chair. "No matter how
expensive his clothes were or what kind of car he drove,
he was nothing but an upstart."

"What makes you think that?" I was beginning to
think the same thing myself, but I was curious how
Nadine had come to that conclusion.

"Because unlike the rest of this town"—Nadine
gave an elegant snort—"I am able to tell the genuine article from the imitations." Her voice was thick
with disgust. "Benedict claimed to be from old oil
money, but he was too eager to flaunt his wealth. He

I winced at hearing the dead man being maligned. I hadn't known Jett very well, and even if, as I suspected, he wasn't who he'd alleged to be, he *had* been my stepfather. For Nadine to dismiss him with a wave of her perfectly manicured fingers was annoying.

Nadine must have taken my silence as a sign of weakness, one she was quick to exploit. "On the other hand"—her smile was like an ice pick—"the new physician who's joined Noah in his practice is the genuine article. Dear Elexus's ancestors were Spanish royalty *and* she's exquisite. A dead ringer for Vanessa Lorenzo."

I hadn't met Dr. Rodriquez yet, and no one had mentioned that she looked like a supermodel.

Refusing to take Nadine's bait, I thrust away the flicker of jealousy and drawled, "Any other reason you were suspicious of Jett?" I saw her countenance darken when I didn't fall apart at her innuendo that Noah had hired Elexus for her beauty and used Nadine's displeasure to my advantage. "Like perhaps what you were referring to when you said my stepfather was sticking his nose where it didn't belong."

"I don't owe you any explanation." Her eyes flashed in outrage.

"Then I suppose I'll have to tell Noah you've been stirring up trouble for my family." I played my ace in the hole. Noah had informed his mother that if she caused me any problems, he'd cut her out of his life. After she'd maneuvered to break us up when we were in high school, he'd felt he had no other choice but to issue the ultimatum.

"But that's a lie," Nadine yelped, gasping and clutching her chest.

"Is it?" I enjoyed how astonished she seemed that someone would fib about her. She did it to others frequently enough that she should expect it.

"As a law enforcement agent, sworn to uphold truth and justice, you wouldn't allow her to do that, would you?" Nadine appealed to Jake.

"Sorry, ma'am. I'm retired." A smile lurked at the corners of his perfect mouth, as he added, "And I don't think anyone can stop Dev."

Nadine looked at me, and I returned the stare. I wasn't backing down.

"Very well." Nadine clenched her teeth. "What exactly do you want to know?"

I quickly reiterated my question before she changed her mind.

"Your stepfather purported to be interested in Shadow Bend's part in the Civil War, but all he really wanted to do was drag the name of one of the heroes of the Confederacy through the mud."

"Who?" Was that what Jett had been researching? If so, there were lots of folks in town who wouldn't have minded sticking a knife into his heart.

"He questioned the part my late husband's great-great-great-grandfather played in the war." Nadine's fingers clenched the arms of her chair so hard I was afraid she'd leave gouges in the wooden surface.

"Questioned how?" I needed to brush up on my Civil War history.

"He wasn't specific. But he came here demanding that I give him access to our private records and said that he'd destroy our family's good name if I refused."

Jake and I exchanged a puzzled glance before I said, "Did he speak to others about their ancestors? Threaten them as well?"

"Not that I'm aware." Nadine shrugged. "But I

warned the members of the Confederate Daughters of Missouri not to allow him in their homes or to talk to him." She frowned at me as if I had disagreed and stated dramatically, "They had a right to be prepared."

Not knowing what else to ask, I looked at Jake, who shook his head, indicating he didn't have anything, either. "Where were you Monday between twelve thirty and one thirty? And can you prove it?"

"Are you accusing me of murder?" Nadine's self-control snapped.

"Not if you have an alibi." I smiled sweetly and crossed my legs.

"If you must know, I was at a luncheon with our esteemed mayor and several other prominent citizens." Nadine's words were confident, but I could sense her relief when Jake and I stood. And when we said good-bye, she couldn't get us out the door fast enough.

CHAPTER 15

After saying good-bye to Nadine and exiting her palatial estate, Jake and I headed to the Mexican restaurant. It had just opened up by the highway, and neither of us had eaten there yet. A Dos Equis and a basket of tortilla chips with guacamole later, I had finally gotten rid of the sour taste in my mouth from talking to Nadine.

After ordering the rest of our meal, we discussed the results of the evening's investigation. Eventually we exhausted that topic, and as we enjoyed combo platters of deliciously spicy food, Jake said, "So what did your mother mean about your parents' little deception?"

"Mom was by herself when she discovered Jett's body. She called my father, who stupidly came running over, and Dad called me," I reluctantly explained, knowing Jake wasn't going to be happy with my actions.

"And you kept all this from the police?" Jake's eyebrows disappeared into his hairline, but his voice was deceptively mild. "What else did you do?"

"I told my father to leave, wiped away his finger-prints, and ditched Mom's cell phone so the cops couldn't see that Jett had been texting her for more than an hour to come to the library."

"Why in the hell did you do all that?" Jake gritted his teeth. "Tampering with evidence. Leaving the scene of a crime. You all could be arrested."

"Dad's on parole." I swallowed a lump in my throat. "I couldn't risk him being sent back to prison."

"You could end up in jail." A muscle ticked in Jake's jaw, and he took both my hands. "You need to be more careful."

"Probably," I admitted. "But what else could I do?"

After a long lecture on obeying the law, Jake grudgingly admitted that if Dad had stuck around and we hadn't gotten rid of my mother's disposable phone, my parents would be in a lot more trouble than they were.

Finally, he said, "If the chief finds out about your lies before the real killer is found, all three of you might be in real trouble."

I needed another beer to get over that idea. Once I had calmed down, Jake and I moved on to consider-ing our next steps. We both agreed that delving into Jett's finances and following up on what he had been researching were the two most promising leads.

As we lingered over the last bites of chile relleno and chicken chimichanga, the restaurant door opened and my friend Ronni Ksiazak strolled in with Coop McCall. She and the fire chief had been dating for the past month or so and seemed to be settling into a steady relationship.

When Ronni spotted me, she led Coop to our table and said, "Hi, you guys! Looks like I'm not the only one hankering for an enchilada tonight."

"Who can resist all that cheesy goodness." I smiled at the lively B & B owner.

Coop and Jake hadn't met, so while Ronni made the introductions and the men chatted, I studied Shadow Bend's fire chief. He and Jake shared the same powerful physique, but instead of Jake's sapphire blue eyes, Coop's were a warm golden brown. He and Ronni seemed to make a good couple, but it was hard to tell if they were really into each other or just friends. I didn't sense any chemistry, but that didn't mean it wasn't there.

Glancing at Coop, I found him staring at me. His heated gaze made it clear that he was still interested in me, and I quickly looked away. Two men were more than enough for me to juggle.

Finally, Ronni and Coop said their good-byes, but as they walked away, Coop turned, and the sharp planes of his face made him look almost predatory. I kept forgetting that behind his slight Southern drawl was a man who had been a marine and who was a self-proclaimed adrenaline junky. Certainly not the type to give up easily.

Before I could shake the impression that Coop had been sizing up his competition, Jake's cell *ping*ed with an incoming text.

He glanced at his phone and frowned, then said, "The health aide says that Meg is having a meltdown."

"I see." Losing my appetite, I pushed my plate away and wiped my mouth with a napkin. "I'm ready to leave whenever you are."

As I started to move out of the booth, Jake got up from his side and slid in next to me.

He stroked his thumb along my inner wrist and said, "Do you want to know why I'm itching to talk to the aide?"

"Well, it's the first time you've left Meg with a stranger," I answered slowly. His touch stole my breath, and I fought to keep my voice steady. "I'm sure you're worried about her."

"Nope." Jake continued to caress my arm. "It's because before I left, I set up a little test to gauge Meg's true mental state, and I want to know the results."

"Oh." I reached down and smoothed the faded Levi's that lovingly molded the muscles of his thighs. "What kind of experiment?"

"I made sure Meg heard me tell the aide that I was going into Kansas City to have drinks with some guys I had worked with as a marshal."

"Okay." I wasn't sure where this was leading. Did Jake think his ex-wife would want to see her old friends, too? "And?"

"And I added that I planned to be back by nine, since that was when your store closed." Jake lifted my hand to his mouth and kissed my palm.

"Uh-huh." Because I was distracted by the feeling of his lips, it took me a second to figure out his plan. "And Meg was fine until just now?"

"Exactly." Jake narrowed his eyes. "The aide said she started screaming at precisely eight fifty-seven. Up until then she'd been quietly watching television with him and had been fine all evening."

"So she's been faking it all along?" I asked, trying to put all the pieces together.

"I don't think so." Jake shook his head. "I'd swear she truly was in a near catatonic state when I brought her down here from St. Louis. What I think happened was that when she started getting better, she kept it to herself."

"To try to get you back?" I laced my fingers with his. "Which I totally understand."

"Not because she loves me." Jake winked. "My guess is that after her experience with the Doll Maker, she's afraid to be alone."

"But you never leave her on her own and she still appears to be scheming to keep us apart." I wondered if Jake was just being modest.

"I reckon she's worried that if you and I are together and you're upset with her being here, and I think she's better, I'll ship her back to St. Louis, where she will be by herself," Jake explained. "Remember, the reason I brought her here to begin with was because she really has no close friends or family."

"Do you think if we both reassure her that she can stay as long as she wants, she'll behave herself?" I asked.

I wasn't thrilled with the idea. However, I was unable to ignore my sympathy for the poor woman. I couldn't imagine what it would be like to be tortured by a serial killer, then afterward having no one in your life but an ex-husband to take care of you.

"Let me talk to Meg and make sure my theory is right. And I have to check with Tony." Jake's smile was rueful. "He's never forgiven her for dumping me when it looked as if I wouldn't be able to walk again. And he really wants her gone from the ranch."

"Absolutely," I agreed, knowing that I tended to rush in and take over.

As Jake paid the bill and drove me back to my car, I was silent. Something was trying to break free from my subconscious. I didn't know if it had to do with Meg's situation or the murder.

I could tell Jake was in a rush to get back to the ranch and confront Meg, because his good-bye kiss was hurried and his pickup tires squealed as he sped out of my parking lot. I had intended to go straight home, but as we pulled into the alley, I'd noticed that the lights were still on in the dime store.

I shook my head. It looked as if the sewing circle ladies had bamboozled Dad into letting them stay late. I had a strict out-the-door-by-nine policy, but the members of the club liked to linger.

Using my key, I let myself in the rear entrance and strolled into the crafting area. As I suspected, the ladies were still sipping coffee, munching on cookies, and chatting. Several of them were fluttering around my father as if he were the only boy at the prom who knew how to dance, and Dad was eating up the attention.

Zizi Todd, a young woman in her early twenties with carrot red hair, was patting my dad's arm and laughing hysterically at something he had just said. Zizi was the spitting image of a grown-up Pippi Longstocking and people often underestimated her. She came off like a space cadet, but in fact, she was in graduate school studying to become a clinical social worker. And was at the top of her class.

I greeted Zizi, who had the grace to look guilty as she grabbed her bag and said, "Dev, we were just packing up to go."

Winnie Todd, Zizi's mother, threw her arms around my neck, nearly smothering me in her long, frizzy curls. While she hugged me, she murmured, "Dev, you have my deepest sympathy on the loss of your stepfather."

Winnie may have been an aging hippie, but like most other native Shadow Benders, she'd taken Miss Ophelia's etiquette classes and could trot out good manners with the best of them.

Extracting myself from her clutches, I inhaled

and said, "Thank you. I didn't really know Jett, but he seemed like a nice man."

Having dispensed with the social niceties, Winnie gestured to my father and said, "Kern is a riot. He was telling us some of his prison adventures. Did you know that he taught math to the other inmates?"

"I didn't." I raised my eyebrows at my father. Anytime I brought up his incarceration, he changed the subject. I wondered why he suddenly was willing to share stories with relative strangers.

Winnie smiled fondly at my father. "I'm so impressed that although he was falsely imprisoned, he still was willing to come to the assistance of his fellow detainees."

Winnie had inherited a sizable estate from her grandparents and used her wealth to help others. She thought of herself as Wonder Woman, fighting oppression at every turn, but mostly she did things that just made people wonder.

Both Winnie and Zizi cared deeply for their fellow human beings, and together they had cofounded the sewing circle. They dedicated the club to supporting the county's homeless shelter and the local hospital's free clinic. It was too bad that both these facilities were more than forty miles away from Shadow Bend and difficult for our poorer citizens to reach unless they had a car.

Currently the group consisted of twenty or so women ranging in age from sixteen to eighty-three. Each member paid for her own materials, and they all donated their finished products either to the shelter for their use or to the clinic's resale shop.

As soon as they noticed me, most of the sewing circle members shot me guilty looks, then immediately said good-bye, gathered their things, and left. However,

Winnie, Zizi, and Cyndi Barrows were made of sterner stuff and continued to dawdle.

Cyndi might be one of the wealthy country club-bers, but she had shown up for the first Blood, Sweat, and Shears meeting and had faithfully attended all the subsequent ones. In my observation, she seemed more comfortable with the local women than with her country club friends.

As she slowly packed up her materials, I said to her, "I understand that some of the newer people aren't too thrilled that the library is reopening. Have you heard anything about that?"

Cyndi shook her head. "I don't spend much time at the club anymore."

"Why?" Winnie joined our conversation, her un-conventional features rearranging themselves into an inquisitive smile. "Did something happen?"

"Well, sort of. Nothing big or dramatic." Cyndi's voice sank to a whisper. "It's just that . . . actually . . . my new boyfriend doesn't like the group that hangs out there. He says they're shallow."

"New boyfriend?" Zizi frowned. "I thought you were engaged to Frazer Wren."

"I was, but . . ." Cyndi blushed and continued. "Five years is just too long, so I gave him an ultima-tum, and he broke up with me. Frazer had a fifteen-year mortgage, a five-year car loan, and a lifetime country club membership, but he told me he was afraid of commitment."

"What an ass!" Zizi touched her arm. "I'm glad you found someone better." Turning to me, she demanded, "What's this crap about people not wanting the library to open? What kind of idiots are they?"

I noticed Winnie had drifted over to where my

father was cleaning up. As I explained to Zizi what I'd overheard, I watched them laughing and joking around. There was something about Dad that attracted the opposite sex the same way Starbucks drew caffeine addicts.

"What a bunch of bullshit!" Zizi's angry expression changed her usual sweet face to a much scarier countenance. "How can people not understand the value of accessible books and knowledge?"

"In my experience, most folks have trouble seeing beyond what's best for them versus what's best for everyone," I said mildly.

I stuck my hands in my pockets. Zizi was still an innocent, but the cynic in me suspected that a few years in her chosen profession would wear some of the naïveté off of her. The thought made me sad.

Cyndi had lost interest in the conversation, and as she headed toward the exit, she waved good-bye.

Zizi watched the other woman walk away, and with a rueful smile, said, "Cyndi's a sweetie. She's not the quickest horse on the track, but her heart is in the right place." Zizi frowned. "I hope her new boyfriend is a good guy. Did she say who he was?"

"Nope." I joined my father and Winnie by the register, and Zizi followed me.

I was about to shoo the women out of the store when I thought of something and asked, "Hey, do either of you know who around here is an expert in Shadow Bend's Civil War involvement?" I qualified, "Not just their family's, but the whole area's history."

"Why?" Winnie's gaze sharpened, and she hitched her patchwork backpack higher on her shoulders. "Is that what your stepfather was researching? Are you and the gang investigating his murder?"

Winnie had it in her head that Poppy, Boone, Noah, Jake, and I were some sort of Scooby-Doo gang. I was pretty sure Poppy was Daphne and Boone was Fred, which left Velma for me. But I wasn't sure if Noah was Shaggy and Jake was Scooby or vice versa.

"Uh. I'm not sure what Jett was looking into." *Crap!* I should have thought of an excuse before I asked. "Someone just made a remark about the war that sounded interesting, so I wanted to know more."

Yes. I lied. But the fewer people who knew about the Civil War connection the better.

"Wait a minute." Winnie scrunched up her face, evidently replaying what she'd heard the past few days. Then she gave me a triumphant look. "You're asking about the Civil War because of the aliens, right?"

"Possibly." I pasted a mysterious expression on my face. "But I can't say."

It was all I could do not to burst out laughing. What in the world would ET have to do with a war that occurred a hundred and fifty years ago? Only Winnie could make that kind of leap of logic. Did she think that Robert E. Lee had been an extraterrestrial?

"I understand." Winnie nodded. "Anyway. Miss Ophelia is the town authority. Hell! She's so old she might have been there when it started."

"Very funny." I chuckled, adding a visit to the etiquette expert to my to-do list. "Thanks for the info." Taking Winnie and Zizi by the arms, I steered them toward the front, opened the door, and gently urged them over the threshold. "See you next week."

Locking up behind them, I turned to Dad, who was carrying the cash drawer around as he shut off

the lights, and said, "The sewing ladies are supposed to be out of here by nine."

"They were having a good time." He headed toward
the storage room. "I figured since I didn't mind hanging around, I'd let them spend their money."

"I don't want to set a precedent." I could just hear
them saying "your father let us stay" the next time I
tried to get them to leave on time. "But thanks for
working the extra hours."

"Did you see your mother?" He deposited the
drawer inside the safe.

"We stopped by around six. Didn't you see my
text?" He shook his head, and I opened the back door,
waiting for my father to walk through. "She was fine.
Chief Kincaid reinterviewed her, but she said she
stuck to her story. She was waiting for take-out delivery when we left her." I paused, then asked in as
casual a tone as I could manage, "Do you know if she's
been seeing any friends while she's been in town?"

"Why?" Dad stopped and stared at me. "What
makes you ask that?"

"It just seemed as if she might have been expecting someone other than the delivery guy." I pressed
the fob on my key ring, unlocking the door to my
BMW. "She was really anxious to get rid of us."

"That's odd." Dad's Grand Cherokee was parked
next to my car. He leaned against the rear bumper.
"Why wouldn't she want you there when whoever she
was waiting for arrived?" When I didn't answer, he
wrinkled his brow, thinking it over, then sighed and
said flatly, "You think she was expecting a man."

"Maybe." I shrugged, hating to see the hurt in his
eyes but unable to hide my disapproval. "Judging
from her appearance . . ."

"Yvette is different from you, Dev," Dad said, his shoulders slumped. "She needs constant attention and excitement."

"Whatever." I decided it was time to change the subject . . . slightly. "Speaking of my mother, has she said anything to you about Jett's finances?"

"Only that he was wealthy." Dad tapped his chin. "Something about old oil money."

"Interesting." I moved to lean next to him. "Nadine was sure Jett was nouveau riche."

"Nadine thinks the Kennedys' fortune is new, too," Dad joked.

"Did Mom tell you what Jett was researching?" I needed to check Yvette's story.

"Does this have to do with what you were asking Winnie?" Dad asked.

"Jett was poking around the town's Civil War history," I admitted. "Nadine seemed to think he was going to reveal something shady about someone's family. The current theory is that someone might have killed him to protect their ancestor's good name."

"Then you might want to talk to Boone," Dad suggested slowly. "That boy has always been mighty proud that his great-great-great-great-grandfather gave up his own life to save the town from the Yankees. But I recall, back when his mother was up for membership in the Confederate Daughters of Missouri, there were some questions raised about her family's part in the war."

"What happened?" I asked. Mrs. St. Onge had been a member in good standing for as long as I could remember.

"I think a rather large contribution was made to the Lee Mansion fund and the talk miraculously disappeared. But I remember when you and Boone were in high school, he damn near came to blows with some kid who made a remark about Major Boone's 'supposed' heroism in during the Civil War." Dad put his arm around me. "I know how close you and Boone are, so you'd better think about it carefully before you stir up that hornet's nest."

"It can't be Boone." I laid my head on my dad's chest. "He'd never murder anyone. I've seen him relocate spiders rather than kill them."

"Let's hope you're right." Dad gave my shoulder a squeeze. "For all our sakes."

CHAPTER 16

When Jake had dropped me off at the store, I'd been ready for an early night, but after Dad's bombshell about Boone, I was too wired to sleep. I needed to talk things over with someone. Jake was busy, and although I'd received a text from Noah saying that he was home and he'd pick me up for our lunch date at twelve thirty tomorrow, his adversarial relationship with Boone made him a poor choice. He'd try to be fair, but I didn't want to give him more ammunition in their ongoing rivalry.

Which was how I found myself driving down the dark country road that led to Gossip Central. I could share my concerns about Boone with Poppy without having to worry the information would somehow be used against him.

When I walked inside the club, I noticed a new sign pointing to the restrooms.

GUYS TO THE LEFT. GALS ARE ALWAYS RIGHT.

I snickered and continued down the hall into the main area. There were only a few die-hard drinkers parked on stools at the bar, a man and woman shoot-

ing pool in the back, and a giggling couple in one of
the alcoves. Otherwise, the place was empty. Week-
nights were usually slow after ten o'clock, and as I
had hoped, Poppy wasn't busy.

When Poppy looked at me, I jerked my thumb over
my shoulder, indicating that we needed to talk in private. After she made sure everyone had a full drink,
she told them to yell if they needed her, then grabbed
a bottle of wine, a corkscrew, and two glasses.

She escorted me to a booth that was far enough
away that we wouldn't be overheard, but near enough
to the action that she could keep an eye on her customers. We slid onto opposite benches, and Poppy
opened the Shiraz.

As I watched her pour the ruby red liquid, I recalled the beers I had guzzled at the Mexican restaurant and wondered if consuming more alcohol was a
good idea. Back when I had been a hotshot investment consultant, I had been used to martini lunches,
cocktail parties, and dinners with wine accompany-
ing every course. But in my new life, I was usually
less of a drinker.

"What happened?" Poppy kept her voice low as
she slid the full glass to me.

I told her about Jake showing up, our stops at the
police station, Mom's condo, Nadine's place, and the
Mexican restaurant. When I got to the part about
Jake's suspicion that Meg was exaggerating her current mental state, I paused for a sip of wine.

"I knew it." Poppy's tone was gleeful. "When Jake
left Meg here with us the other night, I saw that she
kept checking her watch. I told Boone she was planning something, but he said it was a nervous tic."

"Seriously?" I relaxed against the back of the

upholstered seat. "I would have sworn she seemed completely catatonic that evening."

"Only as long as you and Jake were around." Poppy scowled. "Once you two were out of sight, the crazy act faded and she just sat there sipping her pop and biding her time."

"Why didn't you say anything?" I demanded. "You never mentioned a word to me."

"Jake has to figure it out himself." Poppy slugged back a gulp of Shiraz. "If I told you and you told him, we both would have looked like jealous shrews with no compassion for the poor lunatic."

"Well . . . she did go through an awful ordeal with the kidnapper." I was trying to be fair. "And Jake thinks she's just scared."

"Maybe." Poppy finished her Shiraz and poured another glass. "But you didn't come here to tell me about Jake and his ex."

"Why do you say that?" I asked, curious. "You and I gossip about men all the time. Speaking of which, what's the scoop on you and Tryg?"

Tryg Price, Poppy's current boyfriend, was an Illinois attorney. Although they saw each other only one or two weekends a month, she'd dated him longer than I could remember her being with anyone else.

"He's history." Poppy crossed her arms. "He's lucky I didn't kill him."

"Why?" To the best of my knowledge, she hadn't seen him in a couple of weeks, and she hadn't said anything about his imminent demise when she'd gotten home from her last visit to Chicago. "What in the world did he do?"

"I got an invitation to his wedding in today's mail," Poppy ground out between clenched teeth. "I knew we weren't exclusive, but seriously?"

"Oh. My. God!" I took Poppy's hands and squeezed her fingers. "Are you okay?"

"Of course. You know me. I've never needed a man to make me happy." She saw the doubt in my eyes and teased, "But a maid would sure cheer me up."

"Have you talked to Tryg since you got the invitation?" I was kind of surprised she hadn't texted me.

"Yeah," Poppy muttered. "I called him to see if it was his idea of a joke."

"And?"

"And he said that about six months ago his old high school sweetheart had contacted him on Facebook. She was teaching in some small town south of Chicago and they got together. Turns out, back when they were teens they had never had sex and she still hadn't. He claims he couldn't resist the chance to be her first."

"Why do men go for that whole virgin thing?" I asked, recalling my own experience in college.

"Because they don't have to worry about being compared to another guy and found lacking." Poppy smirked. "Anyway, Miss Innocent got pregnant, and Tryg claims he had no choice but to do the right thing."

"The right thing would have been to use a condom, and barring that, at least be man enough to call you rather than send you an invitation to the wedding."

"I knew Tryg was a Colonel Sanders when I started dating him."

"Huh?" I had no idea what she was talking about.

"A typical male only concerned with the freshest legs, breasts, and thighs."

I chuckled and asked, "Where do you come up with that stuff?"

"The secret to happiness is a good sense of humor." She giggled, then added, "And a dirty mind."

When I stopped laughing, I asked, "Want me to get a gun and shoot him?"

"As tempting as the offer is"—a smile tugged at Poppy's Cupid's-bow lips—"I'll pass this time." She shrugged. "I have a few texts and snapshots he'd prefer his bride not see. Since she was under the impression they were an exclusive item, he's sending me a pair of two-carat diamond earrings and agreed to provide free legal services to me for the next five years. So I'll call our account square and chalk the experience up to live and learn."

"You threatened to blackmail an attorney?" I couldn't believe she'd gone that far.

"Hey." Poppy smiled wickedly. "I had to choose between two evils, beating the crap out of him or extortion. I picked the one I had never tried before."

"Who did you assault?"

"Some drunk who thought paying his bar tab gave him the right to rape me." Poppy flexed her muscles. "It's amazing how quickly a stun gun and a baseball bat can sober a guy up."

"Men." I sighed and drank some more wine. "Anyone new on the horizon for you?"

"No." Poppy's gorgeous heart-shaped face turned as red as the sole of her Louboutin pump. "Not really. There is this one guy. He's not at all my type. We're too different for even a fling, *and* he's in love with someone else."

"Who?" I was intrigued. First, Poppy never blushed. And second, she'd always said if the man wasn't married, then he was available, and third, she never cared about differences before. In fact, she'd often stated that having nothing in common was a plus because then there wasn't any possibility of becoming emotionally involved.

"Never mind. Sometimes the stuff in my head gets bored and makes a run for freedom through my mouth. Forget I said anything. Since it's not going to happen, I don't want to discuss it." Poppy waved away my question and changed the subject. "So you talked to the chief. Did he admit that suspecting your dad was stupid?"

Poppy's relationship with her father had been rocky since she entered puberty, but something happened last Christmas that had pushed both of them over the edge. She wouldn't tell me what had caused the final estrangement. All she would say was that it was a difference in their personal philosophy, which I took to mean that her wild lifestyle had clashed with the chief's unbending view of the world. My best guess was that one of them finally did or said something the other couldn't forgive.

"Not exactly," I said, then hastily added, "But the chief did agree to interview my dad in the back room of the store rather than bring him into the station, in order to keep down the gossip."

Damn! I'd forgotten to tell my father that. I quickly dug out my cell and sent him a message. I definitely didn't want the chief to surprise him and have my father blurt out something he shouldn't.

While I was at it, I texted the chief about what Nadine had said about Jett poking around in people's pasts. Having done my civic duty, I looked up.

The veins in Poppy's neck were bulging, and she snapped, "Dad shouldn't have to talk to Kern at all. They're close friends. He should trust him."

Attempting to distract her before she had an aneurysm, I quipped. "I'm pretty sure your father goes by Reagan's 'trust but verify' tenet."

"Yeah." Poppy blew out a long breath. "I sort of live by that rule myself."

"We both do." I squirmed, trying to get comfortable. "Or we should."

"I hate it when I agree with my father about anything." Flinging her arms wide, she said, "Do you think I'm getting old and conservative?"

I had just chugged the rest of my Shiraz and nearly choked at her question. When I could breathe, I said, "I'm pretty sure you're safe for now."

"Are you laughing at me?" She narrowed her eyes. "I'm not kidding around here. First I don't do Tryg bodily harm, then I'm attracted to a Goody Two-shoes, and now I'm agreeing with my father."

"None of the above is exactly a bad thing." I put my hands on my hips.

"Yes, they are." Poppy put her own hands on her hips, mirroring my position.

"Oh, for crying out loud." My patience was wearing thin. "Not assaulting someone, liking a nice guy, and having one freaking thing in common with your dad does not constitute a major life change."

"Fine." Poppy tossed her platinum curls behind her shoulder. She was quiet for a second, and then out of the blue asked, "Since Jake has been so preoccupied with his ex, has that given Noah a lead in the race for your heart, or are they still neck and neck?"

"Noah's been fairly busy himself." I examined my cuticles. I really needed to do something about the jagged mess my lack of manicures had produced. "I thought when he finally hired a second doctor for his clinic, he'd have more free time, but I think all it did was double the amount of patients who go there."

"He is a truly dedicated man." Poppy's expression was fond. "How about the fire chief? Is he still stopping by with extra pizza?"

"You know darn well that I fixed Coop up with Ronni," I retorted, then remembered the heated look we'd exchanged in the Mexican restaurant and felt color creep up my cheeks.

"Hey, that doesn't mean he isn't still interested in you. I haven't heard they're engaged or anything." Poppy grinned, then once again completely changed the subject. "How did Jake take it when you told him the truth about who really discovered Jett's body?"

"About like you'd expect." When I'd told Poppy about my visit with my mother, I'd mentioned that I'd had to come clean with Jake.

"Ticked off?" Poppy guessed. "Did he go all U.S. Marshal on you?"

"Not quite." I shrugged. "He wasn't happy, but he could see my side."

"Too bad your mom spilled the beans." Poppy scooted closer to the table. "The fewer people who know, the better chance to keep the secret."

"True." I glanced around, but no one was paying any attention to us. "On the other hand, if he's going to be of any real help figuring out what happened and who killed Jett, he needed to know."

Jake made three people I'd told and sworn to secrecy, and although I would never admit it, Poppy was the one I was most worried about leaking the information. Not that she would purposely do anything to hurt my parents, but she tended to blurt things out first and think about the consequences later.

I truly hoped I hadn't screwed up the police investigation by keeping my father's presence at the crime scene a secret or by getting rid of Mom's disposable cell phone. But if there was one thing I'd learned from my previous altercations with the law, it was to look out for my family, my friends, and myself before helping the cops.

No matter how much I liked and respected Chief Kincaid, I knew that first and foremost he was a policeman, and his prime concern wasn't protecting us. He'd do what he needed to do to find Jett's killer. Even if it meant dragging my parents through the court system.

A cheer went up at the bar, and we turned to see what looked like a father and son trying to reach the Budweiser tap and help themselves.

Poppy hurried to her feet, muttering, "The beer can doesn't fall far from the keg."

When Poppy got back from quieting the rebellion, she said, "You still haven't told me why you're here."

"Maybe I just wanted a drink with my best friend," I hedged. I knew in my heart of hearts that Boone would never kill someone. Now that I was here, I realized that I really didn't suspect Boone. Still, I did want to hear Poppy's take on the situation and talk to Boone to see if he had any idea what Jett was up to regarding Shadow Bend's Civil War heroes.

"Bull." Poppy tapped the tabletop with her long nails, the shiny black polish gleaming in the low lights of the club. "Spill."

"Fine." I refilled my glass, vowing this was the last one. "Not that I suspect Boone for one little minute, but when I talked to my father about the Civil War connection Nadine mentioned, he said that

Boone was extremely proud of his great-great-great-great-grandfather's part in saving the town from the Yankees."

When Poppy motioned me to continue, I added, "And apparently, back when his mother was up for membership in the Confederate Daughters of Missouri, there were some questions raised about her family's part in the war."

"Boone does go on and on about his namesake, Major Boone, dying gloriously in the last battle of Shadow Bend," Poppy mused.

"I don't remember hearing anything about Mrs. St. Onge having trouble being inducted into the CDM." I frowned. "Do you?"

"Not a peep." Poppy shook her head. "But then again, my family was on the other side in the war, so we aren't involved in the CDM."

"After all those years, what could have surfaced to cause a problem?"

"You know those history buffs." Poppy rolled her eyes. "They're always finding some new letter or diary that changes things."

"Always?" I teased. Poppy's tendency to exaggerate was legendary.

"Often enough to be annoying," she countered. "Anyway, I can't see Boone sneaking into a grubby basement and conking Jett on the head."

"Of course not. As I said, I don't suspect him." I chuckled at the image of a less-than-perfectly-neat-and-tidy Boone. The man hated it when the wind blew his hair out of place. Getting his hands filthy or having a smudge on his shirt would give him hives. "Boone does equate getting dirty with the eighth deadly sin."

"It just occurred to me." Poppy wrinkled her brow.

"Noah and Boone were the ones who brought Jett to town. Surely Boone must know what your stepfather was researching and wouldn't have endorsed him if he was worried about keeping something regarding the major a secret."

"Excellent point." I mulled over what Poppy had said, then grimaced. "Unless Jett either wasn't completely truthful or stumbled onto something like one of those letters or diaries you mentioned."

Before Poppy could comment, there was a commotion by the pool table. We both watched as the woman screamed something at the guy she was playing against, grabbed her cue stick, and brought it down on the man's forearm.

Poppy flew from her seat, and I watched as she expertly disarmed the combatant. When the woman tried to smash Poppy over the head with a beer bottle, Poppy grabbed her wrist and did some sort of judo kick. Her victim fell to her knees, clutching her stomach and threatening a lawsuit. Poppy jerked the woman to her feet and ushered her out the door.

As Poppy slammed the door, she said, "Regina, you need to remember that I'm a badass, but you're just an ass."

While Poppy dealt with the woman's boyfriend, I finished my wine. Just another Wednesday night at Gossip Central.

Once Poppy returned to the booth, she and I discussed the best way to approach Boone. We didn't want him to think for a second that we suspected him or didn't trust him. There was no way we were willing to risk a lifelong friendship on the long shot that in some crazy fit of passion Boone had actually hit Jett over the head.

Eventually we decided to start with asking Boone

what he knew about Jett's intended research and to ease into the conversation about his mother's difficulties with the CDM initiation.

The witching hour was well under way by the time I pulled into my driveway. There were no lights on in Dad's apartment, and I could hear Gran's snores as I let myself inside the quiet house. Tiptoeing past her room, I could see Banshee's eyes glowing from the foot of Gran's bed, and the cat hissed when I walked by.

I hissed back and headed to my own room. Exhaustion and booze inspired me to forgo my usual nightly ritual. Instead of washing and moisturizing my face, I kicked off my shoes and socks, stripped off my jeans, shirt, and bra, and crawled under the sheet.

In the few seconds before I entered dreamland, I thought about Jake and wondered how his encounter with Meg had played out. Had she admitted her subterfuge? Did she break character, or continue to pretend to be more emotionally distraught than she really was? Would Jake's ex continue to come between us?

CHAPTER 17

Because Thursday was the slowest day at Devereaux's Dime Store, Taryn had the day off and we closed at noon. I had almost forgotten Chief Kincaid was planning to reinterview my father, so when he strolled in at ten, my heart skidded into my stomach. He approached me, and after asking me a few questions about my text to him regarding Nadine, he nodded to Dad and discreetly slipped into the storage room. A second or so later, my father followed him.

They were gone for nearly an hour, and when Dad returned, he whispered in my ear, "I let Eldridge out the back way. Everything went fine. I answered his questions as you and I discussed, and he told me not to worry. But he also said not to leave town."

"Yikes!" I squeaked. "That doesn't sound good." Then, trying to make us both feel better, I hugged Dad and said, "No need to stick around the store. I can handle the few remaining customers myself."

Kissing my cheek, Dad headed for the exit, and for the next forty-five minutes I restocked shelves. At twelve I bagged the last shopper's purchases—a bottle

of Old Spice aftershave and a roll of Necco Wafers—
said good-bye, and locked the door behind him.

Hurrying into the back room to freshen up for my
lunch date, I grabbed my tote bag and headed into
the staff bathroom. After combing my hair, brush-
ing on some blush, and applying lip gloss, I changed
into a pair of white jeans and an aqua silk T-shirt.
Next I got rid of my sneakers and socks and slipped
on a pair of sandals.

I noticed I had fifteen minutes before Noah was
due, so I took a seat at the soda fountain, grabbed a
pen and pad of paper from my purse, and made a
list of what I needed to do regarding Jett's murder.
I'd received a text from Jake saying his confrontation
with Meg had gone as well as could be expected and
that he had asked a friend from his law enforcement
days to look into my stepfather's financial situation.
He'd call me later.

Poppy and I had arranged to get together with
Boone at his house for pizza and drinks at six. I'd
suggested we make him supper, but Poppy claimed
that the only thing domestic about her was that she
lived indoors, so we'd compromised by agreeing to
bring takeout for dinner.

We were going to ask Boone about Jett's research,
then ply him with pepperoni and booze before we
delved into Mrs. St. Onge's difficulties with the Confederate Daughters of Missouri initiation.

I chewed on the end of my pen. Who else did I
need to interview? *Ah. Yes.* Miss Ophelia. I had a
vague memory that she was somehow related to
Noah. Maybe a second or third cousin twice removed.
I hoped he'd have time to go with me to see her after
we ate.

Before I could come up with anyone else to question, I saw Noah's car pulling into the space in front of the store. Stuffing the pen and paper into my purse, I ran to the entrance, disengaged the dead bolt, and let myself out, then relocked the door behind me.

Like Jake's darkly powerful truck, Noah's taiga green Jaguar mirrored his character. The Jag was as sleek and sophisticated as its owner.

As Noah hopped out of the driver's side and hugged me, he said, "I am so sorry about your stepfather's death. Are you and your mom okay?"

"I'm fine," I assured him. "I barely knew the man, and Mom seems more interested in his will than what happened to her husband."

Letting my comment go, Noah opened my door and handed me inside. Once I was seated, he smiled and said, "You look gorgeous."

"Thanks." I tilted my head. "You look pretty darn terrific yourself."

As always, Noah was perfectly turned out. His chinos fit as if they'd been tailored just for him, and the crisply starched, striped button-down shirt showed off his broad shoulders.

While he walked around the Jag and settled in behind the wheel, I allowed myself a tiny contented groan. I loved the whole luxury-car experience. The ivory leather seat felt heavenly, and the burled walnut veneer dashboard gleamed richly in the sunlight.

Breathing deeply, I inhaled the scent of Noah's signature aftershave. It permeated the interior, and I was brought back to our first date. I had felt like the luckiest girl in the world. The hints of Brazilian rosewood and cardamom in the Amouage Dia Pour Homme would forever remind me of Noah and that idyllic time.

I was still a little surprised at how easily we had slipped back into our old relationship. After the initial awkwardness when we'd first started seeing each other again, we'd picked up where we'd left off so long ago. It was almost as if we'd never broken up in high school. As if the past thirteen years had just been a bad dream.

Of course, if that were true, Noah and I would probably be married and Jake wouldn't be in the picture at all. My chest tightened. How was it possible that I cared for both men? I had never been one to date more than one guy at a time. What had gotten into me?

Noah had been silent as he concentrated on driving through the bustling downtown area. With people on their way to and from lunch, Shadow Bend was really hopping, and I noticed the alien hunters that had been at the police station were now marching around the village square. Their odd costumes and posters made them hard to miss.

When Noah merged onto the highway, he said, "I hope you don't mind. I thought we'd head into Kansas City for lunch."

"Sounds good to me." I smiled and asked, "Where are we going?"

"Webster House." Noah put the Jaguar on cruise control and smiled broadly. "You mentioned once that you wish you'd gone there when you worked in the city, so I took a chance and made a reservation."

"Wow!" I grinned back at him. "I can't believe you remembered that."

"Well, you did go on and on about it being built in 1885 and being one of the oldest public school buildings in Kansas City and on the National Register of Historic Places." He chuckled. "And you may have mentioned once or twice that it's full of fabulous antiques and has great food."

"Oh. Right." I felt heat flooding my cheeks. "I guess I did rhapsodize over it just a little. Anyway, thanks for taking me there."

"You are very welcome." Noah laced his fingers with mine and said, "I can't imagine a better way to spend a sunny afternoon."

We rode hand in hand until Noah said, "By the way, why did you and Del Vecchio go talk to my mother last night? What in the heck did Nadine say about your stepfather that made you suspicious?"

"Well . . ." I hesitated. I hated to sound like I had thought Nadine was a murderer, but I couldn't think of a way around it, so I said, "Tony heard your mom say that Jett had better stop poking his nose where it didn't belong, and I wanted to know what she meant by that."

"Did my mother even let you in the door?" Noah put on his turn signal, accelerated, and passed a slow-moving Kia Sorento. "I'm guessing Nadine wasn't too thrilled to see you."

"She was reluctant, but I didn't give her much of a choice," I admitted. "Although the only thing she would tell us was that Jett stopped by her house wanting to see some private papers regarding your dad's great-great-great-grandfather's part in the Civil War. When she refused to show him the documents, he threatened her with some unnamed humiliation if she denied him access to those records."

"Damn!" Noah shook his head, then steered the Jag around a tractor trailer that had just merged onto the highway from the entrance ramp. "I sure hope Nadine has an alibi, because that gives her a hell of a motive."

Had Noah seriously just said his mother was a suspect? I jerked my gaze from the road to his face and saw that his eyes were twinkling.

"You can relax." I crossed my arms. "Nadine was at a luncheon during the official time of death." I pursed my lips. "Unless you think she might have hired a hit man to do the job for her."

"Nah." Noah grinned. "I see all of her financial transactions, and I haven't noticed any large withdrawals or suspicious checks."

"That's a relief." I watched the countryside whiz by for a few minutes, then said, "But speaking of Jett's research, when you and Boone worked with him to reopen the library, did my stepfather say what archives he was interested in viewing or why he was in such a rush?"

"Boone handled most of the communication with Benedict." Noah shrugged. "I think your stepfather said he was on deadline for a book he was writing about Missouri's part in the Civil War."

"And that information leads me to a favor I need to ask of you."

Before I could even finish my request, Noah said, "Anything."

My heart warmed at his sweet response. I was touched that Noah was so willing to help. "You're somehow related to Miss Ophelia, right?" When Noah nodded, I continued. "Do you have time after lunch to go with me to ask her what she knows about the Civil War in regards to Shadow Bend?"

"That depends." Noah grinned. "Can you narrow down what you're interested in? Otherwise we'll be at Miss Ophelia's for the next week or two. She's a living encyclopedia on that subject."

"I think I can do that."

"Then I'd be happy to visit Miss Ophelia with you." Noah winked. "Since I knew your store was closed for the afternoon, I arranged for Elexus to cover my patients and I took off the rest of the day, too."

Without any warning, Nadine's comments about Noah's beautiful new hire popped into my head, and I suddenly blurted out, "I hear Dr. Rodriquez is gorgeous. That she looks like a supermodel."

"Uh." Noah glanced at me with a puzzled frown. "Who told you that?"

For a split second, I'd considered claiming that the beautiful young physician's appearance was the talk of Shadow Bend. But I only fibbed if I was fairly certain that I could get away with a lie, and Nadine would probably relay last night's discussion to Noah in excruciating detail, padded with a few embellishments of her own.

"Nadine may have mentioned that Dr. Rodriquez was attractive," I muttered.

"Ah." Noah's lips twisted into a cynical smile. "I'm guessing that Mom was bragging about Elexus's royal ancestry, too."

"Uh-huh." Why had I introduced this subject? It made me look like a jealous idiot. And I had no right to that emotion. Not with the whole Noah/Jake situation. Neither man owed me exclusivity.

"I don't suppose Mom mentioned that Elexus is engaged?" Noah asked.

"We didn't really get into it." I truly wished the Jag's floorboards would open up and swallow me. I hated this whole conversation.

"Mom was just trying to stir up trouble." Noah groaned. "As usual."

"What a surprise." I patted his knee. "Sorry I mentioned it."

"I bet Mom was thrilled to see you with Del Vecchio." Noah grimaced.

"Not especially." I shook my head. "She did try to get him to take her side, but otherwise she mostly ignored him. She's sort of hard to figure out."

"You're telling me." Noah's gaze met mine, and we both sighed.

For the rest of the drive we ignored both the murder and our families and caught up on what we'd been doing since we'd last seen each other. We both were reading books in genres that were new to us. Noah had discovered Michael Crichton's early medical thrillers and was engrossed in *Drug of Choice*.

I was testing the romance waters, literally, with a novel set on a cruise ship. I'd picked it up because the heroine was an Alpha Sigma Alpha alumni and I wanted to support my sorority. I wasn't sure I believed the premise of happily-ever-after, but it was a fun read.

Noah parked in the restaurant's garage, and we walked across the street. The front entrance of the Webster House's Romanesque-style building was impressive. Steps led to red double doors, which swung open on well-oiled hinges. And, as promised, the interior was filled with amazing antiques. Noah patiently waited as I paused to examine several that caught my attention.

We were seated at a table for two with a fabulous view of Kansas City's downtown. Once we were settled, the hostess handed us the menus and told us that our server would be with us shortly.

As I studied the selections, I enjoyed the restaurant's warm ambience. It reminded me of an English country home. Or at least the image of an English country home presented by the PBS programs I watched.

When our server approached, Noah asked me, "Is it too early for wine?"

"Probably." My pulse jumped at his mischievous little grin, and I said, "But let's have some anyway."

After sending the waitress off to get a bottle of 2009 Santa Margherita, Noah took both my hands and said, "This is so nice. It seems like something always comes up to keep us from being alone."

"That reminds me. Are mother and baby okay?" I felt guilty that I hadn't asked about his patient earlier. "Did they make it to the hospital in time?"

"She's fine." Noah's eyes lit up. "And she had a healthy baby girl. Her husband is deployed, so I stayed with her until her ob-gyn showed up. Dr. Barnes was in St. Louis, so the patient was lucky she got there in time." He chuckled. "Although I doubt the new mother felt fortunate at the time. Six hours of labor is not fun."

Before I could respond, I heard a female voice behind me say, "Dr. Underwood. You're just the man I've wanted to talk to."

"Hi, Kiara." Noah greeted the owner of the voice. "Fancy meeting you here."

Kiara Howard walked up to our table. She was the event coordinator for the Shadow Bend country club. As always, the striking African-American woman was beautifully turned out. Today she wore a gorgeous peach silk suit, and suddenly I felt underdressed.

When she noticed that it was me with Noah, she said, "Dev, nice to see you."

"Always fun to run into a familiar face." I smiled at her. "What brings you into the city?"

"I'm waiting for a couple who are considering holding their wedding at the country club." She glanced at her watch. "They requested an interview before driving all the way to Shadow Bend."

"It is quite a jaunt." I shrugged. "Would you like to join us until they arrive?"

"No, thanks." She checked the time again. "They should be here any minute."

"How are things at the club?" Noah asked. "I wasn't able to make the last meeting."

Noah was a member of so many boards, I sometimes wondered how he managed them all.

"That's what I wanted to talk to you about. We had a bit of a problem the other night." Kiara tapped the toe of her high-heeled pump. "That professor investigating the alien sightings burst into the ballroom during our monthly dinner dance, claiming that everyone needed to come outside and use their collective energy to help him communicate with the extraterrestrials."

"What happened?" I asked. Chief Kincaid would blow a gasket if this guy kept bothering people.

"Our security guard escorted him out of the building," Kiara answered. "He was told that if he returned we'd call the police."

"Has he been back?" I asked, noticing that the event coordinator seemed nervous.

"Not exactly." Kiara fingered the stack of gold bangles on her right wrist. "However, I did receive a phone call from one of our members asking that we allow the professor access to our grounds. I told her I'd have to take the issue to the board."

"That's the correct procedure." Noah seemed perplexed that the event planner was discussing it with him now. "Which member made that request?"

"Your mother."

"Oh." Noah rolled his eyes at me, then said to

Kiara, "Please disregard Mom's call. I'll speak to her and take care of the matter."

"Thank you, Doctor."

The three of us were silent for a few seconds; then Kiara noticed a couple entering the restaurant and said, "I think that's my bride and groom." She fluttered her fingers and said, "Have a nice lunch."

After Kiara left, our waitress served our wine and took our food orders. Noah and I decided to share the olive oil crostini with pimento cheese, rosemary deviled ham, and pickled shrimp spreads, but while he selected the Monte Cristo Panini for his main course, I went for the Frutti di Mare, a combination of campanelle pasta, bay scallops, shrimps, and mussels in a corvina and tomato cognac cream sauce. For the kind of money the restaurant was charging, I wasn't eating a fancy grilled cheese and ham sandwich. Gran would be happy to cook that for me anytime.

The food was delicious, but I could tell Noah was worried about something.

As we finished our coffee, he said, "I really need to figure out who is riling Nadine up about the aliens. Do you think it's that professor?"

"I doubt it." I set my cup down. "He's not at all attractive or charismatic. Unless, of course, he's from old family money."

"Who else could it be?" Noah signaled the server for our check.

"No clue." I toyed with my spoon while I thought about who would be able to influence Nadine. "Maybe it's one of her CDM friends."

"There are one or two who get involved in some weird causes." Noah wiped his mouth on his napkin and sat back. "You know how it is. Too much time and money on their hands and husbands or children who neglect them."

"Maybe you could make some calls," I suggested. "I can keep an ear out in the store for any sign of who might believe in ET."

"Let me know if you hear anything." Noah took care of the bill.

We walked back to where we'd parked and Noah helped me into the Jag, then headed the car back to Shadow Bend. Noah was clearly still concerned about his mother's interest in the professor.

After several miles of silence, I joked, "Maybe it was the aliens who killed my stepfather."

"Right." Noah snickered. "Try selling that theory to Chief Kincaid."

CHAPTER 18

As we parked in front of Miss Ophelia's, I admired the modest turret-covered front porch. Unlike most of the more elaborate Victorian homes built in Shadow Bend during the nineteenth century, this house's stick and spindle work was minimal, but the irregular roofline classified it as a Queen Anne.

We walked up a short flight of steps to the front porch, and I admired the four white posts with their gingerbread trim supporting the arched roof. The pale yellow exterior was in pristine condition, but the period feeling of the house had been retained.

Miss Ophelia answered the doorbell, and after Noah explained our visit, she invited us inside. We followed the tiny old woman as she led us into the hallway and then waved us into the parlor.

Slowly seating herself on a gorgeous Heywood-Wakefield wicker chair, she gestured to the carved mahogany rope-twist settee across from her and said, "Please make yourselves comfortable."

"You have a lovely home." Although I had attended etiquette classes here, the students always entered through the back door. We then used the rear staircase to access the second-story classroom and dance studio. We were never allowed anywhere on the main floor. Miss Ophelia's personal living space was strictly off-limits, and we'd all been too terrified of her to test that rule.

"Thank you. It's all original to the house." Miss Ophelia's straight spine never touched the back of her chair. "It's exactly as my great-great-great-grandmother decorated it a century and a half ago. Her husband had everything shipped from New York."

"Impressive." I gazed at the Oriental carpet and the flocked wallpaper, neither of which showed any indication of wear.

"May I get you something to drink?" Miss Ophelia asked. "I was about to put the kettle on for a pot of tea when you arrived."

Noah glanced at me, then answered for us both. "No, thank you. We just had a wonderful lunch at Webster House in Kansas City."

"An extremely fine establishment." Miss Ophelia smiled. "Or so I've been told. I no longer travel into the city." She inclined her head. "Now, you indicated an interest in Shadow Bend's part in the Civil War. Is there any specific event you'd like to discuss?"

"Yes." Noah's leg nudged mine as he said, "The information we're most concerned with would involve the ancestors of local families."

"Ah." Miss Ophelia folded her hands. "Anyone in particular?"

"Folks who are still living in the area," I said. "Especially current members of the Confederate Daughters of Missouri."

"I see." Miss Ophelia shot me a sharp glance, then

asked Noah, "What has your mother gotten herself involved with this time?"

"I hope nothing." Noah sighed. "Although if you know why she's suddenly fascinated with aliens, I'd love to hear about it."

"Nadine rarely speaks to me." Miss Ophelia's thin lips curled slightly. "She finds my insistence on facts rather than gossip boring. And she has yet to realize that to acquire knowledge, one must first admit one doesn't already know everything."

Although I agreed with Miss Ophelia's assessment of Nadine's character, I was anxious to get down to business and asked, "Are you aware of any controversy regarding any of Shadow Bend's Civil War heroes?"

"As you are undoubtedly aware from your high school state history class, Missouri sent men and supplies to both sides of the conflict." Miss Ophelia crossed her ankles, evidently settling in for a long story. "We had separate governments that represented each side. And Missourians fought over it, neighbors against neighbors and brothers against brothers."

"Was that the case in Shadow Bend?" Noah asked. "Were we a community divided, or were most of the townsfolks firmly Confederate?"

Miss Ophelia ignored his question and continued her lesson. "Missouri supplied more than thirty thousand troops to the Confederate army and approximately a hundred and ten thousand to the Union."

"Did Shadow Bend families send many of our men to the Union side?" I asked.

My question didn't fare any better than Noah's had, and the elderly woman continued her lecture without deigning to acknowledge it.

"There was fighting all over our state."

When she paused, Noah opened his mouth, but before he could speak, she said, "The best estimates that I've read indicate that twelve hundred separate battles and skirmishes were fought in Missouri." As Miss Ophelia shook her head, her snow-white chignon gleamed in the sunlight coming through the front window. "Only two other states saw more fighting than Missouri—Virginia and Tennessee."

"Wow." I vaguely recalled learning those details in school, but at that time, they hadn't made much of an impression.

Miss Ophelia seemed almost to be talking to herself as she continued. "The first major battle west of the Mississippi River took place at Wilson's Creek, Missouri, and the largest conflict west of the Mississippi River was the Battle of Westport at Kansas City."

"Very interesting, Miss Ophelia." Noah leaned forward and touched her hand. "But is there anything more specific to Shadow Bend?"

"There were two skirmishes in this area," Miss Ophelia answered, appearing to refocus. "In the first, the Union troops outnumbered our local regiment by about three to one and easily routed them. Casualties were extremely heavy, and there were many fatalities. The deaths and loss of limbs of so many of our young men stirred up a lot of strong feelings among the townspeople who, up until then, had been less than passionate about the war."

"And the second battle?" I asked, gathering that that encounter was the more complicated and thus more relevant to our situation.

"The second was later in the war." Miss Ophelia took a lace-edged handkerchief from the pocket of her dress and cleaned her glasses. "Our boys were terribly dispirited by their early defeat."

"How much later?" I asked, squirming a little on the uncomfortable sofa.

"Near the end." Miss Ophelia settled her spectacles back on her face. "It took place in early September of 1864, a week before General Sterling Price, our former governor, led his ill-fated raid. He believed his attack could stir a general uprising for the Confederacy."

"But it didn't." I remembered that much from our Missouri state history class.

"Shadow Bend's regiment, along with many others in Missouri, had been ordered to create a diversion for General Price's troops." Miss Ophelia neatly folded her hanky and returned it to her pocket. "This time, before the big battle, our men used guerrilla maneuvers to weaken the enemy."

"Like what?" Noah asked.

"Ambushes, sabotage, and hit-and-run tactics," Miss Ophelia explained. "They used their familiarity with the area and their ability to move quickly against the Union's larger and less mobile troops."

"Which means"—I paused as I thought about the ramifications of that type of fighting—"during the period before the actual battle, the Shadow Bend guys were mostly on their own. Little or no accountability."

"Correct." Miss Ophelia raised a feathery white brow. "Which is perhaps how tales became exaggerated and later questioned."

"Any of our local families' heroes have disputed claims?" I asked. This had to be what Jett was researching. But why would he care about a tiny regiment that had made little impact in the war?

"There were stories about collaboration with the Union and another about an act of cowardice," Miss Ophelia answered. "But nothing was ever proven, and with the passing of years, the rumors died out."

"Do you know which soldiers were accused of what?" Noah asked.

"Thirty-nine years ago, Mindy Hargrove found a box of letters written by her great-great-great-grandfather. In them, several new facts came to light, one of which was a complaint that the only time Major Boone fought alongside his men in the front lines was during that last fatal battle." Miss Ophelia tented her fingers. "But that wasn't unusual for officers."

Could that have been the issue that nearly kept Mrs. St. Onge out of the CDM? It hardly seemed like enough, but I had no idea the stringency of the membership requirements.

"Who else was mentioned in the Hargrove letters?" I asked.

"Hargrove wrote that Captain Sinclair reported that the Union train his unit was sent to raid never showed up." Miss Ophelia gazed at me. "He speculated that the Sinclairs were Union sympathizers."

"Interesting," I murmured. That was what Nadine had alluded to at the city council meeting. Since my family wasn't too rah-rah about their ancestors' past glories during the war and my initiation into the CDM had been halted due to my father's imprisonment, I'd never heard about the issue until Noah's mother had thrown the accusation at me. "And ironic considering that my great-great-great-great-grandfather was killed in that final battle, along with Major Boone and Colonel Underwood."

"What about Colonel Underwood?" Noah broke in. "Any dirt on him?"

"Our ancestor's name has never been besmirched." Miss Ophelia straightened her already rigid spine, then winked. "But Nadine has never allowed me to examine the papers pertaining to his service."

"So we have a possible coward, an accused Union sympathizer, and an unknown," I summarized, wanting to make sure I had everything straight. "And three of the founding families are represented."

"That is precisely why the allegations were never examined." Miss Ophelia scowled. "No one was interested in stirring up that kettle of fish." She tapped her fingers on the arm of her chair. "Outside of the members of the CDM, who only want to flaunt their status, few people care about the past anymore. Which is why I was surprised when Mr. Benedict requested a meeting."

"Did you agree to see him?" Noah asked, his shoulders stiffening.

"I did." Miss Ophelia tilted her head toward me and said, "You have my deepest sympathy on the loss of your stepfather. He was a charming man and extremely well versed in Civil War history. It was a shame that we'd barely begun chatting when we were interrupted by a call from his lawyer. He excused himself and immediately left. He and I were supposed to meet again the next afternoon. Unfortunately, he was killed before that happened."

Noah and I glanced at each other, and then I asked, "Was there anything in particular Jett asked you? Anything that stood out as unusual?"

"His interests were similar to the ones you and Noah have expressed."

"Did you tell him what you told us?" I asked. I held my breath. Were we on the same track? "Or was he called away too soon?"

"Mr. Benedict already knew what I've relayed to you." Miss Ophelia smoothed her skirt over her knees. "What he wanted from me was an opinion on a set of documents he'd recently run across."

"At the library?" I asked.

"He didn't say where he'd located the documents."

"What was in those papers?" Noah asked.

"I never got to examine them." Miss Ophelia frowned. "He was called away before he produced them and declined to leave them with me."

Something about Miss Ophelia's answer rang a bell in my head, but before I could figure out why, Noah said, "Thank you so much for seeing us." Noah got up and hugged his cousin. "If you think of anything else about issues regarding the local families and the Civil War, please give me a call."

"I will." Miss Ophelia stood and showed us to the door. "But I suspect the documents your mother won't allow me to study might be what you really need to see."

CHAPTER 19

As Noah opened the Jaguar's door for Dev, he glanced at his watch. It was almost five. "I need to stop back home to walk Lucky. Why don't you come with me, and afterward we can take a dip in the pool?"

"First, I don't have a swimsuit." Dev slid into the passenger seat. "Although that wouldn't be a deal breaker." She smiled naughtily, and Noah felt himself harden. "Second, I need to talk to Dad and Gran about our ancestor's possible Union leanings." She put her purse on the floor and buckled her safety belt. "Third, I'm meeting Poppy at Boone's for pizza at six." She gazed at Noah through her lashes as he climbed behind the wheel. "And I have a hunch that if I went to your house, I'd be late." She paused, then added softly, "Or I wouldn't make it there at all."

The suggestive note in her voice and the gleam in her eyes sent a lightning bolt to his crotch. He wanted to ignore her arguments and drive them to his place just as fast as the Jag would take them. Unfortunately, she had a determined expression on her face that said no amount of coaxing would change her mind.

He put the car in gear and pulled into the street. It took all his self-control to maintain a pleasant expression as he said, "Are you free Sunday afternoon? It's supposed to be clear and in the eighties. We can laze in the water and have a picnic."

"Sounds fun." Dev put a hand on his leg. "I'll bring the food."

"Great." He struggled to keep his tone even. Her fingers on his thigh were not helping calm his arousal. "Does two o'clock work for you?"

Dev fished her phone from her purse and checked her calendar. "That would be perfect."

They were both silent for the few minutes it took Noah to drive from Miss Ophelia's to the parking lot behind the dime store. As soon as he stopped the Jag, Dev leaped out. Shouting that she'd see him later, she waved, hurried over to her own car, and hopped inside.

As he watched Dev reverse the BMW, he accepted defeat. *Hell!* Forget about an evening of fooling around; he hadn't even gotten a good-bye kiss. Driving away, he snarled. Why was it that whenever he was around Dev, he lost every damn bit of his famous willpower?

Noah groaned. It was probably a good thing Dev had jumped out of the car so fast, because a single touch of her lips would not be enough. He wasn't certain anything short of forever would be enough to stop the ache inside of him.

Taking things slow and trying to prove that he was the sure and steady guy for her wouldn't work. Not when every time he and Dev finally had a chance to be together some crisis got in their way.

If he'd been smart, instead of the lame excuse of needing to walk his dog, he should have kept his mouth shut, driven her to his place, swept her into his arms, and carried her to his bedroom. Noah chuckled. Too bad Dev would have probably kneed him in the balls if he tried that kind of caveman stunt.

Taking a deep breath, he forced himself to put his desire for Dev aside and concentrate on the matter at hand. Once he had walked Lucky, he'd drop by his mom's. Nadine was acting crazier than usual, which meant she might be heading for some real trouble.

As much as he'd like to wash his hands of his meddling mother, Noah was honor bound to take care of her. He'd promised his father, and he considered himself a man of his word.

Still, as he pulled the Jaguar into his garage, the memory of Dev's sea green eyes, velvety skin, and lush red lips interfered with his breathing. Emotionally, she consumed him, and for one irrational moment he wanted to turn his car around, drive to Dev's place, and kidnap her for a night of wild sex and a morning of sweet kisses.

Noah took another deep breath. Then, having regained his common sense, he took care of his dog and drove over to his mom's. He parked in the driveway and got out.

The place never changed. His mother had always insisted on keeping both the exterior and interior in museumlike condition, and it was still the cold, imposing pile of bricks it had been when he'd lived there. He'd never felt comfortable in his parents' home, and he had escaped to college as soon as he could, vowing never to spend another night under his mother's lavish roof.

Now that he'd finally found a reliable health aide, Noah limited his visits to a once-a-week wellness check. Every Sunday morning after church, he and

Nadine suffered through an uncomfortable, often silent, brunch, where each of them searched for a neutral topic of conversation. He was relieved when the obligatory two hours were up and he could say good-bye. And Noah suspected his mother was, too.

Nadine's aide, Beckham Janson, answered the door-bell and said, "Mrs. Underwood is on the patio."

The handsome young man had become more of a majordomo to Nadine than health care worker. At first Noah had been alarmed at the guy's growing influence on Nadine. Noah had been concerned that Janson would take advantage of his position and try to bilk her out of her fortune, but there had been no sign of duplicity.

The aide seemed perfectly happy to live rent-free in a beautiful house with comparatively light duties. For the most part, Janson provided more compan-ionship than actual physical assistance. His pres-ence was as much a safeguard as anything else.

Because Noah handled all the financial aspects of his mother's life, he would know immediately if there was the slightest hint of inappropriate transac-tions. With that in mind, he'd resolved to count his blessings and be thankful for Janson's help.

Nadine's miraculously improved physical condi-tion, but questionable mental health, made Noah grateful that Janson kept him thoroughly informed regarding Nadine's whereabouts and her activities. At least the ones the young man was around to observe.

"Mrs. Underwood is having cocktails." Beckham stepped aside. "May I bring you one?"

"No, thanks." Noah nodded to the aide. "I'll be with my mother for the next couple of hours, so you can take a break."

"Cool. I'll run to the gym and get in a workout." He flexed his arms. "You don't get guns like these by slacking off." He held out his hand. "By the way, thanks for picking up the membership fee. That was really awesome of you to include that perk in my contract."

"My pleasure." Noah shook the man's hand, then walked down the hall, across the kitchen, and opened the patio doors.

Stepping outside, Noah saw that Nadine was sitting on a chaise lounge, sipping a martini and idly flipping through a fashion magazine. Her chair faced the immaculately landscaped backyard, giving him a view of her profile.

He studied her for several minutes, watching as every once in a while she put her drink down on the nearby glass table, gazed over her kingdom, and sighed. It was rare to see his mother so pensive. Her usual expression was complacent. What was she thinking?

Finally, clearing his throat so as not to startle her, Noah walked over to his mother and said, "Hi, Mom. Enjoying the nice weather?"

"Noah." Nadine looked up at him and shaded her eyes. "I wasn't expecting you." Her voice faltered. "Was I?"

"I thought maybe we could have dinner together." Noah smiled. "Unless you're busy."

"Not at all." Nadine closed her magazine. "Would you like a drink?"

"Maybe later." Noah lowered himself onto the chaise lounge beside his mother's and said, "I told Janson he could have a couple of hours off. I can whip up an omelet and a salad and we can eat out here."

"That would be nice." Nadine's mood was difficult to read.

"Are you still happy with Janson?" Noah asked, thinking that might be a good lead-in to the subject of the aliens. "Is he helpful?"

"As I've said before, I don't really need anyone." Nadine's tone was martyred. "I only keep him around since you said it made you feel better to have him here. Now that I seem to have stopped having those silly little spells, I'm perfectly capable of taking care of myself."

"I'm glad you're feeling so much better," Noah said slowly. "But especially now that Mrs. Fowler has retired and you haven't found another housekeeper, I think it's a good idea to hang on to Janson's services."

"If I must." Nadine patted her hair. "Beckham is amusing and very helpful." She took a sip of her drink. "My friends like him."

"That's always a big plus with household employees," Noah commented dryly.

"Of course." Nadine's voice held a note of uncertainty. She had never been one to appreciate sarcasm.

Noah kicked himself for baiting his mother. When would he learn?

As he berated himself, Noah realized that the introduction of Nadine's cronies' opinions was his opening, so he asked, "What's the new hot topic among all your CDM pals?" He needed to find out who was planting the alien crap in her head so he could stop it.

"Jett Benedict's murder was all anyone could talk about for the last few days."

"And before that?" Noah used his best bedside manner. "What was it?"

"Well . . ." Nadine finished her martini. "Janice St. Onge is enthralled by Professor Hinkley's work. She's the one who originally told me about what was going on around here with the teenagers."

"Did Janice get that information from the professor?" Noah asked as casually as he could manage. If his mother felt like he was interrogating her, she'd stop talking faster than a criminal who had just been Mirandized.

"I'm not entirely sure of the chronology." Nadine tilted her head.

Noah made a noncommittal sound to encourage her to continue.

"However, I believe Janice saw the funny lights several weeks or more before the professor spoke to the city council." Nadine wrinkled her nose. "She'd mentioned the UFOs to me previously, but the afternoon before the meeting, she came over here and told me the whole story."

"That was when she said the aliens were abducting the teenagers?" Noah asked, leaning toward his mother. "And replacing them with copies?"

"Janice claimed that half the children were already replicas, or maybe that the teenagers were still themselves with parasites inside of them controlling their actions." Nadine's tongue traced her lips. "I think the latter is her current theory."

"If that were true, don't you think their folks would have noticed that their kids were different?" Noah asked with a frown.

"It depends." Nadine put her empty glass down on the table and grabbed both of Noah's hands with hers. "The thing is, the aliens are so good at this, no one realizes what's happened until it's too late."

"None of the teenagers I've seen at the clinic

display any unusual behavior." Noah squeezed his mother's fingers. "And physically they have all been normal."

"Janice says that the parasite that controls them is so sophisticated it is undetectable." Nadine let go of Noah's hands and slumped back. "She told me that by the time anyone realizes what's going on, it might be too late."

"How does Janice know all this?" Noah grimaced. His mother was getting all stirred up, and that never turned out well for him. He should drop the subject, but he needed to figure out what was going on, and for once Nadine wasn't evading his questions.

"Janice didn't exactly say how she found out." Nadine licked her lips again. "She just told me that we had to stop it, because once they were done with the children, they'd start on us next."

"So no plan?" Noah asked.

He tried to remember his rotation on the psychiatric ward. Keep the patients talking until they'd shared their concern. Too bad he couldn't recall if he was supposed to encourage their delusions or try to make them see reason.

"Uh . . . I don't believe Janice thought that far ahead." Nadine trailed off, then seemed to catch herself. "No. I'm sure she didn't." Nadine glanced at Noah. "We had quite a bit of wine while we talked, and I was doing the Master Cleanse, so I hadn't eaten." She shrugged unapologetically. "The rest of that afternoon and evening are pretty fuzzy, but Beckham informed me I spoke about the extraterrestrial problems at the city council meeting."

Noah rolled his eyes. As a doctor he didn't see the value of drinking a combination of lemon, maple syrup, and cayenne pepper. He felt that his patients would do better eating sensibly and consuming more water. And unless the person was constipated, the herbal laxative tea that was part of that regime wasn't high on his approval list, either.

"Janson was telling you the truth. You made a vehement speech about the alien menace at the meeting." Noah sighed. "And once he got you home, you tried to phone the media so that they could warn everyone about the threat. Luckily, Janson and I stopped you."

"I see." Nadine paled. "While I do think we should do something about the extraterrestrial situation, I'm glad you intervened and I didn't involve the television people. They're so crass."

"I'm happy to have been of service." He would have to talk to Janice St. Onge to track down who had gotten her embroiled in the impending alien invasion. Clearly, Nadine had been too intoxicated to get any details. "And speaking of not getting people involved, it would probably be best if you withdrew your request that the country club allow the professor access to their property."

"But Janice asked me as a favor." Nadine stuck out her lower lip. "She thought because you were on the board, it would be better coming from me."

"I understand." Noah stood. "Still, I recommend that you don't pursue the matter."

"Fine." Nadine crossed her arms as if in a huff, but her expression bore a trace of relief.

"Thank you." Noah pecked his mother on the cheek. "Now, why don't I go start dinner?"

"It's a little early to dine," Nadine said, frowning up at him. "I usually eat closer to six thirty, a much more civilized hour. I like to have another cocktail or two in order to help stimulate my appetite."

Which was precisely why Noah wanted to get some food into his mother. Nadine claimed she was never hungry, but he suspected her quest to stay a size two might have something to do with her disinterest in nourishment. He'd told her many times that there were more calories in one of her giant martinis than in a grilled chicken breast with a baked potato and vegetables.

"Well, I'm hungry," Noah lied. He was still full from lunch, but he was willing to perjure himself if it would get his mother to eat. "How about you have another *small* drink while I'm cooking?"

"That would be nice." Nadine adjusted her watch so the diamond-encrusted dial was centered on her wrist, then looked at Noah from under her eyelashes. "I always have such a better appetite when you and I dine together. Maybe we could do it more often."

"Maybe." Noah felt a tug of guilt. His mother was lonely, and although she liked her health aide, Janson wasn't family or even a friend.

"I'll keep you company while you prepare our meal." Nadine rose from her chair, picked up her empty glass, and followed him inside.

Noah watched through the doorway to the dining room as his mother poured herself a martini from the pitcher sitting on the bar cart against the sidewall. Then, balancing the full glass, Nadine joined him in the kitchen and perched on a stool at the granite counter.

Biting his tongue to keep from commenting on the size of his mother's *small* drink, Noah took six eggs from the fridge and placed them in warm tap water. While the eggs came to room temperature, he found a skillet and heated it over medium-high heat.

As he worked, Noah kept an eye on his mother. He'd managed the minefield of one difficult subject— the alien invasion—but he still had to maneuver her into discussing his ancestor's Civil War experience. Normally, Nadine loved to talk about either her family's brave officers or her husband's great-great-great-grandfather, the Confederate hero, but the information Noah needed wouldn't be as easy to get from her. She'd never willingly disclose any dishonorable acts Colonel Underwood might have committed.

Once the pan was hot, Noah added the butter, and when it melted, he swirled it around the surface of the frying pan. As he cracked the warmed eggs into a bowl, added salt and blended with a fork, he rehearsed how he was going to introduce the topic.

Finally, Noah commented, "I saw Miss Ophelia this afternoon. She mentioned that you had some papers from my great-great-great-great-grandfather's service. I would love to read them."

"They're not very interesting." Nadine looked away from Noah's gaze. "Mostly lists of supplies and men, and who was assigned where."

"Still." Noah poured the eggs into the center of the pan and stirred them with a rubber spatula. "I'd like to know more about my history so that when I have children I can tell them about it."

"Children," Nadine said sharply. "I hope you aren't counting on Devereaux for that. She seemed fairly enamored with that U.S. Marshal."

"Dev hasn't made up her mind yet." Although Noah's stomach clenched, he kept his expression neutral. "But I'm sure she'll choose me."

"Not if there's a God in heaven," Nadine muttered, then took a sip of her drink.

Ignoring his mother's comment, Noah lifted the pan and tilted it until the excess liquid was under the cooked part of the eggs. "So, do you have those papers handy? I'd like to take them with me tonight."

"I don't think that's a good idea." Nadine played with the stem of her glass.

"Why is that?" Noah used the spatula to loosen the omelet's edge.

"The thing is"—Nadine gave a high-pitched, mirthless laugh—"there might be some unflattering material in those documents, and I wouldn't want you to think any less of your heritage because of something you might misinterpret or fail to understand in context."

"I promise to keep an open mind." Noah wondered what his mother had been hiding all these years. Seeing Nadine's lips tighten, he knew she was about to refuse, so he brought out the big guns. "After all, I am the last male Underwood. It's time for me to assume the family mantle of responsibility. It's not as if I'll share the information with anyone."

He mentally crossed his fingers. Finding a man's killer was more important than keeping a secret about something that had happened more than a hundred and fifty years ago. And if it had nothing to do with Benedict's death, Noah trusted Dev to keep the information confidential.

As if reading his mind, Nadine narrowed her eyes and said, "This has something to do with that awful man's murder, doesn't it?"

"Only inasmuch as hearing about his research has piqued my interest." Noah hadn't lied this much to his mother since he was a teenager.

"You know, Mr. Benedict visited me, asking about those same papers."

"Uh-huh." Noah couldn't remember if his mother had told him about the guy stopping by or if it had been Dev who'd shared that information, so he kept his response noncommittal.

"Initially, he was charming. He even offered to make drinks for us." Nadine smiled reminiscently. "He mixed the best cosmopolitan that I've ever tasted."

"Then what happened?" Noah minced a couple of slices of ham for the omelet.

"At first he was really upset when I refused to let him see the Civil War papers, but then he made us another cocktail and we chatted about other things."

"So he just gave up?" Noah added cheese and meat to the omelet.

"Well . . ." Nadine refused to meet her son's eyes. "I must have dozed off, because when I woke up later that evening, Mr. Benedict was gone."

"Janson wasn't here?" Noah wanted to scream at his mother about her drinking, but he knew it would do no good. He needed to have her doctor talk to her. She might listen to her physician, but certainly not her son.

"I'd given Beckham the night off," Nadine answered. "I had planned to go to the country club dinner dance, but Mr. Benedict delayed my departure."

"Was anything missing?"

"No." Nadine pressed her hand to her chest. "I was worried Mr. Benedict might have stolen the documents he wanted while I slept, but they were still here." She sighed. "It did look as if the contents of the file might have been gone through, but nothing was missing. I checked the inventory."

"Speaking of those papers, as I mentioned, I'd like

to see them." Noah figured that Dev's stepfather had photographed the documents. Nadine would have had to be out for hours for the man to read them, and Benedict wouldn't have risked Janson returning early or his hostess waking sooner than expected.

"Customarily"—Nadine toyed with the pearls around her neck—"the male heir gets the journals and the trust fund on his fortieth birthday. It was felt that at that point a man would be mature enough to handle the confidential information in the diaries."

"I recall the trust-fund age restriction when Dad's will was read, but I don't remember about the papers."

"That part isn't in writing. It's a tradition." Nadine tossed down the rest of her martini, then leaned forward and said, "But since it means so much to you, I'll make an exception." She sighed again. "I may be sorry, but I'll give you the box."

"It'll be fine, Mom," Noah reassured her. He folded the omelet, cut it in half, and slid it onto two dishes.

"I hope so." Nadine's tone was querulous. "Just remember your duty is to the family, not to a woman who may or may not love you."

While his mother fetched the documents, Noah carried their supper out to the patio table. When his mother joined him, she silently handed him a carton containing bulging accordion folders. As they ate, he noticed that her attitude toward him had subtly changed. She seemed almost apprehensive, which wasn't like her at all.

Just as Noah and his mother finished their meal—at least Noah had eaten; Nadine had pushed the food around her plate—Janson returned. The aide offered to clean up and do the dishes, so Noah stood and said good-bye to his mother.

As he reached for the box, Nadine grabbed his

wrist, her nails biting into his skin, and said, "I really wish you wouldn't do this."

"You worry entirely too much about the past and what others will think." Noah freed his hand. "Most folks don't judge people's worth by their ancestors' behavior."

"You have no idea how hard I've worked to keep the Underwood name one that people admire in this town," Nadine snapped. "Now, if you'll excuse me, there's a television show that I want to watch on the History Channel, and it comes on in a few minutes."

"Sure." Noah kissed his mother on the cheek, then teased her, "Are you sure it isn't *The Bachelor* or one of those other reality shows?"

"Certainly not." Nadine pinned him with a cold glare. "I only watch educational programs. Otherwise, I spend my lonely evenings reading important literature."

Noah swallowed a chuckle. The only novels in his mother's house were the ones in his father's office, and the last time he'd been in there, the books were exactly as his dad had left them.

Before Noah could leave, Nadine clutched his arm and warned, "Think twice before you decide some woman is worth flushing everything the Underwoods stand for down the toilet."

As Noah walked away, he wondered just how rotten the family skeleton would be.

CHAPTER 20

After Noah dropped me at my car, I went home and filled Dad in on what we knew so far about Jett Benedict and what leads we were pursuing regarding his murder. Once he was caught up on my investigation, I asked about Captain Sinclair's part in the war.

Dad assured me that as far as he or Gran knew, our ancestor had been firmly on the side of the Confederacy. But since neither he nor any of our more distant relatives had ever been very interested, there was no written history, and any stories had died with Grandpa Sinclair.

When my father said he was taking Birdie and her friend Frieda to the VFW's spaghetti dinner, I was relieved that he was staying away from Mom. Telling him to have a good time, I retreated to my room.

I had half an hour before I had to head back into town, so I stretched out on the bed and checked my cell. There were two missed calls from Jake, but he hadn't left a message.

I dialed his number, but when it went straight to

his voice mail, I disconnected. I hated playing telephone tag. Instead, I texted him, asking what was up, and saying that I was busy the rest of the night.

The remaining e-mails, texts, and messages were business related, and after answering inquiries from vendors, bidding on some vintage lingerie that I wanted for my erotic gift baskets, and deleting a lot of spam, I glanced at the clock and saw that I needed to go.

Having volunteered to bring the food, I stopped at the local pizza joint and picked up an unbaked super supreme. I'd ordered an uncooked pie so that we wouldn't have to worry about it getting cold if Poppy was delayed. My dear friend wasn't known for her promptness, and a quarter of an hour late was actually on time for her.

After shelling out nearly thirty bucks for the extra-large and an antipasto salad, I drove to Boone's. He lived near Nadine in the old-money part of town. His neighborhood was full of majestic houses, none of which had been built anytime in the past hundred to hundred and fifty years.

When Boone's parents made it clear to the older Mrs. St. Onge that they preferred their contemporary residence, she had left her grandson her Prairie-style home. Boone adored the place, showering it with both the contents of his bank account and his attention.

He had kept the original building intact, but had enlarged the master bathroom and had annexed one of the adjoining rooms for a walk-in closet. He'd also added a detached garage in the rear, claiming that his Mercedes couldn't possibly sit out during the Missouri winters.

When architectural purists criticized him for the

changes he'd made, Boone was quick to point out that while vintage was wonderful, there was no need to go crazy. After all, he loved *Gone with the Wind*, but he had no desire to live during a period when people bathed only once a week and there was no deodorant.

When I arrived at Boone's, I parked in his narrow driveway. As always, I was the first to get there. One of the reasons I was inevitably early was due to Birdie's influence. She felt tardiness was rude and had made sure I felt guilty if I wasn't wherever I needed to be at least ten minutes before the appointed hour.

But a big part of my motivation was that if Poppy made it to Boone's before me, her humongous Hummer would take up the entire driveway. Then I'd be forced to leave my Z4 on the street, where it would be vulnerable to all the idiot drivers who might sideswipe it.

I had minimal auto insurance and a sky-high deductible, which meant if the car got dented, having it repaired was a luxury I couldn't afford. And call me superficial, but it would crush me to drive a battered vehicle. I know, pride cometh before a fall, but I'd already suffered several falls, so pride was all I had left.

As I got out of my BMW, I gazed at the house. No matter how often I visited Boone, I always stopped to admire the grouping of multipaned windows that were the focal point of the second floor. Boone kept them illuminated, and the result was stunning.

My BFF was waiting for me when I got to the door and ushered me into the foyer. Boone greeted me, then stood back to examine my outfit. I still wore the aqua silk T-shirt and white jeans I'd put on for my lunch date. When he frowned, I peeked in the mirror opposite the coat closet and cringed. My top was a mess.

Smoothing the shirt over my hips, I said, "Guess I should have changed. I was lying across my bed answering e-mail, and my clothes must have gotten wrinkled."

Now that I could see my full-length self, I noticed that the silk top hugged my generous curves more tightly than I liked. With a body type more often seen in a Rubens painting than in a fashion magazine, I tended to wear looser clothing. As I was prone to comment, the only thing that should cling was plastic wrap.

As Boone tried to brush out some of the creases, he *tsk*ed. "Girl, don't you ever look at yourself before leaving the house?"

"Of course I do." I narrowed my eyes in mock outrage and retorted, "Just not as often as you. But then again, you're much prettier than I am."

"True." Boone took the pizza box and salad container from the small table where I had placed it and led me into the kitchen. "But I prefer the word *handsome*."

I followed him, biting my thumbnail. It would be tough asking Boone about the ancestor he was so proud of without sounding as if I suspected him of murdering my stepfather. And the last thing I wanted to do was offend one of my oldest and best friends.

Boone had always been there for me. When my father went to prison, my mother abandoned me, and Noah broke up with me, Boone had gathered the shattered pieces of my heart and glued them back together.

I watched Boone place the pizza carton in the refrigerator, and keeping my tone casual, I asked,

"How are your folks?" It was lame, but it was the only thing I could think of to say, and I wanted to wait for Poppy before getting into the evening's real topic. The one that would be so difficult.

"Same old, same old."

"Still not talking to each other?" I asked.

Although Mr. and Mrs. St. Onge lived in the same house, except for a brief respite during a crisis, they hadn't spoken for years. With the advent of modern technology, they utilized e-mail and texting for all their communication needs. Before that they'd made Boone their messenger.

"As far as I know." Boone peered into the open fridge and said, "Do you want—"

"Wine?" I interrupted. "Yes, please."

"How did you know what I was going to ask?" Boone grabbed a bottle.

"Because there comes a time in every day that whatever the question, the answer is wine."

Boone chuckled, then said, "I'm surprised neither Dr. Dreadful nor Deputy Dawg are joining us tonight. I'd expect both your beaus to want to help you figure out who killed your stepfather."

"I thought we needed a BFF night." I hedged, reaching down to pet Boone's cat, Tsar, who had materialized out of nowhere and was rubbing against my calf. "Besides, Jake is busy, and I know you aren't all that fond of Noah."

"What can I say?" Boone shrugged. "To quote Winston Churchill, Noah has all the virtues I dislike and none of the vices I admire."

I rolled my eyes, then glanced at the wall clock. "Poppy should be here soon. Maybe you should pre-heat the oven."

"Sure. It'll take at least ten minutes." Boone spun

the dial. "I think I heard her Hummer roar to a stop a couple of seconds ago."

"That would mean she's only eleven minutes late." I pulled out a wooden slat-back chair from the matching square-leg table and sat down. "I think that just might be a record for her."

Boone sniggered as he headed toward the foyer and let Poppy in.

Poppy hugged us both, then deposited a bakery box on the table.

Without asking, Boone poured us each a glass of merlot, grabbed a cheese and cracker tray that had been sitting on the counter covered in waxed paper, and said, "Shall we adjourn to the study?"

Poppy nodded, and I got to my feet, following her, Boone, and Tsar into my favorite room of his house. Its large windows were framed in golden brown curtains that brushed the shiny hickory floor, and an assortment of brass lamps were scattered throughout the space. An oak library table behind the sofa held a crystal vase full of fresh alstroemeria accented with pussy willows, and best of all, there were books everywhere.

Poppy and I shared the nutmeg leather couch, and Boone sat on a club chair to our right. No one spoke as we all sipped our wine.

Finally, Boone grabbed a cracker, spread a bit of Camembert on it, and asked, "So what did you two want to talk to me about?"

I opened my mouth, glanced at Poppy, and said, "We told you we want to go over the clues we've gathered about the murder."

"What else?" Boone fed Tsar a sliver of cheddar and crooned to the cat, "Aunt Dev and Aunt Poppy are up to something."

Poppy shot me a look, then turning to Boone, she admonished, "You're always so suspicious. We wouldn't ambush you."

"Don't give me that malarkey." Boone adjusted the creases in his khakis. Pointing to Poppy, he said, "*You* didn't hire a bartender just to have a pizza party with me." He smiled sardonically and gestured at me. "And if we were really only discussing the murder investigation, one or more of your devoted swains would be here."

I started to protest, but the oven buzzed, indicating it was ready, so I jumped to my feet and ran into the kitchen. By the time I got the pizza cooking, set the timer for twenty minutes, and disposed of the cardboard box in the recycle bin outside the back door, I had almost figured out how to bring up the subject of Boone's ancestor.

When I returned to the study, Boone was plying Poppy with liquor and ruthlessly grilling her for information. He had replaced her wine with a martini and was shooting questions at her faster than an Uzi.

Poppy narrowed her eyes and snapped, "Stop it right now, Boone St. Onge." She fingered her white Giuseppe Zanottis and said, "Your boots may be made for walking, but mine are for kicking ass, and you're about to become my target."

Deciding to stay out of the debate, I stepped over to the brimming bookcases that covered three of the four walls. Tsar joined me, and we perused the shelves. I ran my fingers across the spines as my two BFFs competed in a battle of wits.

Finally, Poppy took a sip of her drink and said to Boone, "Do you want to keep interrogating me, or should we actually discuss the case?"

"I suppose thumbscrews are out of the question?" Boone pursed his mouth in a pout. "Or how about Chinese water torture?"

I looked at Poppy and said, "Your attitude is contagious."

"So I've been told." She smirked. "But I hear that the CDC is looking for a cure."

I shook my head, took my seat, and said. "Let me summarize what Jake and I learned at the police station, then go from there." Leaning forward, I made a face. "Basically, the cops are stumped."

"What did they find at the scene?" Boone sat back in his chair.

"They haven't processed all the trace yet. There was tiny bit of magnesium there, but nothing obvious, like fingerprints or what was used to bash in his skull," I answered. "Time of death is between twelve thirty and one thirty."

"Unless my dad is lying," Poppy sneered. "You know you can't trust him."

"Jake got most of the information from the dispatcher." I rolled my eyes. I sure wished Poppy would give the evil-father thing a rest.

"Humph." Poppy grabbed a cube of Monterey Jack and stuffed it in her mouth.

"What else have you found out?" Boone asked, evidently having decided that he couldn't rush what we had come to discuss.

"The country clubbers oppose the library." I reached for my glass and was surprised to find it empty. When had I finished my wine?

"All of them?" Poppy raised a brow. "And how did you find that out?"

After explaining about the overheard conversation and the lack of actual names, I got up and refilled my glass with merlot.

Boone's lawyerly logic appeared. "Hard to pin something like that down, which means it's too vague to be very useful."

"Unfortunately," I agreed. Now was the time to ease Boone into the subject of Shadow Bend's possibly-not-so-honorable war heroes. "But Jake's uncle Tony overheard Nadine tell one of her cronies that Jett needed to stop poking his nose in places it didn't belong, so Jake and I went to talk to her about it."

"Oooh!" Poppy yipped, causing Tsar, who had been sitting at her feet, to run out of the room. "That must have been an interesting visit."

"*Yeah.*" Boone drew out the word. "But I bet she was overjoyed that you were with a handsome guy that wasn't her son."

"Strangely, not so much." I shrugged. "I doubt anything I could do would make Nadine Underwood happy. On the other hand, she did talk to us."

"You blackmailed her into having that conversation by saying you would tell Noah she upset you," Poppy guessed.

"Hey." I held up my hands in mock surrender. "It's my parents' lives on the line. I did what I had to do to get Nadine's cooperation."

"Who cares how you got her to talk?" Boone bounced on his seat. "Just tell us what she had to say before my head explodes."

While I was happy to see Boone focusing on the case, I knew I was approaching shaky ground and carefully considered how to phrase my description of the interview Jake and I had had with Nadine.

Finally, I said, "It turns out that Jett's research had

to do with Shadow Bend's part in the Civil War." I turned to Boone and smiled. "But you probably know more about that, since you were so active in bringing him to town and working with him to fund the library."

"Actually, your stepfather said his research was top secret. He was afraid some other scholar would beat him to it and publish a book before Jett could get his out. I knew it concerned Missouri in the Civil War, but not Shadow Bend in particular." Boone's expression was puzzled. "I wonder why he didn't mention that."

"According to Nadine, Jett was planning to expose one of the town's heroes."

I watched as a variety of emotions chased across my friend's face.

"How did she come to that conclusion?" Boone asked, wrinkling his nose.

"Because Jett demanded to see some super-secret papers about Colonel Underwood and threatened her if she didn't produce them." I took a deep breath. Now for the hard part. "In fact, Noah and I spoke to Miss Ophelia, who is apparently the foremost authority on Shadow Bend's part in the Civil War."

"Oh?" Boone mumbled noncommittally, clearly beginning to see where I was going.

"She told us that several of Shadow Bend's Civil War heroes might not be as wonderful as we were led to believe." I licked my lips. "Although she didn't have any dirt on Colonel Underwood, she said Captain Sinclair claimed that the Union train that his unit had been sent to raid never showed up, but the speculation was that the Sinclairs were Union sympathizers."

"Who else did she mention?" Boone asked, his brow wrinkling.

"Some folks thought it was odd that except for the final battle, Major Boone never fought with his men in the front lines and they claimed he was a coward." I put my hand over Boone's. "But not being in the front lines wasn't unusual for officers."

Boone froze for a solid minute, then abruptly shook off my fingers and shouted, "And you and Poppy are wondering if I killed your stepfather to keep that information out of the history books?"

"No!" I yelped. This was exactly what I was afraid would happen. "Did you even know about those rumors concerning your great-great-great-great-grandfather?"

"Of course I did. My parents told me about them when I did a paper on the major for a history class." Boone slumped in his chair. "The rumors had surfaced before I was born, just about the time Mom was in the process of joining the CDM. However, there was no other evidence that the major had acted in a dishonorable manner, so the matter was dropped." Boone narrowed his eyes at me and said, "Do you also suspect one of your relatives of trying to stop Jett's research? Your ancestor's name might be muddied, too."

"Nope. None of the Sinclairs really ever cared about that stuff." I twitched my shoulders. "Mom was the only one who gave a damn about joining the CDM. And she doesn't exactly have a Prada in that fashion show anymore."

"That's true," Poppy said. "And Nadine has an alibi."

"And so do I," Boone snapped. "I was over in the county seat in court during the TOD." He looked at me and bared his teeth. "Are you satisfied, or do you want me to give you the judge's name so you can check?"

"No. Neither Poppy nor I ever suspected you. We

just wanted to see what you had to say on the matter." I could hear the pleading in my voice and didn't like it. "We thought maybe you knew about someone else who Jett might have antagonized with his research."

"Well . . . Okay." Boone sighed. "And no, I haven't heard anything about other families having issues with him investigating their ancestors."

The three of us were silent as we processed the near hit to our friendship. A few seconds later, the timer beeped, and we all trooped into the kitchen for pizza. As we ate, the conversation turned to other subjects, and I hoped that Boone had truly forgiven us.

CHAPTER 21

A t nine o'clock, full of pizza and reassured that Boone had forgiven us, Poppy and I said good-bye. She sprinted down the front walk to her Hummer, blew a kiss at me, and hopped inside the giant SUV. Waving back at her, I headed toward my Z4 in the driveway.

Just as my hand touched the BMW's door handle, a shadowy figure moved toward me. I squealed and jumped back, half convinced that my stepfather's killer had decided to eliminate the whole family.

Before I could unglue my feet from the cement and make a run for safety, the would-be murderer emerged into the streetlamp's pool of light and said, "Sorry to startle you. It's just me."

"Noah Underwood, don't you ever sneak up on me like that again." Taking a deep breath, I waited for my heartbeat to slow before adding, "What in the world are you doing skulking around my car?"

"I am so sorry." Noah wrapped his arms around me. "I didn't realize that it was too dark for you to recognize me until you screamed."

Leaning back, I studied Noah's face. He seemed

sad—no, that wasn't quite right. Dejected. Uh-uh. Maybe *discouraged* was the word I was searching for. I noticed all this while I continued to yell at him for scaring me half to death.

Finally, once I'd calmed down enough to think, I said, "Has something happened?"

"I had dinner with my mother." Noah continued to hold me loosely in the circle of his arms, but his expression was unreadable.

"Oh," I said cautiously. Had Nadine finally persuaded Noah to dump me?

"She's drinking a lot more than I realized." Noah rested his forehead against mine. "And I think her obsession with staying thin might be getting out of hand as well. She hardly ate anything, and when I texted her aide after I left, Janson reported that her appetite's been poor for the past few weeks."

"Depression, even situational depression, could account for both the increased alcohol consumption and the decreased appetite," I pointed out. As a doctor, Noah probably knew that better than I did, but when it's your parent, sometimes it's hard to have the emotional distance needed to make that kind of diagnosis.

"I need to spend more time with her." The muscles in Noah's jaw were clenched. "But truthfully, we have so little to say to each other . . ." He trailed off, then admitted, "And she drives me nuts."

"It seemed as if she was getting better after you hired Janson." I smoothed the crease between his brows with my finger. "Right?"

"Yes." Noah scrubbed his face with a fist. "She started seeing her friends again and stopped having those 'spells' of hers."

"So maybe the depression is related to Jett's research. It could be that she's afraid that whatever she's hiding about your father's great-great-great-grandfather will come out and ruin your family name." I cleared my throat. "Nadine is nothing if not proud."

"That could be it." Noah nodded, then told me about Jett's visit to Nadine, finishing with, "So I think he drugged her drink and photographed the documents."

"Oh. My. God!"

"Yep, and I guess I'm about to find out what the big secret is." Noah stared unseeingly over my shoulder. "Mom gave me the papers."

"Even with the possibility that Jett saw them and made copies, I still never expected Nadine to hand those over without a fight," I said warily. "How did you convince her to give them up?"

"Uh . . ." Noah hesitated, then muttered, "I said I wanted to fully understand my heritage so I could pass it along to my children."

Children! I met his gaze, then quickly looked away. We had never discussed kids. *No.* That wasn't true. When we'd dated in high school, we'd talked about having a boy and a girl. We'd even picked out names—Kyle for the boy and Danielle for the girl.

Breaking into my reminiscing, Noah said lightly, "Nothing like the promise of producing an heir to motivate Mom to cooperate."

Chuckling, I asked, "Did Nadine demand to know the identity of your future kids' mother?"

"Not exactly." Noah's cheeks turned red. He was silent until I raised a brow. Finally, he gritted his teeth and added, "But she did warn me not to count on you. Was it really necessary to bring Del Vecchio with you when you went to see her?"

"Sorry." It hadn't crossed my mind that Nadine would use that against Noah, but it should have. The woman didn't care whom she hurt. "It was just that it was *his* uncle who overheard her warning to Jett."

"I understand." Noah rubbed a weary hand over his eyes and sighed.

"You're tired." I stepped away from him. "I should let you go."

"Wait." Noah grabbed both my hands and pulled me toward him.

"Why?" The smoldering heat I saw in his eyes startled me.

"Because . . ." He trailed off, dropping my fingers to cup my chin.

The feeling of his thumb caressing my jaw sent my pulse skittering. I had to draw in a breath of much-needed oxygen before I could ask, "Because why?"

"I am tired, but I know I'll never be able to fall asleep." Noah stared into my eyes, and I could see the electricity arcing between us. "So. I either could go home and lift weights or . . ."

"Or?" I knew I sounded ridiculous repeating his words, but the intense attraction between us was making it hard to concentrate.

"We could go back to my place and look over the Underwood family documents."

"Oh." I must have looked disappointed, because he gave me a rueful smile. "Actually, I'd like to take you home and . . ." He whispered a suggestion that made me blush. "But I know you're determined to wait until you've made your choice, and I don't want to rush you."

"Thank you." I was barely able to squeeze out those two words as the sensual images of what he'd just suggested we do to each other zoomed through my mind.

"Not that I wouldn't love to hustle you into my bed." Noah drew me back into his arms—and then, with his mouth inches from mine, he said huskily, "But I want to make sure when we finally get to that point, you know you love me and don't have any regrets."

His voice washed over me like honey, and my breath caught in my throat.

"Because"—his whisper was ragged as he stroked my cheek—"once we're together like that, I'll never be able to let you go."

I could feel his heart thudding against my fingertips. There was such an incredible pull between us, but I knew I should leave now or we wouldn't be able to stop. Noah was right. Until I made a decision, this wasn't fair to either of us, or to Jake. But before I could force myself to move, I closed the gap between our lips.

His kiss felt like fire, and as I pressed closer to him, he licked into my mouth. When he wrapped his arms tighter around me, I admitted defeat.

I knew that with the murder and the situation with Jake, Noah and I shouldn't be doing this, but I had longed to be in his embrace for so many years that I couldn't stop myself from responding. When he pushed me back against my car, I could feel how much he wanted me. Then suddenly, a bright light blazed into my face, and I squinted in pain.

As I jerked my head in the direction of the street, it took me a long second to understand what had blinded me. When I did, I groaned. A car was backing into the driveway across the road, and Noah and I had just been caught by Boone's neighbor necking like a couple of teenagers. I was sure Nadine would hear all about it in the morning.

A shudder traveled through me, and I forced myself to ease my hold on Noah and step away from him.

After the incident, as I liked to call it, there was no way I was going to sleep anytime soon, so I followed Noah to his house. He put on a pot of coffee, and we spread the contents of Nadine's file across the kitchen table. A part of me nagged that, considering what had almost happened, it was silly to be alone with Noah. But the mood had been broken for both of us, and discovering who had killed my stepfather would get me that much closer to figuring whether it was Jake or Noah whom I loved.

As the coffee perked, Noah told me about Janice St. Onge's part in stirring up Nadine regarding the alien invasion. Because I had a good relationship with Boone's mom, I offered to call her the next day to find out whether her interest in ET and the professor's arrival in town were linked.

With steaming mugs of motivation at our elbow, Noah and I sifted through the mountain of documents we had pulled out of the carton.

After a few minutes, I said, "It really is sweet of you to risk finding out something bad about your family in order to help me."

"Not at all." Noah shoved his fingers through his hair. "I'm sick of secrets. It's about time whatever skeleton is hidden in the Underwood closet comes out and gets a decent burial."

I made a noncommittal noise. I was a firm believer that denial was often the best option. Still, I was glad

Noah hadn't come to that conclusion, or I might never figure out who murdered Jett.

We spent the next hour sorting papers into three piles. Innocuous letters to family members. Boring military documents concerning supplies, lists of soldiers, as well as other everyday workings of the regiment. And half a dozen diaries. It seemed that Colonel Underwood had fancied himself quite the memoirist.

I arranged the journals chronologically, with Noah taking the last one and me starting with the first. I skimmed through the initial pages where Colonel Underwood described raising, organizing, and paying the meager salaries of Shadow Bend's regiment.

Evidently, the customary infantry regiment was comprised of ten companies consisting of a hundred men each. The companies were led by a captain. Which explained where my relative fit into the hierarchy.

Shadow Bend's regiment averaged only four hundred men, so there would have been only four captains. They would have answered to a major, who was Boone's ancestor, and the major would have been controlled by Noah's great-great-great-great-grandfather.

Now that I had the chain of command straight, I continued to scan Colonel Underwood's first diary, but found nothing irregular. As I put it aside and reached for the next volume, I noticed Noah scowling at the journal he was reading. He was furiously flipping back and forth between the pages and muttering to himself.

Not wanting to interrupt him, I got up and poured another cup of coffee for us both. If my suspicions were correct, we were in for an all-nighter, and I reminded myself that I needed to be home in time for breakfast or Birdie would send out the National Guard to find me. And, as it was, we were already up to our necks in Civil War military and didn't need any more troops muddying the water.

I was about three-quarters of the way through volume two, when Noah said, "I think I might have something here. Most of it seems to be in some sort of picture or symbol encryption, but from what I can tell, Colonel Underwood, Major Boone, and Captain Sinclair conspired to hide something extremely valuable."

"Yep, that would go under the scandal column, all right." I pushed aside my empty coffee mug and held out my hand for the journal. "Especially since it's my understanding that by the end of the war, the people around these parts were penniless and starving."

As I opened the diary, a memory flickered through my mind and I said, "Grandpa used to tell me a bedtime story about the Treasure of Shadow Bend. Before Captain Sinclair was killed in that last battle, he told his wife that no matter how the war turned out, they would be okay financially. His optimism turned out to be unfounded, as the family had a real struggle to survive."

"Colonel Underwood, Major Boone, and Captain Sinclair all died that day." Noah raised his brows. "Although they may have hinted to family members about the loot, obviously they didn't confide in anyone where it was concealed. Which meant that after their death, there was no one left to retrieve whatever they'd hidden."

"Wouldn't the colonel have confided in his wife?"

"I remember my father saying that his great-great-great-grandmother had a stroke when she heard her husband had been killed in battle and had difficulty communicating from then until her own death a few years later."

"And Colonel Underwood's journals were probably boxed up and never really examined until much later," I said, thinking out loud.

"Knowing my family"—Noah wrinkled his brow—"when the diaries were finally read, my ancestors were more concerned with keeping the colonel's less-than-honorable actions a secret than with finding any possible treasure."

"Because your family regained its fortune pretty quickly after the war?" I asked. When he nodded, I said, "And without those papers, neither Major Boone's nor Captain Sinclair's kin had any clue to the location of the treasure."

Shaking my head at all the past errors in judgment, I began reading. Noah had flagged the relevant sections of the diary with Post-its, and I paged between them. Colonel Underwood had written about a wounded Union soldier who had been captured and held somewhere secret for interrogation. The soldier revealed that a Union train would be passing nearby carrying treasure vital to the war efforts. The young man had passed away from his injuries before revealing what exactly was being transported.

After that entry, the rest of the references to the incident were crude drawings. Frowning, I grabbed a pen and one of the legal pads Noah had put on the table and painstakingly sketched each symbol and made a tally of how often they were used.

While I was doing that, Noah transcribed the whole segments. Then we both scanned the remaining journals for any other instances of the cipher.

When we found none, we replaced all the diaries in
the carton and put it aside. By the time we finished,
it was nearly two a.m., and we were beat.

I yawned and stretched, then said, "My mind is
fried. I can't see a pattern."

"We'd better call it a night." Noah stood, pressed
his palm against his back. "I'm on call at the clinic
from eight until noon, but we can get together tomorrow night after you close the store and try to figure
this code out."

"We're so close." I got to my feet. "I know this has
something to do with Jett and why he was in Shadow
Bend."

"Maybe Jett was writing a novel instead of a history book." Noah moved closer. His silky voice filled
my ear.

"More likely, if whatever is hidden is still valuable,
he was after that." Why was I having trouble breathing? I was too tired to be turned on. "I'm convinced
there was something shady about my stepfather."

"We'll just have to decipher the code and find
out." Noah took my hand, his thumb caressing my
palm, and I felt goose bumps form on my arms. "At
least it looks as if our ancestors worked together on
this. Maybe that's why my mother is so anti-Sinclair.
She thinks the captain was a bad influence on Colonel Underwood."

"Uh?" I croaked, losing my train of thought as
Noah moved his fingers upward, stroking my inner
arms. "Oh. Right. No. Nadine had a thing for my
father, and he dumped her. That's why she hates us."

Oops. I hadn't meant to blurt that out. I really
needed to leave before I said something even more
foolish than that last bit.

Noah was silent, looking at me strangely, so I

quickly added, "But Dad assures me they didn't have an affair, so we aren't related."

"Good to know." Noah grinned, then frowned. "When did you find that out?"

"Gran told me a few months ago." I had decided not to tell Noah about this, but it had slipped out. "When my father was about to be released from prison, Gran was afraid your mom might do something to mess up his parole. I asked why Nadine would care enough to interfere, and she told me about my dad dating your mom back before he met Yvette."

"Interesting. And for sure not something my mother would have ever mentioned to me." Noah shrugged, then asked, "So tomorrow night? Do you want to come back here?"

"No. I mean yes, I want to meet you, but I can be here in the afternoon at twelve thirty instead of waiting until later," I explained. "The store doesn't have any craft groups scheduled, so I can ask Dad to adjust his hours, and he can handle the place without me."

"That's great. I'm glad you've got him to take some of the load off your shoulders." Noah followed me out of the kitchen. "That will give us more time to figure everything out."

When I got to the front door, I said, "I'll bring lunch, and would you mind if I asked Boone, Poppy, and Jake if they are available to join us? It sounds as if Boone has a stake in this, too. And Poppy is really good at puzzles."

"And Del Vecchio?" Noah's jaw was clenched. "What's he good at?"

Ignoring Noah's displeasure, I answered calmly, "I'd like to have Jake with us because he's getting the info on my stepfather's finances."

"Can't he just hand them over and leave?" Noah muttered.

Apparently, at that point my lack of sleep overcame my good sense, because I kissed Noah lightly on the lips, then said, "And FYI, Jake is good at everything."

CHAPTER 22

Friday morning as I waited on customers, my mind replayed last night. Why in the hell had I told Noah that Jake was good at everything? Up until that moronic moment when I'd opened my big mouth and taunted Noah about Jake's awesomeness, I'd been doing everything I could to discourage any rivalry between the two men. After all, Noah was equally amazing, so what had gotten into me?

I chalked it up to the stress of worrying that Dad might end up returning to prison and vowed never to say anything like that again to either guy. The thought of my father back behind bars, but this time with my mother and me in the next cell, sent a shiver down my spine. I needed to figure out who killed Jett before the cops discovered that we had tampered with evidence. I did not want to be on the wrong side of Eldridge Kincaid.

When Dad showed up at the store at eleven forty-five, I brought him up to speed on the deliveries I was expecting that afternoon, then told him to call me if he had any problems. After combing my hair and putting on some lip gloss, I headed to Little's Tea Room to collect the box lunches I had ordered earlier.

I was in luck and nabbed a coveted parking spot in front of the restaurant. Before going inside, I checked my cell. I had texted Poppy, Boone, and Jake as soon as I woke up that morning, asking them if they could meet me at Noah's house at twelve thirty to help decipher the encrypted passages of Colonel Underwood's journal.

My two BFFs had immediately replied that they'd be there, but Jake hadn't answered until now. He said that he'd been doing chores and hadn't seen my message. Unfortunately, he couldn't make it to Noah's, as he was getting together with his contact regarding Jett's finances. The forensic accountant didn't trust the Internet and would only give him the documents in person. Once Jake was free, he would come over and share the information.

After picking up the food, I checked my watch. I still had a few minutes, so I sat in my car and phoned Janice St. Onge. She answered on the first ring, and we chatted about Shadow Bend's upcoming Apple Festival. Janice was the chairwoman, and I had agreed to host some of the events in my store's newly renovated second floor.

When Janice ran out of festival news, I said, "Nadine Underwood mentioned that you were one of the first people around here to see the suspicious lights hovering above the town."

"Actually, I was the very first one. I saw them in early July, during the Cupcake Weekend." Janice's voice rose in excitement. "I've always been extremely interested in the idea of UFOs. I've watched the night skies religiously for years."

"Really?" I knew Boone's mother was more than a little eccentric, but I'd had no idea about her hobby. Did her son know? "Nadine also shared that you believe aliens are taking over the bodies of the town's teenagers."

"I was at the city council meeting when she spoke. It would have probably been better to approach that another way." Janice sighed. "I didn't realize how upset Nadine would get when I informed her about the children being turned into pod people, or I wouldn't have told her. Or, at least, not when she was drinking."

"What makes you think the kids are being possessed?" I asked.

"Initially, it never occurred to me," Janice answered. "But after my first sighting, I began posting on the Friends of Space bulletin board. I described the formation of seven blinking lights that hovered for hours in the sky over the old drive-in theater to the east of town, and a couple of weeks later, Professor Hinkley contacted me. We e-mailed back and forth for a while, and then he asked me to arrange for him to speak to the city council. He warned me that the particular species of extraterrestrial observing Shadow Bend was known to use human adolescents as hosts for their parasites."

"You might want to tell Nadine you were mistaken," I suggested. "Just to calm her down a bit until the professor actually verifies his theory. Noah would consider it a real favor."

"Well . . ." Janice hesitated. "I think all will be revealed tomorrow when Khrelan Naze appears in the town square and tells us his plan."

"Right." I had forgotten the professor's claim that

the alien leader was bringing mankind a gift. "But if Khrelan Naze is a good guy, why would he be taking over Shadow Bend's children?"

"He isn't," Janice protested. "It's the other aliens. He's going to help us fight them."

"Ooo-kaay." I drew out the word. Why did this whole scenario sound familiar? Mentally shrugging, I said, "Good talking to you, Janice. Bye."

I quickly disconnected and headed toward Noah's. He'd be relieved to know that his mother wasn't the only nut in the town's fruitcake batter.

Boone and I pulled into Noah's driveway at the same time, and Noah met us at the front door. Fifteen minutes later, Poppy arrived, and I distributed the box lunches, putting the extra one for Jake in the fridge. He could eat it when he showed up. Noah poured soda for everyone, and as we ate, he and I explained what we'd found out so far.

Using the Xerox machine at his clinic, Noah had made several copies of the coded passages he and I had reproduced from the journal. Once the four of us were finished with our meal, Noah passed out those pages, and we all studied the encryption. There were dozens of reoccurring symbols, but we concentrated on the ones in the first encrypted segment. There was a silhouette, a new moon, a winding river, two crosses—one lying on its left side and the other on its right—and what looked like a handsaw that tapered to a gradual point.

Noah and I believed this paragraph indicated the hiding place of whatever our ancestors had concealed. After a couple of hours with little success, Boone's groan interrupted the silence.

"What?" I asked, scrubbing my face with my fists. "Giving up already?"

"Never." Boone bent back over the pages he'd been studying.

We were all getting tired, and I was afraid everyone had about had it. It was time for my secret weapon. I got up from the table, ran out to my car, and came back with the world-famous pink-and-brown box. Flipping open the lid, I presented each of them with the Kizzy Cutler signature cupcake—vanilla rosewater with honey-lavender icing.

Because I had saved her life, Kizzy had given my dime store exclusive distribution rights for the Kansas City area. This flavor was my favorite because a portion of the profits from the sales was donated to an anti-bullying foundation.

Boone glanced into the carton and said, "I thought you'd have health food for us."

"Cupcakes are health food," I retorted. "Mental health."

Poppy immediately peeled off the paper liner and licked the frosting off her fingers. Moaning, she devoured the pastry, then glanced down at the pages in front of her. Suddenly, she squealed, jumped up from her chair, and pumped her fist in the air.

"I think I figured it out!" Poppy danced around the kitchen. "Or at least part of it." She darted to the fridge and grabbed a can of Coke.

"Are you going to share with the rest of the class?" Boone asked.

"I suppose I should." Poppy pointed to each symbol in turn and said, "A silhouette is also a shadow, and the winding river is a bend."

"Great." Boone rolled his eyes. "We now know the cache is hidden in Shadow Bend. That really narrows it down a whole heck of a lot."

"I wasn't finished." Poppy thrust her lower lip

out. "The only place in town that I can think of with a crescent moon on it is the library's windows."

"How about the crosses?" Noah asked. "Are there crosses anywhere inside the building?" He looked at the three of us, and we all shrugged.

"Any clue as to what the saw thingy might mean?" Poppy asked.

"Maybe." Noah tilted his head and squinted. "You all know the library was originally Colonel Underwood's medical offices, right?"

"How could we forget?" Boone drawled. "His name is above the door."

"In which case"—Noah continued as if Boone hadn't spoken—"I think that symbol might be a bone saw. I vaguely recall that that the colonel used the basement as his surgery."

"We need to get into that building," I said as I paced the length of the kitchen. "But when I picked up lunch at Little's Tea Room, I noticed that the crime scene tape was still across the alley."

"So we'll duck under it." Poppy twitched her shoulders. "We'll just have to wait until it gets dark and make sure we aren't spotted."

CHAPTER 23

In Missouri, it didn't get completely dark in early September until almost nine p.m., so Noah, Poppy, Boone, and I decided to go our separate ways and reunite for a late dinner at seven. Once our plans were in place, I checked my phone, and seeing nothing from Jake, I texted him to meet us at the Spur and Feather, a steakhouse twenty miles south of Shadow Bend.

Poppy and Boone had suggested the Golden Dragon, but Noah and I figured our group would be less likely to cause gossip at an out-of-town restaurant than if we went someplace local. At the Spur and Feather, we'd have more privacy to go over Jett's financial records and plot our search for the colonel's treasure. Because both Noah and Boone had keys to the library, we weren't technically breaking and entering. The only sticky part of the maneuver would be the crime scene tape.

After my BFFs left, I told Noah what Janice St. Onge had shared about the aliens. He was relieved that all the nonsense would be over by the next day

and his mother could return to her regularly scheduled craziness and leave ET to phone home without
her assistance.

Giving Noah a quick kiss good-bye, I took a ride
by the dime store. It was past five o'clock, so the
after-school crowd would be gone. And since there
was no smoke or sirens, I assumed Dad was doing
fine.

Poppy had offered to drive since her Hummer
was the only vehicle that held four people comfort-
ably, and I had an hour before she was picking me
up. I hadn't spent much time with Gran lately, so I
wanted to get home and see how she was doing.
Birdie had been so much better since Dad's release
from prison, I sometimes forgot how poorly she'd
been when I'd first quit my job and bought the dime
store to be around for her more.

I also needed to change into a black shirt and
jeans. Boone had insisted we all wear dark clothes
for the raid on the library. I just hoped no one at the
restaurant mistook us for the Johnny Cash fan club
or a Goth heavy metal band.

Poppy pulled into the restaurant's parking lot and
eased her Hummer into a spot next to a Shadow
Bend police car. What was a Shadow Bend cop doing
here? Maybe the officer was assisting a neighborhood jurisdiction and was on his or her supper
break. Whatever. As long it didn't have anything to
do with Jett's murder, I didn't really care.

The Spur and Feather was your typical old-
fashioned steakhouse. There was a lot of wood and
nothing fancy. As the four of us pushed through the
weathered oak door, the hostess, who was dressed

in jeans and cowboy boots, smiled and asked, "How many, please?"

"Five," Jake answered, stepping forward from the wall he'd been leaning against. He moved to my side and added, "We'd like a quiet booth."

"I have the perfect spot for you." The hostess fluttered her lashes at him and said, "Right this way."

When she paused to gather menus and silverware wrapped in paper napkins, I commented, "So you made it on time after all."

Jake had texted that his contact lived in Kansas City and they'd met downtown, so he might be late for dinner.

"I was motivated." He shot a look at Noah and slipped an arm around my waist.

"Good thing you didn't get a ticket." Noah immediately took my free hand and added, "It would have been a real shame if you were delayed."

Oops! Maybe getting Noah and Jake together hadn't been one of my more brilliant ideas. I wiggled free of both of them and followed the hostess.

She led us to a corner three-quarters circle booth, where I made the mistake of sliding in first. Instantly, Noah slipped in next to me and Jake did the same on my other side, bracketing me like scowling bookends. Boone and Poppy giggled and took the remaining aisle seats. Poppy by Noah and Boone by Jake.

Once we were settled and the hostess left, in a rush to distract Jake and Noah from glowering across me at each other, I said to Jake, "Did your contact come through with Jett's financials?"

"Yep." Jake slapped a folder on the table. "I've got them right here."

"We've been busy, too." Noah took a copy of the encrypted diary passages and smacked it down.

"So Devereaux has informed me." Jake's expression darkened. "Breaching a cordoned-off crime scene is not a good idea." He arched a brow at me and muttered, "Bad enough omitting the presence of a witness."

"I explained about that," I protested. "I had to protect my father."

"Dev had no other choice." Noah's jaw tightened. "Wouldn't you do the same for your parents?"

"Not in a million years." Jake crossed his arms, then whispered in my ear, "But maybe for Uncle Tony."

Poppy interrupted the men's bickering. "Good news about the crime scene thing. I reached out to my source at the PD, and he tells me that the tape is coming down tomorrow morning. There's one more area the techs wanted to check, but by noon the library will be released."

"So we wait and do our search tomorrow at twelve fifteen?" Boone asked.

"But if we go during the day, people will see us," I pointed out.

"We can approach it from the other end of the alley," Boone explained. "The entrance off of Denison Street, rather than on the square."

"Okay," I agreed, knowing it was better to wait rather than cross the tape, but I was still impatient. I was sure whatever we found hidden would lead us to Jett's killer, and I was anxious to get Chief Kincaid's attention away from my family before he found out what we'd done. "Are you scheduled at the clinic, Noah?"

"Only until noon," Noah answered. "Elexus has the rest of the day."

"Poppy? Boone?" I asked, deliberately excluding

Jake, as I wasn't sure how he'd feel about participating in a questionably legal act.

Once Boone and Poppy assured me they were free, Poppy picked up one of the menus from the pile and said, "Now that we've settled that, we should figure out what we're ordering."

A few seconds later, a waitress appeared to ask us what we wanted to drink. We asked for a pitcher of beer, and she hurried away.

Not wanting the server to overhear our conversation, we agreed to wait until we had placed our dinner orders before studying Jett's financial information, and the conversation stumbled to a halt. Poppy glanced at the two silent men on either side of me, shot me a "got your back" smile, and immediately began to describe to Jake how she'd cracked Colonel Underwood's code.

When Poppy finished, Jake grinned at her and said, "You're a pistol."

She retorted, "Only when I'm loaded."

As my friends bantered back and forth, I was surprised to spot my mother at a cozy table for two near the back wall. Suddenly, I realized the real reason for the Shadow Bend squad car in the parking lot. The cop was keeping an eye on Yvette.

Excusing myself, I told Poppy what I wanted to eat, asked her to order for me, and then waited for her and Noah to let me out of the booth. Once I was free, I strolled over to the engrossed couple.

As I got nearer, Yvette glanced up and trilled, "Dev, darling, what are you doing so far away from Shadow Bend?"

My mother and her attractive escort looked out of place at the homespun restaurant. Both were dressed more for an evening at a fine-dining establishment in the city than a meal at a small-town steakhouse.

"The better question is what are you doing here with a man?" I gritted my teeth. "Didn't we discuss how bad it would look if you, a widow of three days, were to be seen dating? You do know that a police officer is here watching, right?"

"Of course." Yvette's lips curled up in a smug smile. "I informed him that my attorney and I were going to dinner and where we'd be." She wrinkled her nose and simpered, "I wouldn't want him to get fired for losing sight of me."

"Your lawyer?" I studied the man with her. Why did he look so familiar?

"Well, actually, he was Jett's attorney, but now he's mine, too." Yvette gestured to me and said, "Sebastian, this is my daughter, Devereaux Sinclair. Dev, this is Sebastian Hinds."

"Nice to meet you." As I shook his hand, I continued to examine the lawyer. I definitely knew him from somewhere. "Are you from around these parts?"

"I'm from Texas, ma'am." He fiddled with the stem of his wineglass. "I hurried up from Dallas when Yvette informed me of Jett's death. With a large estate such as his, there are a lot of details to settle."

"I see." I knew he wouldn't tell me what was in Jett's will, so I didn't waste my breath. Instead, I turned to my mother and asked, "Has Chief Kincaid contacted you again?"

"Eldridge stopped by the condo yesterday afternoon." Yvette shrugged. "He asked the same questions as the previous times, and I gave him the same answers." She shook her head. "He clearly doesn't have a clue."

"Maybe." I sincerely doubted the chief was clueless. More likely, he was just holding his cards close to his vest, waiting to pounce. "Well, I'd better let you two get back to your supper."

When I returned to the booth, our beer had arrived and Jake had my stepfather's financial records spread across the table. As the money expert, I dove in, and by the time our food arrived, I had figured out Jett's fiscal picture. It wasn't a pretty one.

"He was broke," I announced after the waitress left. "Jett was in debt up to his eyeballs. Using one credit card to pay off another. His house has a second mortgage, and his car payments are way overdue."

"So how in the heck could he fund the library?" Boone demanded, slicing into his New York strip and popping a piece into his mouth.

"He never intended to give the town any money," I said, cutting open my baked potato to add butter and sour cream. "Now that we know about Colonel Underwood's treasure and that Jett's not the rich guy he pretended to be, his plan is pretty obvious. He promised the cash so he could get into the archives, find what he needed to figure out where the treasure was hidden, and get out of town before we realized that no dough was ever going to materialize."

"What an asshole," Poppy sneered. "Getting everyone's hopes up like that."

"But how did Benedict even know about the hidden treasure?" Noah asked. "Hell, I had no idea about it, and my ancestor was involved."

We were silent for a few seconds, and then I hit my forehead with my palm. "Yvette. Remember when I told you that my grandpa Sinclair used to put me to sleep with bedtime stories about the Treasure of Shadow Bend? My mother probably overheard those tales and repeated them to Jett. I don't recall the details of Grandpa's story, but I bet Yvette did." I turned to Jake. "Didn't my mom say that Jett encouraged her to talk about the town and its people?"

"She did." Jake forked a piece of dry-aged rib eye into his mouth.

"Then that's it." I took a long drink of beer, swallowed, and said, "Mom told Jett about the legend. He was broke, so he did some research and somehow decided that the library archives was his best bet for finding the answer as to where the treasure was hidden. But the library was closed. In order to gain access, he made up the whole endowment scheme."

"Benedict had to have been getting close to discovering whatever the colonel hid," Noah said. "I'm pretty sure he drugged my mother and made copies of the colonel's journals. He must have figured out the code, too. He might not have known the basement was used as a surgery, but the fact that the library building was originally the colonel's medical offices would have been easy to figure out."

"And that knowledge got him killed," Jake countered. "We should turn this all over to the police."

"We will." I refused to meet Jake's stare. "As soon as we know the murderer's identity."

"I can't talk you out of searching the library tomorrow?" Jake asked. When we all shook our heads, he sighed and said, "I wish I could go with you, but I have to take Tony to the doctor tomorrow at eleven thirty. He's been having chest pains, and we need to find out if it's his heart. If I don't go with him, he won't tell me the truth about what the cardiologist has to say."

"I understand." I patted his arm. "Between the

four of us, we should be able to figure out the hiding place."

"It's not finding the treasure that I'm worried about." Jake pressed his lips together. "What concerns me is making sure you all aren't the killer's next victims."

CHAPTER 24

When I got home from dinner, I asked my father if he could work at the dime store from twelve to closing the next day. He agreed, but I could tell he was curious. This past week, I'd asked him to switch shifts and been absent from the business more than at any other time since I'd hired him. Unwilling to make Dad an accessory to our actions, I told him that a bunch of my friends were getting together and I wanted to join them. Which was not exactly a lie, just not the whole truth.

The next morning, the store was unusually busy, and it wasn't until I overheard a man and a woman arguing about the best spot on the square to see the alien leader land that I remembered Khrelan Naze was supposed to arrive at noon with a gift for mankind.

By twelve, when my father hadn't arrived yet for his shift, I worried that something had happened to him. Had Chief Kincaid brought him into the station for more questioning? Or worse, found out that Dad had been at the crime scene and arrested him? If so, Mom and I were probably next on the chief's list.

To distract myself from the image of Dad, Mom, and me in adjoining jail cells, I pondered my encounter with Yvette and Jett's lawyer. What was it about that guy that bothered me? There was something he'd said that had set off my BS meter.

I went over the conversation in my mind, and the discrepancy came to me just as Dad walked into the store. Miss Ophelia had told us that during Jett's visit with her, he had received a phone call from his attorney and left to meet him. Sebastian had claimed that he'd arrived in Shadow Bend only *after* my stepfather's death. Why had he lied about his whereabouts?

Before I could come up with an explanation, Dad hurried over to me and apologized for being delayed. Before agreeing to work at the store this afternoon, he had promised Gran that he'd drive her to the county seat to shop. They'd left the house early, but the checkout line in Walmart had been longer than they'd expected.

I assured my father that it was okay, then hurried out the back exit. In order to approach the library from the rear, I wound my way up the side streets. Boone had agreed to get to the building first so he could use his key to open the side door. Noah, Poppy, and I were to sneak inside one by one, making sure no one saw us.

As I trotted the last couple of blocks, I continued to think about Sebastian Hinds. There was something else about Jett's lawyer that was nagging at me.

Whatever was disturbing me about Hinds was on the tip of my tongue when I entered the alley between the library and the movie theater. I slowed, trying to retrieve the elusive notion, but before I could dredge the idea from my subconscious, I heard the crowd in the square chanting their displeasure. Evidently, ET was running behind schedule and hadn't landed yet.

With one last glance behind me to make sure I wasn't being observed, I eased the metal door open a few inches, slipped inside, and quickly shut it behind me. Once again, the hallway was pitch-dark.

But this time I was prepared, and I unhooked the flashlight I had clipped to my belt. The pepper-spray gun Jake had made me promise to have at the ready was in my pocket. Switching on the Maglite, I looked around. The door to the storeroom to my right was closed, but I could see a faint illumination shining up the basement staircase.

It was twenty after twelve. The rest of the Scooby Gang must have already assembled and were waiting for me in the archives.

I hurried toward the steps, but just as I reached them, there was a loud uproar outside. I hesitated. What was happening? I'd better find out before I went into the basement. Once I was down there, I wouldn't be able to hear anything. And if the commotion near the library involved the police, we needed to abort our mission.

Turning around, I sprinted to the front of the building. From where I stood, I had a good view of the square and could see that the mob was growing restless waiting for the alien kingpin to arrive. The mayor stood on the bandstand, and the crowd was advancing. Hizzoner had a bullhorn, trying to sweet-talk the throng, asking them for their patience and suggesting they enjoy all the shops and restaurants that Shadow Bend had to offer while they waited.

Careful to keep out of sight, I edged away from

the window. As I walked back to the staircase, I wondered why Professor Hinkley wasn't the one speaking to the crowd. Which was when it hit me.

Sebastian Hinds had seemed familiar because he was the image of Professor Hinkley. Take away the picket-fence teeth, Albert Einstein hairdo, and Mr. Magoo glasses, and the two guys could be twins.

Or, the same man—one wearing theatrical makeup in one persona and unembellished in the other.

But why would he put on a disguise and pretend to be someone else?

I answered myself. Because he was neither a professor nor a lawyer. He was Jett's partner. My stepfather wouldn't have wanted to admit to Miss Ophelia that he had a partner, which smacked of commerce rather than scholarly research, so he said that his attorney had called and he needed to meet with him. And Hinds or Hinkley or whoever he was had used that same lawyer role on my mother.

With that piece of the puzzle in place, I realized that the story Mrs. St. Onge had told me about evil space invaders taking over Earth children and being saved by the good extraterrestrials was the plot of *Falling Skies,* a television show my dad liked on TNT.

I leaned against the wall. It was all becoming clear to me. If the professor was a fake and had been working with Jett, the whole creatures-from-outer-space routine had probably been a distraction. The UFO story had been Hinkley's way to stir up the town and divert their attention from what he and Jett were doing. Being an alien hunter gave Hinkley the perfect excuse to poke around and trespass.

Major Boone and Colonel Underwood had both lived in town. Digging a hole in their lawns would have caused a lot more talk than Captain Sinclair burying something in his fields. No wonder Hinkley wanted to be on the Del Vecchio property so badly. Tony had bought most of the Sinclair acreage, and where better to search for the treasure than on the land of the one officer most likely to have hidden it?

The only remaining question was whether Hinkley had killed Jett. Had my stepfather found the treasure and refused to share it with his partner or vice versa? Had the two con men fought over the cache? Maybe if we located the treasure the colonel had written about in his diary, we'd have our answer.

Excited to have figured out so much of the mystery, I dashed down the stairs. But as I entered the dimly lit room separating me from the archives, I heard the sounds of a scuffle and froze.

Before I could move, a voice inside the archive room yelled, "Bitch, you have one minute to tell me what I want to know or I'll shoot you!"

I didn't have to wonder who was speaking or to whom. It had to be Hinkley screaming at Poppy. Undoubtedly, like the Scooby Gang, he'd been waiting for the police to take the crime scene tape down from the library, too. He must have come in after my friends arrived and surprised them.

Inside my head Jake's voice was telling me to leave, to get the police, but I ignored it. What if Hinkley went through with his threat and killed Poppy before the cops got here? I'd never forgive myself.

I couldn't risk the professor overhearing a call, so I texted Chief Kincaid and copied Jake. Praying that one of the men would see my message and be nearby, I gave my location and said that Poppy, Boone, and Noah were being held at gunpoint. Then, making sure my phone was on vibrate, I set it to record, put it in my bra, and crept toward the archives. I was relieved to see that the door was slightly ajar, which meant it wasn't locked.

I peered into the gap between the hinged side of the door and the frame. Noah and Boone were seated back-to-back on two wooden chairs. They were duct-taped together at the ankles, chest, and wrists. Hinkley stood near the back wall with a gun pressed to Poppy's head.

Even though it was cool in the basement, Hinkley was sweating. He mopped his brow with his left arm and said, "You all wouldn't be here if you hadn't figured out that damn code, so quit telling me you don't know where the gold is hidden."

"All we know is that one passage in the colonel's diary seems to indicate that the library is the key," Poppy said.

"Then why did I find you down here?" Hinkley ran his fingers through his hair and sneered, "Unless you want to end up like my late two-timing partner, you better tell me what you know."

"What we know is that you killed Jett Benedict," Poppy snapped.

"You may be aware of that, but no one else is." Hinkley's finger stroked the gun's trigger. "If you tell me where the treasure is, I'll leave town and some-one will eventually find you down here alive and well." He narrowed his eyes. "I'm going to count to three, and if no one tells me what I want to know, I'm going to spray this bimbo's brains against the wall."

I felt as if I couldn't breathe. I had to save Poppy. Hoping that the hinges wouldn't squeak, I grabbed my pepper-spray gun from my pocket and eased the door open wide enough for me to slip through. Once again the dim bulb hanging from the ceiling was the only light, and I edged inside, keeping in the shadows.

Hinkley's attention was riveted on Poppy, and I tried to figure out how I would get within firing range without him noticing me. Exactly how far would the pepper-spray gun shoot? And how accurate did my aim have to be?

Unfortunately, my ability to estimate distances was about on par with my ability to sing. And let's just say that I wasn't allowed at Poppy's bar for karaoke night.

While I was trying to decide how close I had to get to Hinkley, he said, "One."

"I swear," Poppy pleaded. "We don't know."

With no real plan, I scoured the room for inspiration. Hinkley's walking stick was lying abandoned near where Boone and Noah were bound to their chairs. He must have put it down when he was taping them up. Unless it was just a prop for his Hinkley character, he'd be unsteady on his feet. Perhaps a weakness I could use to my advantage.

As I stared at the cane, I realized it was the murder weapon. The glass ball on the handle was the exact size and shape of the indentation I'd seen in Jett's head. Certainly, there would be DNA evidence where the globe was connected to the wooden staff. Now I just had to get us all out of here alive so we could hand over the walking stick to Chief Kincaid's crime scene techs.

"Then I guess you all die," Hinkley sneered, bringing my gaze back to him. "The three of you are as stupid as Benedict. He thought he could keep all the gold for himself."

"So the treasure is gold?" Boone asked.

Hinkley turned his attention from Poppy and

was staring at Noah and Boone with a hungry expression on his face as he said, "Twenty-six fifty-pound gold bars worth a cool twenty million."

"But if Jett found it and wouldn't share, why do you need us to tell you where it's at?" Noah's question kept Hinkley's attention on him and away from Poppy.

I watched as Poppy eased a few inches from Hinkley. She was giving herself some space to maneuver. I knew she'd practiced mixed martial arts for years, but would her skills work against an armed man?

Hinkley's mirthless chuckle was like a seal bark. "Benedict showed me one of the gold bars and bragged that I'd never find the rest. He laughed at me for thinking it was buried and said it was under our noses all along. He gave me the bar and said that was my share. That he was keeping the other twenty-five."

"But how—"

"Two." Hinkley cut off Noah's question. "Where. Is. My. Treasure?"

"We have no idea." Boone shook his head. "We'd give it to you if we could. Not all of us are money-grubbing thieves."

"Enough." Hinkley waved the gun at Boone and Noah.

Poppy, evidently seeing her opportunity, raised her leg and, in a move too fast for me to follow, swept Hinkley off his feet. Knowing this was my cue, I rushed forward and aimed my pepper-spray gun at Hinkley's face. Pulling the trigger, I held it down until the weapon was empty.

Hinkley was screaming and clawing at his eyes, but he still clutched his pistol.

Poppy stepped on his hand and said in a conversational tone, "Let go of the gun, or I'll break your wrist."

I held my breath. Was Hinkley going to cooperate?

When he didn't immediately release his weapon, Poppy said, "I love hearing the sound of bones grinding together as they crack."

Hinkley's shocked expression was almost funny, but I wasn't laughing. Even if the guy couldn't see, he could still fire his weapon and hurt someone.

I caught a glimmer of a movement out of the corner of my eye and saw that Noah had somehow broken free of the duct tape. As he stood up, the chair rattled and Hinkley's head whipped toward the noise. At that moment, I lunged forward and wrested the gun from his hand.

While Poppy called the police, Noah and I shoved Hinkley facedown on the floor, and using the same roll of duct tape he'd used to bind Noah and Boone, we trussed him up like a Thanksgiving Day turkey ready for the oven. Once he was secured, I rushed across the room and freed Boone. Then we all stared as Jett's killer sobbed like a six-year-old.

An officer had already taken Hinkley to the police station, where he would be charged with murder, among other lesser crimes, and we were now being read the riot act by Chief Kincaid.

While he went on and on about why we should have brought our suspicions to him rather than investigate on our own, I felt my cell vibrate and slipped it out of my pocket. It was Jake, and I stepped away from the chief and my friends to answer.

Huddled near the rear wall with my back to Chief Kincaid and the others, I assured Jake that we were all fine and the murderer had been caught. He explained that when I texted, he'd been in the doctor's office, so he had just seen my message. He was on his way back to the ranch and he would call me when he was in the area.

While we'd been talking, my gaze had wandered around the room. On the wall beside a bookcase was a large cross.

Chief Kincaid turned his wrath on his daughter and didn't seem to notice that I had separated myself from the group. Free from the chief's scolding, I examined the cross. I tried to tug it off the wall, but it wouldn't budge. Next I tried to twist it. Nothing.

Suddenly, a cold gust blew up the back of my neck, and I stumbled forward, stopping myself with a hand on the cross. When I heard a click, I continued to press on it, and at the same time, just as the symbols had indicated, I rotated it to the left, then to the right.

A loud creaking noise got everyone's attention, and we all watched in awe as the entire shelf swung inward, revealing a secret room. The five of us crowded into the small space. The paint was peeling and there was a bolted-down bedframe with a rotting bare mattress on the rusty springs. A metal table next to the cot was also fastened to the floor.

But what grabbed our attention was the stack of gold bars against the rear wall. We had found the Shadow Bend treasure.

EPILOGUE

Sunday afternoon, instead of just the good doctor, me, and a pitcher of margaritas lounging on his patio as we'd planned, there was a crowd sitting around Noah's pool rehashing what had happened the day before. I could almost understand how Jake, Boone, and Poppy had been included in the party, but why my parents and Meg were there was a mystery. At any moment, I half expected Nadine, Birdie, Tony, and Chief Kincaid to arrive.

Being the host, Noah had claimed the cushion next to me on the wicker love seat. Jake sat across from us on the matching club chair, glaring whenever his rival's hand touched mine. Boone had taken the second chair and Poppy was doing laps in the pool. This left my parents occupying the couch with a strangely silent but seemingly sane Meg between them.

An assortment of sandwiches and chips were arranged on the central coffee table, but no one had touched the food. On the other hand, everyone had accepted a drink. Deciding that with Poppy out of earshot, this was the perfect time to share what I'd learned from her father, I chugged the remainder of my mojito and tapped the glass with the glass stirrer.

When everyone stopped talking and looked at me, I said, "Chief Kincaid called me this morning. He admitted that the four of us hadn't done anything illegal in searching the library. The crime scene had been released, and as city council members, both Noah and Boone had a right to be on the premises."

"Glad to know he isn't planning to arrest any of you." Jake raised a brow and glanced at my father. "And I'm glad the chief never has to find out who was really there when the body was discovered."

Ignoring Jake's dig, I quickly said, "The chief wanted you all to know that while the city attorney figures out who owns the gold we found, it has been moved to the bank vault for safekeeping."

"The most likely scenario"—Boone leaned forward—"would be that the federal government will claim it, as it appears to be stolen from the Union troops during the Civil War."

"The other possibility," Jake interjected, "might be that Shadow Bend has ownership because it was discovered on town property."

"Do you think we'll at least get a reward for finding it?" I had secretly hoped the Scooby Gang would get to split the treasure.

"I doubt it." Noah chuckled. "Remember, it was our ancestors who stole it in the first place."

"True," I admitted, then continued. "I'm not sure why Chief Kincaid was so willing to talk to me, except that everything he told me will probably be in the paper, but he said that Hinkley's real name is Roy Gabriel and he's got quite a history of fraud."

"What a surprise," Jake muttered, then asked, "Has he ever been violent before?"

"No." I shook my head. "He lashed out at Jett in anger, not with premeditation."

"He seemed like such a charming man." Yvette reached across Meg and clutched my father's arm. "The day after Jett's murder, when he approached me at the coffee shop, he said he was a friend of my husband and had a message for me, but needed to speak to me in private."

"Is he who you were expecting the night Jake and I visited you?" I asked.

"Yes." Yvette sighed. "I guess I should have been suspicious that he only told me he was Jett's lawyer after I said that I had no idea what my husband had been researching."

"According to Chief Kincaid, because of Gabriel's confession, the DNA evidence they expect to find on his walking stick, and his criminal history, his attorney and the county prosecutor are working on a deal." I paused, then added, "It looks as if they'll agree to voluntary manslaughter and drop any charges related to his attacking Poppy, Noah, and Boone."

"How long will he get for that?" Yvette asked.

"With his record, probably the full fifteen years." Boone took a swig of his beer.

Noah stretched his arm on the cushion behind me and asked, "How did Gabriel find out that Boone's mother had been seeing mysterious lights in the sky?"

"He probably Googled Shadow Bend when he and Jett were planning their treasure hunt," I answered.

I could hear Jake's growl, so I moved out of the reach of Noah's caressing fingers. The last thing I wanted was the two of them fighting over me in front of my parents and friends. Although I wouldn't mind Meg seeing Jake's interest in me. I glanced at her, and she shot me a little smile. What was up with that?

"Mom always posted her extraterrestrial sightings online," Boone said. "All Gabriel had to do was type 'Shadow Bend' into a search engine and her stuff would pop right up."

I got up to refresh my mojito, and Jake joined me at the portable bar. I felt his hand on my back as he whispered, "Meg has admitted she's better but not ready to live completely on her own. She'll rent an apartment in Shadow Bend for a while and start seeing a therapist in Kansas City until she feels more like herself."

"Great." I was truly happy that Jake's ex-wife was getting better.

As to her sticking around town, I had mixed emotions. I could understand her fear about returning to St. Louis, but I wasn't convinced that was her only motive.

While I contemplated my feelings, Jake and I returned to the group.

As we sat down, Jake asked, "Did the police ever figure out if that magnesium they found at the crime scene was related to the murder?"

I nodded. "One of the ways the professor encouraged the whole alien-invasion theme was by shooting off fireworks in the distance. The magnesium was residue that had been trapped in his pant cuff and spilled out when he and Jett struggled."

Poppy finally heaved herself from the water and joined us in time to hear my last comment. As she toweled off she asked, "How about that scrap of paper your stepfather was clutching? Did the cops ever figure it out?"

"It was from a handwritten document Jett had found in the archives," I explained. "The crime scene techs discovered similar paper among a group of letters that referred to the Union soldier who had been captured. The letter writer complained that Colonel Underwood allowed only Major Boone and himself to interrogate the prisoner."

"Jett must have put the dates together with the rumors about Captain Sinclair's claim that he failed to intercept the Union train," Noah said. "Which is when Benedict became desperate to see the colonel's diaries."

"And once he drugged Nadine and took pictures of the journal, he was able to figure out the code and find the secret room." I took a sip of my drink. "If he hadn't gotten greedy and decided to keep all the gold for himself, he could have slipped out of town with a fortune, melted the gold down, and sold it with no one being the wiser."

I looked at my mother, who shrugged. She didn't seem at all upset that her husband had been such a scoundrel. I just hoped she wasn't planning to stick around Shadow Bend to try to get her hooks into my father again. Although considering how broke the Sinclairs were, I doubted she'd be interested in renewing her vows with Dad.

As if reading my mind, Yvette got to her feet and said, "Thanks for inviting me, Noah, but I need to get going. I'm catching a plane back to Texas tomorrow morning, and I haven't packed a thing."

"You're very welcome." Noah smiled. "Have a good trip."

She walked over to me, bent down, gave me a hug, and whispered, "Don't let him get away this time. Jake may be a hunk, but Noah is the whole package."

Before I could respond, she said her good-byes and was gone. I was glad to see that Dad hadn't left with her. Maybe I could finally relax.

After Mom's departure, we snacked and chatted. Just as I popped a chip into my mouth, a question occurred to me, and I hurriedly swallowed, then said, "What I don't understand is why the mayor allowed Gabriel carte blanche around town."

"I can answer that." Boone rolled his eyes. "My mother made a large campaign contribution to ensure Egger's cooperation."

"That explains it." I grinned. I knew there was some way Hizzoner had lined his pockets. "Has Janice learned her lesson?"

"Who knows?" Boone shrugged.

"What I don't understand is how Dev figured out the secret way into the hidden room," Poppy said, then stuffed a taco chip full of salsa into her mouth.

"I . . ." I paused, not really sure how I'd done it myself. Suddenly, that same cold gust of air that I'd felt in the library archives surrounded me, and I shivered.

Meg stiffened and shot to her feet. She pointed to a spot near me and screamed.

"Son of a bitch!" Jake swore. "What's wrong?"

We all looked to where Meg was staring, but there was nothing there.

As abruptly as she'd stood, Meg sagged back onto the couch. She blinked and asked, "What happened?"

Jake explained and then said, "I'd better get her home."

We all nodded, and after pressing a hard kiss to my lips, Jake led Meg away. After they left, the rest of us said our good-byes, too. Part of me wanted to stay behind with Noah, but I was exhausted and needed some time alone to recover from the past few days.

Noah put his arm around me as he walked me to my car. He opened the door, gave me a sweet kiss, and waved as I drove away.

On the way home, I thought about what had just happened. I wanted to believe that Meg was pulling another stunt to keep Jake away from me, but a nanosecond before she'd screamed, I had felt something cold tap my neck. And considering that I'd been standing alone in eighty-degree sunlight, I had no idea what had touched me.

A thought flickered through my head that perhaps Captain Sinclair had been trying to help me, but then I laughed. I had never believed in ghosts or messages from beyond, and I had no intention of starting now.

Read on for a sneak peek
of the next book in Denise Swanson's
Scumble River Mystery Series,

Murder of a Cranky Catnapper

Available in September 2016.

As school psychologist Skye Denison Boyd hiked
down the main hallway of Scumble River Ele-
mentary School, she juggled her purse, a bulging
tote bag of files, an old shoe box containing reinforce-
ment rewards, and a cup of heavily sweetened and
creamed decaf coffee. Passing the front office, she
glanced through the window of the closed door.
There was still no sign of her visitor.

Not that she'd really expected to see him. Although
he wasn't due for another fifteen minutes, she'd hoped
he'd arrive early enough for her to greet him and explain a few things.

Skye hesitated, wanting to wait for her guest, but
then walked on. The boys in her fourth-grade counseling group would show up any second, and she couldn't
risk not being in the room when they got there. Rule
number one in any educational setting was to never
leave children unsupervised.

Hmm! She should start writing that type of information down for next year's school psych intern.

Rule number two had to do with the secretary and the custodian. The first day of Skye's own internship, her supervisor had sat her down and explained that those two individuals had the power to make her job a heck of a lot easier or nearly impossible. He had advised her to find out their preferences, then provide them with a steady stream of treats.

And although her internship had been almost a decade ago, Skye had always remembered his words of wisdom. She'd quickly discovered that as an itinerant school staff member, more often than not, she needed the custodian or secretary's assistance on a daily basis. And keeping on their good sides was a matter of self-preservation.

Which was why Skye had made a mental note when she'd overheard Fern Otte, the grade school secretary, tell someone that she loved Chicago's famous Garrett popcorn. Fern had confided that the caramel-and-cheese combination was her one gustatory weakness.

So today, when Skye had stopped by to ask Fern a special favor, she'd dropped off a canister of the costly snack. It was a small price to pay for having her visitor escorted through the warren of corridors instead of left to wander through the labyrinth alone.

Speaking of which, Skye paused at the T intersection leading to the building's oldest wing. This was where the real maze began. She sighed and turned the corner.

Instantly, the smell of mildew hit her full force and she sneezed, then sneezed again. *Great!* Now her eyes would water and all the effort she'd spent putting on mascara, shadow, and liner would be wasted.

Skye didn't generally bother with much makeup, usually settling for a quick dusting of bronzer—and if it had been a late night, a dab of concealer. However, this morning, when it had taken her three tries to find a pair of slacks that zipped, and when none of last spring's blouses would button over her baby bump, she'd decided that in order to face the day, she needed everything in her cosmetics case.

Intellectually, she knew that her clothes were tight because she was pregnant, and that she should buy some maternity outfits. But emotionally she just felt fat, so she needed the ego boost that only perfectly styled hair and full makeup could provide.

In her teens, Skye had struggled to fit into single-digit sizes. She'd starved herself, eating less than eight hundred calories a day, trying to look like the women she saw in the movies and in the magazines. Then when she had finally exited the dieting roller coaster, it had taken her a long time to come to terms with being larger than what was considered attractive. Now that those curves were expanding again, she was having trouble accepting her new silhouette.

Determined to stop fretting about her blossoming figure, she reminded herself that while she couldn't stop the bird of sorrow from flying over her head, she could prevent him from building a nest.

Smiling at her silly thoughts, she descended the final stairs into the original school building. Immediately, the humidity enveloped her like a spiderweb. Beads of sweat formed on her upper lip, and she could feel her hair start to frizz. Any hope of saving her smooth curls or makeup melted away with her foundation. It was the first Monday in May, and Illinois was experiencing a preview of the coming summer.

Skye grimaced. She was not fond of heat, and the soaring temperatures would be even less fun carrying an extra twenty-five or thirty pounds. It was a good thing that school would be over in less than a month and she could ride out the most blistering parts of June, July, and August planted in front of her home air conditioner.

As Skye continued down the corridor, she noted that evidence of the wing's previous occupants was still present. The space had been rented out to a church group, and although the religious objects had been removed, their outlines in the faded paint remained. Anywhere but Scumble River, Illinois, a town with a population hovering around three thousand, an image of a cross in a school would cause a parent protest. Here, no one seemed to notice.

The church had found a better facility and moved, but four years later, the school board was still trying to figure out whether to bring the wing up to code for classroom use or to tear it down.

It wasn't the best location for a counseling session. Not only was it stifling in the warmer weather and freezing in the winter; it was dreary and cut off from the rest of the school. However, Caroline Greer, the grade school principal, had assured Skye that other than the psych office, it was the only available area in the building for her to meet with her group.

With those being the only options, Skye wisely chose dilapidated over jam-packed. There was no way she could squeeze five lively nine- and ten-year-old boys into her refrigerator-carton-size office, and the kids wouldn't notice the annex's shabby decor.

For someone working in public education, conditions were rarely ideal. As always, she'd have to make do with what was available. Another pearl of wisdom Skye needed to write down for her future intern, because whining about the spaces they were assigned to use would only make things worse.

On the bright side, this wing's isolation was what

had helped convince Caroline to allow Skye to try a new type of therapy with her counseling group. Initially, the principal had been reluctant to grant permission for anything so unconventional, but Skye had provided Caroline with data that persuaded her to authorize six pilot sessions.

Skye was determined to give the innovative therapy every chance for success. Which was why today, instead of using her normal spot, the pastor's old office, she had moved the group to one of the larger rooms. She'd spent most of last Friday afternoon making sure the walls were bare and the blinds on the windows worked. Then, with the exception of seven chairs placed in a semicircle, she had removed all the other furniture and had vacuumed the ancient gray carpeting.

A lesson Skye had learned early on was that when attempting a group-counseling session, it was best to have an area free of visual or auditory distractions. And this afternoon's meeting would be stimulating enough without any extra diversions.

Skye was relieved to see she had made it to the room before the boys, and she quickly settled into the center chair. Taking a sip of her coffee, she waited for her group to arrive. After a couple of swallows, she became aware of the silence. Usually schools were full of noise, but in this unused annex, she was totally alone.

Before she could enjoy the quiet, the boys burst into the room with the teacher's aide hurrying after them. The aide had a harried expression on her reddened face and was breathing in short gasps. Evidently the kids had had her running most of the way.

She wheezed hello, then waved, turned on her heels, and fled. While her charges were with Skye, the woman was able to take a much-needed and well-deserved break, and she clearly wasn't wasting a minute of that precious time on small talk.

Skye yelled her thanks at the aide's disappearing back, then studied the five boys exploring the unfamiliar room. Three of them had Individual Education Plans that specified the counseling goals they were working to achieve. The other two were in the group mostly as role models. Their parents had noticed some mild attention issues and had asked that they be included.

The boys with IEPs were among the most unusual with whom Skye had ever worked. Although Clifford Jirousek had tested out of the stratosphere on every intelligence test he'd ever been given, he was so obsessed with books that he had isolated himself from all social interactions.

He carried a book with him at all times, and his mother reported that he hyperventilated if she removed a single volume from his bedroom. Normally, liking to read would be considered a positive trait in a student, but Clifford refused to do anything else. Left on his own, he wouldn't listen to instruction, participate in class, or interact with his peers.

Each session, Skye had worked on including Clifford in the rest of the boys' play, but today, as always, the moment he came into the room, Clifford separated himself from the others. He sat on the chair farthest from Skye, and opened an enormous all-in-one edition of *The Lord of the Rings*.

Christopher Hardy, another member of the group, walked over to him and asked, "What ya doing?" Clifford ignored him, and the boy persisted. "It's really thick. I bet you're not going to read the whole thing."

Peering over the book, Clifford sneered, "I'm not

saying that you're stupid." He glanced at Skye. "Because Mrs. Boyd told me that I can't call kids that. But you sure have bad luck when it comes to thinking."

Christopher's hands fisted and he snapped, "Well, my imaginary friend thinks you have some serious problems." He opened his mouth to continue, but when he looked over at Skye, she made a motion for him to walk away.

Once he complied, she got up and gave him a token. Then she went over to Clifford and tapped the front of his novel. Glaring at her, he closed the cover and clutched it to his chest. She held out her hand and after a long moment, he placed the book in her palm. She deposited it in her tote bag and gave Clifford a token. When he earned fifty, he could cash them in for lunch with the librarian.

Skye then went to check on the others. While she had been busy with Clifford, Alvin Hinich, the second boy with an IEP, had gotten down on all fours and was crawling around the room's perimeter. He sniffed the corners and made excited yipping noises. When he raised his leg, Skye hurried over to him and touched his nose with her finger, then pointed to the circle of chairs. He growled, but scuttled over and took a seat.

Alvin insisted he was a dog by the name of Spot, and when Skye had begun working with him, he'd refused to speak. After a year of counseling, he would now talk, but he still preferred barking to communicate, and he had to be constantly reminded to use words.

When Skye continued to stare at him, Alvin mumbled, "Hello, Mrs. Boyd."

"Hello, Alvin." Skye reached into her pocket and gave him a sticker for his behavior chart. When he filled all the squares, he would earn playtime with the

PE teacher. Skye frowned. She needed to check to make sure Mrs. Lake wasn't going to allow Alvin to turn their activity into a game of fetch or retrieving Frisbees with his mouth.

The third boy with an IEP in place was Duncan Canetti—or, as the kids called him, Mr. Clean. Duncan liked everything to be perfectly orderly and hygienic. When Skye had first met him his head had been shaved. His mother had explained it was because her son couldn't stand to have even a hair out of place. He'd also insisted on wearing disposable gloves to school. Skye still couldn't believe Mrs. Canetti had gone along with either of those notions.

After some intense negotiation, Skye had convinced Duncan to forgo his bald-headed look for an extremely short buzz cut. She had also asked the teachers and other staff to intervene if they heard any of the children using his nickname. She was pleased with Duncan's progress. He no longer sprayed a can of Lysol in front of himself as he walked into a room, and he had stopped wearing plastic gloves out on the playground. Now she had to work on getting the hand sanitizer away from him.

During the first year of counseling, Clifford, Alvin, and Duncan hadn't been able to make any friends outside of the group. This had concerned their parents, as well as the school personnel. And while each had made some headway on their more unusual issues, they still had difficulty joining the rest of the children's play during recess.

Last spring, at their IEP conferences, after much discussion about the boys' lack of social skills, Skye had suggested including a few regular-education students in their group. Which was how Gavin Girot and Christopher Hardy had become members. Both of the boys' parents had signed permission, with the understanding that Skye would concentrate on improving Gavin's and Christopher's attention spans and on-task behavior.

Skye looked over the assemblage and said, "Okay, boys. Everyone take a seat so we can get started. I have a surprise for you."

Gavin immediately obeyed and Skye gave him a coupon for five extra minutes of art time, but Christopher seemed mesmerized by the black cord hanging from the projector screen. He flicked it, watching it swing back and forth. Duncan stood frozen by a shelf, staring at a dust bunny the size of a Chihuahua. He whimpered and reached into his pocket for his Purell.

Skye exhaled noisily. Obviously, she still had her work cut out for her.

Walking over to Duncan, she closed the lid on the sanitizer bottle and pointed to an empty chair. Then in a mild tone, she said to Christopher, "Please take your seat so we can be ready for our surprise."

Once the boys were all sitting, Skye joined them and said, "Today we're going to have a visitor. His name is Dr. Quillen and he's—"

"No doctors!" Duncan screamed, jumping to his feet and backing against a wall. "They touch you and poke you with dirty needles."

"Please return to your seat, Duncan," Skye said. "Dr. Quillen isn't a people doctor. He's a veterinarian. He's going to help us—"

"No!" Alvin dropped to his knees, then tilted his head toward the ceiling and howled.

"Alvin, use your words." Skye checked her watch. The vet would be here any second. She had to get control of the session. With one boy cowering in a corner and another baying at the moon, she wasn't sure which behavior to address first.

As she considered her options, the door swung open and Dr. Linc Quillen strode inside. He had a beautiful Maine Coon cat in a Pet Taxi and a Siberian Husky on a leash.

"Wolf! It's a wolf!" Clifford screamed. "He's going to eat us."

"It's only a dog." Skye jumped to her feet, trying to calm the boys and herd them back into their chairs. "He's a nice doggy. Really."

But it was too late for reassurances. Group hysteria took over, and the boys scattered. Alvin, Duncan, Gavin, and Christopher huddled against the far wall, but Clifford skirted around Dr. Quillen and the animals and ran out the door.

"Sorry!" Skye yelled, dashing after the escapee, adding, "Keep an eye on the boys. I'll be right back."

Skye sprinted down the hallway, then realized the others might try to follow her. Just as she twisted her neck to look, she heard footsteps in front of her. Before she could swing her head toward the sound, she slammed into what felt like a brick wall. Flailing her arms for balance, she lost her footing. But before she could fall, hands gripped her arms and steadied her.

Skye's gaze shot to her rescuer's face. *Shit!* The man holding her upright was Palmer Lynch, the school board member who was running against her godfather, Charlie Patukas, for the presidency. She was so screwed.